The Train

The Train

Dacia Maraini

Translated by Dick Kitto and
Elspeth Spottiswood

Camden Press

Published in 1989 by
Camden Press Ltd
43 Camden Passage, London N1 8EB, England

First published in Italy as Il treno per Helsinki
Copyright © 1984 Giulio Einaudi editore s.p.a., Torino

Translation © Dick Kitto and Elspeth Spottiswood

The translators wish to thank Dacia Maraini for her help
with the translation

Set in Baskerville
by Photosetting & Secretarial Services Yeovil
and printed and bound by
BPCC Wheatons Ltd, Exeter

British Library CIP Data
Maraini, Dacia
The train.
I. Title II. Il treno per Helsinki. *English*
853′.914[F]

ISBN 0-948491-50-7 Pbk

ABOUT THE AUTHOR

Dacia Maraini is one of Italy's best known women writers. Her novel The Age of Discontent (L'Eta del Malessere') won the Prix Formentor in 1963 and has been translated into twelve languages. She has written nine novels, four volumes of poetry and nine plays.

OTHER WORKS BY DACIA MARAINI

Novels

La Vacanza (1962); published in Britain as 'The Holiday'
L'Eta del Malessere (1963): winner of the 'Prix Formentor' in 1963; published in Britain as 'The Age of Discontent'
A Memoria (1967)
Memorie di Una Ladra (1968); published in Britain as 'Memories of a Female Thief'
Donna in Guerra (1975); published in Britain as 'Woman at War'
Lettere a Marina (1981); published in Britain as 'Letters to Marina'
Isolina (1985)

Poetry

Crudelta all'aria aperta (1968)
Donne mie (1974)
Mangiami Pure (1980)
Dimenticato di Dimenticare (1983)

Theatre

Riccato a Teatro e Altre Commedie (1968)
Don Juan (1976)
La Donna Perfetta (1974)
Viva l'Italia (1976)
Dialogo di una Prostituta con un suo Cliente (1978)
I Sogni di Clitennestra (1981)
Suor Juana (1980)
Lezioni d'Amore (1982)
Mary Stuart (1984)

I AM peeling a potato. I stop with the dripping knife in one hand and the half-peeled potato in the other. Out of the little black box comes the voice of Miele. He is talking about peace. His voice is nervous and husky full of hesitations and reasonableness.

I can't take in what he's saying. The sound of his voice enters my ears and goes straight down into my belly following well-trodden paths that are long-since past and forgotten. Many years ago. Almost fifteen. I don't remember... the past has the consistency of thick vegetable soup.

Yes it's many years since I last went down that path from my throat to my guts. That slippery slope where the sound of Miele's sibilant 'esses' acted as a cushion and a bridge into the chaos of my emotions.

I sit there with my mind a blank my hands paralysed my gaze fixed on the radio. From what bloody awful corner of the world does this ghostly voice emerge? From what dark cave of memory?

I nibble Alice's mushroom. I shrink. I become minute. I pass through the looking-glass and slide down a black funnel into a cave whose soft damp walls plunge me down down through the roots of my innards towards the narrow passage of my anus that contracts and shits me out of myself into a perfumed garden. I look around stunned.

Miele is there waiting for me. He looks a little fatherly a little indecisive. He is wearing white linen trousers and a cotton pullover with pale blue stripes. Paolo has met up with him God knows where and brought him home.

Paolo gives me a kiss on the cheek. 'Miele's a bastard but he's a genius' he says laughing. He takes off his shoes and flings them down. He glances at his latest painting with its dark raw outlines. He sits down on the floor and starts to beat his drum with his open palm. Miele sits down too looking rather embarrassed. He has the sturdy neck of an athlete sloping shoulders strong ankles sparkling eyes. I pour some red wine into his glass and he thanks me with an intense tender voice that excites my curiosity. Paolo is oblivious of us. He beats the drum bending his fine head down between his shoulders.

'He thinks he's an African' says Miele knocking back his drink all in one breath and giving me a provocative look.

1

'He thinks he's still in his mother's womb' I say conscious of the firmness of his beats on the sealskin. The drum is a call from the primeval darkness the creation of life. It is the heart of the baby trying to adapt to the rhythms of its mother's heart-beat. It is the agony in which the baby weeps for his future birth and for the shame of being brought into the world.

Miele laughs but he doesn't understand. The Paolo he knows is different – his friend from University days. A melancholy painter. Someone with a scarred face shabby clothes and a hatred for his family whom he has never come to terms with. Whose wealth has always been an embarrassment. Someone who arrived at the University in an old broken-down station-wagon with a black mongrel gazing stonily out of the window. A silent person with slightly stooping shoulders and a kind gentle smile. Someone who will stay for hours on end sitting on the pavement confronting a line of policemen with riot-shields and rifles in protest against a far-off war of oppression. Someone who at the right moment will plant himself underneath the waiting horses' hoofs to defy America. The sort of person who will invite home anyone who is hungry or who needs a bed for the night – but who then can't be bothered to talk to them. Someone who married a blonde girl whose body is strangely awkward and who writes plays for the theatre that never get performed.

Two days later I find him waiting for me outside the door of my house in his red Volkswagen Beetle.

'Miele' I call out. He sidles indolently up to me like a sensuous cat.

'Where are you off to?'

'I'm going to the theatre.'

'I'll come with you.'

Testone who always makes a big fuss of everybody keeps his distance with Miele. He sniffs at his shoes and the bottom of his trousers with a bored look. Then he turns round nonchalantly and lifts his leg against a lamp post and sprinkles it with a few drops of urine.

'Where's Paolo?'

'I don't know. He went out this morning at seven. He didn't say where he was going.'

'Isn't that his dog?'

He too sounds disparaging. He reciprocates Testone's antipathy. For a long moment they exchange hostile looks. Then each of them adopts the bored dignified air of someone who for reasons of convenience is obliged to put up with a person they'd prefer to keep at a distance.

So we go to the bar at the tennis club in the Fori Imperiali. Testone quickly slips in among the dwarf cypresses where he sits in front of a colossal white marble gladiator and fixes his gaze on a golden pigeon that is walking calmly across the sculptured curls of the statue. Outlined against the pale yellow sky his muscles bulging with exaggerated realism the gladiator casts his unseeing eyes over a clear still world.

Miele collapses into a deck chair with pink and blue stripes. He is still wearing his white linen trousers with a blood-red shirt. He tends to dress quite smartly but in accordance with his own taste – part of his very private vision of the world. He hates fashion and everything that is obvious and predictable. His body proclaims quietly 'I am a handsome young man. I'm open. I'm genuine. I'm strong and I am here for anyone who wants me but they must one way or another be worthy of me. I haven't got time to waste on idiots and failures.'

3

He is not a failure. He has outsize thumbs ready to grasp the world by the ears and make it his. I try to get him to smile because what really turns me on most about him is his sudden smile – so tranquil and yielding. When he smiles his eyes become a disquieting intense green.

What I want is to penetrate the kernel of that smile. I want to be submerged in those clouded eyes with their lightning flashes of menace and seduction and their emerald depths of tranquillity.

He orders a Daiquiri in a tone of voice somewhere between bravado and shyness. What on earth is a Daiquiri? I know a moment later when the waiter returns bearing a small metal tray. On it a transparent long-stemmed glass with its rim dipped in sugar. A whitish opalescent liquid.

'Can I have a taste?'

'Have you never tried it?'

'No.'

'It's very sweet. It's disgusting actually. I only drink it because it reminds me of a woman I was once in love with.'

When he talks he lets the words fall nonchalantly from his mouth. He throws them away with a gesture of indifference and peevishness.

'Were you very much in love with her?'

'Oh yes very very much.'

'What was she like?'

'Beautiful.'

'Fair or dark? Tall or short?'

'Forty years old with fervid eyes a husband who was some big-shot in the business world and two teenage sons. A villa in Fregene with two footmen and two bodyguards whose jackets were stuffed with guns and ammunition.'

'However did you get mixed up with someone so different from you?'

'Her husband used to run after call-girls so he was hardly ever at home.'

He obviously gets a big kick out of telling me about her. He spins the thread of his silken voice like some greedy spider. He knows how to draw it out of his cunning mouth inch by inch weaving together

4

truth and fiction exhibitionism and paradox.

'She was always alone' he continued running on self-indulgently. 'Her sons were both away at school one in Switzerland and one in America. I used to visit her at night whenever she switched on an orange light in her bathroom. I'd go in through the back gate and climb up the fire-escape. I soon got the measure of those two armed bastards.'

'And then?' I am fascinated by his rapid voice which has the strength of sisal and the softness of a cloud.

'Then one night her husband came back unexpectedly. We didn't hear him. He found me in bed in his place. He was going to hand me over to his two assassins for their breakfast. But his wife threatened to leave him for ever so he had to swallow the bitter pill. He needs her there beside him for when he grows old. He claims he loves her and he believes in family life. In his own way it could be true.'

'And you?'

'A tycoon whose fingers dripped gold. An army of workers to keep in their place. A wife to shut away in the house like a prize sow.'

'So how did it end?'

'The two butchers saw me off. There was no way I could visit her any more. I went berserk. I circled round the villa in desperation leaping from one tree to another like a monkey. But she was never to be seen. I couldn't eat. I couldn't sleep. I'd spend hours and hours looking at a small snapshot I'd nicked from her. I cried like a child.'

'Then one morning I caught sight of her. Leaning out of the window. I hardly recognised her. Hair whiter than white. Skimpy dressing-gown pulled tight round her waist. Not an ounce of flesh on her. Face ravaged. I started to scream. Then I felt something whistle past my ear. I was right at the end of a branch overhanging the garden clinging to it like a monkey. I let go and fell. Four months in hospital with six ribs broken and a fractured arm.'

'The heroic lover!' I throw a dash of cold water on the fire of his words. He laughs and plunges his nose into his Daiquiri.

'It took me four years to get over it.'

'How old were you when all this happened?'

'Nineteen.'

5

'And now?'

'Twenty-six.'

A few moments of silence. I watch him hesitate with the tip of his tongue in the milky liquid. He shuts his eyes dilates his nostrils and drinks with small silent sips.

'You never saw her again?'

'Let's talk about something more cheerful. Do you think I might fall in love with you?'

'What do you think?'

'I think I already have.'

So he has said it all. Flopped in his deck-chair his sunburnt arms folded behind his head his green eyes laughing. He isn't afraid of anything. He throws himself into an adventure quite confident that he'll be able to pull out of it. He scents risk like an old fisherman poaching salmon.

Whereas I am afraid of everything: of my clumsiness of the wounds of love of the future which I see advancing like black suns on a misty horizon. I look at him coldly as if to say: 'Don't try to put me under your spell. I can see through you – fascinating maybe but all on the surface. So cocksure of yourself but lacking in any depth.'

But that was not the whole Miele. I understood that too late when I was already drowning in his mystery like a fly in milk.

After that there is no more talk of love. He disappears for a whole month. I don't despair. Every so often I think about him. Mostly I think about his name. Miele – honey! It's so strange so intangible so transparently sweet. It's almost cloying the way that name slips out the way it trickles down like some scented liquid.

I let myself become absorbed in the routine of a happy marriage. Paolo whom I have held in my arms night after night for four years. His breath on my neck sleeping silent and relaxed like two children on the big mattress that smells of bleach.

I dream of flying. Month after month. I start to fly almost as soon as I fall asleep. I take off my shoes so as to reduce my weight. I stand on tiptoe. I peel off into flight. 'Peel off' is the right expression with its sense of delicate yet decisive separation from the fruit of the orange. I detach myself from that curled-up body of a woman in the embrace of

6

the eternal husband and I rise up into the universe of city roofs. I land on my feet on top of the window ledge and look down. Eight floors of velvety darkness. If I make a slip I shall die flattened against the paving stones below. Fear erupts in my throat. I launch myself forward and at the same time I wave my arms slowly up and down like wings. I paddle my legs as if I were swimming. The air supports me.

When I am tired I grasp the eaves of the roof. I sit with my legs dangling in the wind. Then I fly off again. I aim for another ledge. First the rounded white one of the Banca Nationale and then the red one of the College of Priests. I settle on the eagle's wing at the pinnacle of the gateway to the Villa Borghese. I take a deep breath. I feel good. I decide to continue flying. From there I'll go to the papal orbs that stand poised on the doors of the Piazza Flaminio. Colossal fleur-de-lys of grey stone consisting of two stiff petals and a ball of red granite. I sit on one of the orbs and watch the night traffic as it slides rapidly by. Red eyes flicker. Brilliant green porpoises plunge and twist along the road surface spattering little cascades of liquid blue on the walls of the sleeping houses. I am drawn to the dark mass of a gigantic oak-tree beyond the Muro Torto and that will be my next stop.

The sensation of a heavy weight on my stomach wakes me up. Paolo is trying to thrust himself inside me. With that blind determination I know only too well. I embrace him half-heartedly. He thumps away with the rhythm of a drum. He'd like to penetrate me with his pelvis and with his bottom and with his legs and even by drawing back and thrusting into me with his head.

Not a word. Not a kiss. Only this gross submersion into the black waters of the mother's womb. Half asleep I can just manage a ragged orgasm which comes in fits and starts. I would have preferred to continue flying from roof to roof. Or to take a desperate turn round a television aerial like a flag blown by the wind. A sensation of freedom within me. An irrepressible happiness in which I can lose myself.

I GO to the kitchen to get a glass of water. Lamberto is there sitting at the table dipping furtively into a bowl of custard.

'That custard is for tomorrow's pudding' I say. He jumps. He lifts his head and squints short-sightedly with disappointment. He follows me with wide-open eyes as I go over to the fridge. I bend down to get a bottle of mineral water. I pour some into a glass and drink it. He isn't sure whether to go on eating or not. He stretches out a hand picks up his glasses and sticks them on his nose. He at once takes on a more confident look.

'I see. I see' he says in a paternal sort of way.

'I don't like to hear you speaking like that Lamberto. It makes you sound just like my grandfather.'

Lamberto is twenty-five but because of illness he has remained like a child. He's a spastic with the body of a prematurely aged eleven-year-old. He has moments of great intelligence and tenderness. At other times he is inert and vacuous.

'Get your books and we'll do some geography.'

'Today it's maths!'

'We'll do both.'

Obediently he gets out the books. But he is suspicious: he's afraid that I'm going to tell him off about the custard. He bends his outsize head over his exercise books. He sniffs. He grinds his teeth. Sometimes I feel that his behaviour is becoming like a force that nature has let get out of control. But then he flops. He turns back on himself and coils up into a ball around his weak and weary heart.

'Go on then. Eat the custard. I'll make some more tomorrow.'

His face lightens up with happiness. He seizes the spoon and shoves it violently into the bowl spattering custard everywhere.

The doorbell rings. It is Miele. He has brought a big cake decorated with sugared violets.

'It's Paolo's birthday isn't it?'

'Tomorrow.'

'I'll be back tomorrow then. *Ciao*.' He goes out closing the door quietly behind him.

'Stay if you like. Have something to drink' I say but he's already

8

half-way down the stairs.

'How many times does 3 go into 15?'

Lamberto sighs and swallows. He chews his pen. He laughs. He has the awkward grace of a famished mouse. Every now and then he glances in the direction of the bowl of custard which he hasn't quite polished off.

The thought of Miele insinuates itself between the numbers. It takes the form of a plump round 5 and a slender impulsive 2. I watch Lamberto's stubby fingers gripping his pen in a kind of spasm.

'Shall we go out and buy something for supper Armida?'

We walk along in the sunshine his hand in one of mine a plastic bag cutting into the fingers of the other. A smell of raw fish and bruised cauliflowers in our nostrils. For the first time I ask myself what Miele does when I'm not around. I find a void: an unknown house unknown thoughts unknown activities unknown gestures. I cannot visualise any of them.

The three of us Paolo Lamberto and I are eating in the kitchen. There have been several phone calls already wishing Paolo a happy birthday. Elizabetta was first with her shrill affectionate voice. Then Dida whose laugh is like a waterfall. Then Nico and Cesare and Ada. The little family of friends who are closest to us.

But my thoughts are wandering to that part of today that still separates me from tomorrow. Every so often I go to the fridge to keep an eye on the cake with its violets. The cake reassures me that Miele will be coming. I keep expecting it to reveal something more about him but the white icing hides the cake's inside. And those violets are so shiny, so artificial. They don't tell the truth.

Paolo curls up to play his drum. Meanwhile I cook cut peel butter fry. The interminable day of waiting at last draws near its end. Night arrives with its blind embraces. The time for my solitary flight. The whine of buses in the piazza below the window. Then the brash clamour of the alarm-clock.

Miele arrives early. A curl the colour of brown earth hangs over his bare forehead. He embraces Paolo. He presents him with a silver fountain-pen. He gives me hardly more than an embarrassed handshake.

9

I cook spaghetti with pesto sauce. Lamberto is eating chocolates and watching television. Testone lies on the goatskin rug in the sitting-room keeping a watchful eye on the door.

Dida arrives wearing a filmy dress of pink lace and a long necklace of imitation pearls which dangles down to her navel. She sits down beside Paolo. She gives him a long-drawn-out kiss on the neck. Immediately after her Cesare arrives on the doorstep already grumbling against heaven knows what wrong he has suffered. The whole world is in league against him. Ada follows after him dark and silent as a raven her arms laden with presents.

Miele has eyes for no one but Paolo. I ask him if he would like a Daiquiri. He gives me a sharp look. He doesn't even answer. I don't press him. Nodding his head to the rhythm of the drum he squats down beside Paolo between the record player and his American idol. Ada performs a solitary dance near the window. Nico is drinking a mixture of wine and beer. His eyes are red and he smiles conspiratorially at anyone who comes into his line of vision.

Nico is in love with Dida. Dida is in love with Cesare. Cesare is in love with Ada. Ada does not return his love because she also is in love with Dida. A chain of febrile emotions that spiral in on themselves leading nowhere.

The group has met every evening for years. Miele joined it only recently. It's not clear what his feelings are so he is viewed with some suspicion. Sometimes he is made much of. At others he is kept at a bit of a distance. As a result he finds himself almost by chance the centre of intense morbid curiosity.

I too ask myself what it is that makes Miele tick. I watch him moving his hands like an Indian prince his back flattened against the wall his big feet encased in hefty mountain boots.

The pasta I cooked is demolished in a few minutes. We pass on to a meat dish with cream sauce. Miele chews listlessly and eats very little. Lamberto serves himself greedily to three helpings. Paolo tells him to leave a little for other people. He shrugs his shoulders. Cesare thrusts his fork into his helping as if he were engaged in man-to-man combat. Nico cuts his up on his plate and then savours each morsel slowly and suspiciously.

Miele brings in his big cake with its impenetrable milk-white icing. The polished violets look as if they were made of plastic. Dida opens her eyes very wide. Lamberto works out how big each portion will be. A lighted candle leans dangerously to one side. Paolo fills his cheeks and blows it out with one precise puff. Everyone claps. The knife sinks into the soft cake.

Towards two o'clock Lamberto falls asleep in his chair. I take him up to bed. Dida asks me where the talcum powder is because she has a stain on her dress. Paolo takes her by the hand into the bathroom. Ada has remained transfixed in front of the window for the last hour. She drinks with long slow gestures. Nico is stretched out at her feet. Cesare gathers up the crumbs of the dismembered cake from the table and brings them absent-mindedly to his mouth.

I am tired. I long for sleep. But no one seems to be leaving. I help Lamberto to undress. When he is under the blankets he seizes my hand and imprisons it tightly between his. My head falls forward. I sleep chained to the bed waiting for him to doze off.

When I wake up the city is submerged in silence. No buses whining. No hooting. No stamping of footsteps on the pavements. I go to the bathroom. I lift my skirt. I sit on the toilet. I hear subdued noises. I wonder about mice.

In the sitting-room I find Cesare and Ada asleep back to back. Nico has left. Miele too. And Dida? Her shoes peep out from under the table. I walk on tiptoe to the bedroom. I open the door. Dida is bending over Paolo's lap. I close the door. I go into the kitchen. I sit down at the table. I force myself to look at a glass of milk on which a layer of yellowish fat has congealed.

But the nagging image has stayed in the fissure of my eye: Dida extricating Paolo's short sturdy prick from the open zip of his trousers. Dida smiling with delight. Her plump fingers playing around this bud of flesh. Paolo arching backwards. Dida serious and self-possessed bending down to taste this tempting bud.

And here he is: Paolo. He comes into the kitchen and goes confidently towards the fridge. He sees me but pretends not to. He takes a bottle of mineral water and turns to go out.

'What were you up to with Dida?'

'I ... nothing. We were just playing.'

'What sort of game were you playing at?'

'You know we're like brother and sister. It's absurd to be jealous of someone I was in love with years ago.'

'I'm not jealous.' The fact is I'm not jealous enough. On the contrary I feel euphoric. That scene has released me from an excess of marital intimacy.

He goes off without listening. Meanwhile Lamberto appears having woken from one of his usual nightmares. His nose begins to bleed. Drops of blood run down into his mouth down his chest and pyjamas and on to the floor. I put some ice on his temples and make him lie down. He kicks angrily. He takes my hand between his teeth and bites it until I cry out. Then he gives a contented laugh.

I T is one o'clock in the morning when we set out from the house. Paolo has put on his navy blue gym suit with a long yellow stripe that cuts his hips in half. I am wearing loose trousers and a sweater streaked with paint. I've got my gym-shoes in my hand as I haven't had time to put them on. Dida and Cesare are waiting for us in the street. In Dida's Morris 1000 the colour of egg-yolk. Paolo bends down to kiss her. Cesare beckons me with a nod. I sit with him in the back seat. We set off. Two buckets of wallpaper paste are resting on the floor beside me. One bucket is pea-green and the other bright pink. Behind are two paint-brushes smelling strongly of turpentine.

Dida drives calmly. Eyes moving watchfully. Fair filmy hair falling on her broad shoulders. Freckled arms jutting out of her short tight jacket. Cesare lets his arm dangle out of the car window.

We stop in the Piazza Mazzina. The car draws up close to the pavement and halts alongside a lamp-post. We get out. Dida gets a roll of posters out of the boot. Cesare takes the pink bucket, grabs a paintbrush, dips it into the paste and starts to daub the lamp-post. Dida comes quickly and presses the poster against the lamp-post. Cesare takes the brush and goes over it again – up and across with firm brush-strokes.

I take the other bucket and brush and go on towards the third post while Paolo unrolls the posters. I hear footsteps behind me. I turn round. A man in a white open-necked shirt is watching me with amazement. I glance at Paolo. He shrugs his shoulders. He senses that the man has nothing to do with the police and isn't a fascist out looking for trouble. We continue to spread the paste.

Meanwhile Dida has moved towards the second lamp-post with a poster in her hands. Cesare follows her closely with the bucket of paste. Splashes of sticky liquid. Suddenly the blare of a police-siren. Cesare stops and listens. He gives a nod to Dida and turns quickly towards the car. Dida rolls up the posters. She gets into the Morris. Paolo is still standing there with his arms in the air. Paste drips from my hands.

'Don't stand there you fools! Let's go.'

Paolo drops the poster all smeared with glue and leaps into the car.

I struggle into the back seat with my full bucket. I put it down on the floor beside me. The car leaps forward. The side window is still open. In trying to shut it I put my foot in the bucket.

This time the car stops alongside a long pock-marked wall. I don't know where we are, I've been sitting with my head bent down trying to do something about my sodden foot. I see Cesare getting out. He seizes the brush and covers the wall with big strokes. Dida stands behind him with the roll of posters.

I grab the green bucket and get out too. My foot slips inside my soaking shoe. At each step I run the risk of sticking to the pavement. I jerk my knee up to a right-angle so as to prise my foot off the ground. Paolo giggles. Cesare ticks me off for wasting time. I plunge the paint-brush into the whitish liquid. In the light of the street-lamp it looks like semen. I say that to Dida who shrugs her shoulders with a little laugh. But I stay there unable to move. My eyes are glued to the gelatinous surface. To the bucket of sperm into which I so carelessly plunged my foot.

A hundred pricks all ejaculating at the same moment with a gasp that becomes a sort of rumble and then a gigantic explosion of collective satisfaction – the *mascoliata finale* as they call it in Sicily: a flight of shooting stars cascading downwards against the black sky of the festival night. The spittle of life against the death of all things.

'What's up with you? Get on with it!' comes Paolo's voice sharp and hard. I lift my head from that ocean of semen that dances and ripples like a milky way in the opaque warmth of the city streets impregnating the walls, lamp-posts and pavements.

I follow Paolo's hands as he aligns them square to the wall. The poster falls straight down without creases. I grip the brush and dip it into the bucket. I spread two big brush-fuls of semen over the words *Guerra Multinationale Capitalismo*. The faint black characters become soaked and create minute white blisters. The blood-red background is immersed in a cloud of damp sticky vapour.

Angry voices reach us and I see Cesare rushing towards the car pulling Dida by the arm. 'Let's go Armida! Run!'

I finish giving the last horizontal brush-strokes. Paolo is already sitting beside Dida. Cesare holds the door open for me. I grab the bucket and jump in. Dida has started the engine and presses down the accelerator. The fascists erupt round the corner. They are more to be feared than the cops. A dozen legs in dark leggings and black boots with iron heels black leather belts bulging pockets and pale angry faces. They are striding towards us. One of them stops in front of a half-stuck poster. He lets out a whistle. The others run up.

I hardly have time to pull in my leg when Dida sets off at high speed. The door shuts with a bang. We hear an excited voice followed by a metallic thud. A stone has hit the boot of the Morris. Dida accelerates. The door swings open again hits against the side panel rebounds and slams shut. I am within an inch of having my fingers chopped off.

We fly towards an underpass. I realise we are near the University. We turn sharp right heading in the direction of the Piazza Della Repubblica. We turn down a oneway street. Cesare stamps his feet.

'That's all right Dida you've shaken them off.'

I clutch the seat. The paste slops round my ankles. Dida turns downhill into Viale Regina Elena at sixty miles an hour, her hair flying in front of her eyes. She is gripping the steering wheel tightly in her hands. Cesare protests and fidgets. Paolo holds his breath and digs his heels in.

On the back seat I surrender myself... the sensation of having already lived through this experience. But when? I am nothing but eyes and flesh... in the arms of my mother... then – yes of course! Jolted from one house to another... from one car to another...half asleep I first saw the town framed above and below by the arch of her shoulders that sheltered my body from head to foot. My father driving at break-neck speed towards his 'brilliant future' for ever in a hurry for ever grazing the kerb-stones and overtaking other cars by a hair's-breadth.

My mother always wore dresses of misty silver... greys mixed with pink and an intense shade of electric blue. She was a nomad. I was a nomad too. One embracing the other in her womb. Locked in each others' arms. Unloved through too much love not really knowing where one of us began and the other ended. . . .

Clusters of lights. Mysterious eggs. Huge balloons suspended in the

15

air supporting a whole structure of dark forms. Houses, white walls in the darkness, perpendicular walls always ready to crash on top of us but always mysteriously poised above in space.

Cesare gives Dida a slap. She brakes sharply. She gets out of the car and goes off banging the door. Cesare runs after her. Paolo gives me a despairing look.

I lean my head against the back seat. My gaze rests on the lions' mouths jutting out from the iron bars of the black gate. They are the flowers of the dead. Beyond the gate the rows of tombs in the Verano cemetery can be glimpsed indistinctly.

My feet are soaked with glue. An uncanny silence seizes us by the throat. I close my eyes... I am sitting in the sunshine inside a bus...going with my mother to Milazzo to fetch my father. While the bus fills up we sit waiting next to a big window scintillating in the sun. Children all dressed up in immaculate white stockings and small black patent leather shoes. Velvet hats decorated with flowers. A man in blue clasping an accordion.

They have all just come from a wedding. They carry little bags of confetti hanging from their wrists packets of sweets and bunches of flowers. They look replete and festive.

Suddenly I have a vision of all those mothers and fathers dead – skulls smooth teeth bared arms like small sticks legs dangling soft round pelvises draped in innumerable bits of white cloth on top of which jump coloured skirts and petticoats all reduced to a collection of fragile polished bones like the carcases of sheep I used to see near our house.

This vision intrigues me. Fascinates me. Then a terrible pain makes me shudder violently and for the first time the sense of death erupts in the tender feelings of a child who has no divinity to console her...

I am woken by Paolo putting a paper cup of boiling hot coffee in my hand. I drink it down in one gulp. I know that now I'll be unable to sleep. I am convulsed by feverish shivers.

We kiss each other in the darkness of the car while we wait for Cesare and Dida who are quarrelling round the corner. Bitter taste of coffee on his tongue. My cheek against his cheek.

M IELE comes to see us almost every evening. He hardly greets me. He slips straight into Paolo's studio. He listens while Paolo beats his drum. They talk quietly. I haven't an idea what they talk about.

At supper-time they both emerge cold and hungry. They ask me what I've made to eat.

'Tell Armida what good friends we are.'

'She knows.'

'She doesn't know. She doesn't have a clue!'

Something suspect in this display of brotherly feeling. Something put on for my benefit. Something I don't understand. A punishment? A threat? A banishment?

'You describe it then.'

'Shall I begin with affinities or differences?'

Clasping each other round the shoulders they come into the kitchen laughing.

Lamberto is like Testone: he dislikes guests who take Paolo's attention away from him. At the first opportunity he does something to annoy Miele. But Miele never seems to notice. He is affectionate towards Lamberto. He's gentle with Testone. Only with me is he distant and perfunctory.

Later in the evening Ada and Nico arrive followed by Cesare and Dida. Ada is smoking. She's attached to her cigarette as if it were the fountain of life. As if God knows what mysterious force might emerge from this little white tube. She sucks it she stews it with her lips she devours it while she waits to be flooded with a sensation of divine well-being.

'This evening I don't feel like cooking for everybody' I say.

'Let's go out and eat.'

'Yes we'll go to a pizzeria!' Lamberto puts an outstretched hand to his brother's chest.

'Yes. All right. Let's go' says Paolo.

Dida is wearing a skimpy white sweater embroidered with pearls and an Indian scarf knotted over her shoulders. Cesare follows her looking sulky and frowning. Ada walks beside me her face small and pinched her eyes opened wide with pain.

17

'I dreamt I was going to Paestum with Dida' she says.

'Why Paestum?'

'I haven't a clue! She was sitting next to me in the car and I had my hand in her lap. Suddenly I realised that underneath my hand her trousers were becoming dreadfully swollen. I said:

'But you're a man. You've been conning me!' She opened her trousers and laughingly revealed a baby tortoise which was lying in her lap. 'What do you think it means?'

'I can't imagine!'

'I dream about her almost every night!'

'Have you told her?'

'No.'

'Tell her.'

'It wouldn't be any use. She's completely besotted with that cretin Cesare.'

'And Cesare's in love with you!'

'I'm not in love with him though. What am I to do Armida?'

'I don't know... Wait a bit and see what happens.'

'I've been waiting for two years.'

'All our loves seem to be twisted: Nico loves Dida who loves Cesare who loves you who love Dida.'

We thread our way into the pizzeria on the via Flaminia. Bottle-green neon lights walls papered with fake wooden panelling wooden tables with white plastic tops.

Miele sits next to Paolo. Lamberto comes close to me and leaning his cheek on my shoulder asks me to cut up his meat for him. Every once in a while I look up at Miele. But he never looks at me. And our talk in the tennis club bar? Him saying he was in love? All forgotten – wiped out.

Ada smokes as she eats. She puts the lighted cigarette on the edge of her plate picks up her knife absent-mindedly cuts a slice of pizza and pushes it into her mouth. 'Too hot' she mutters and tears well up into her eyes. The others laugh. Dida hands her a glass of water. Cesare cups his hand beneath her chin and shouts 'Spit it out here. Spit it out!' But she swallows it quickly so that she can get back to her cigarette without a moment's pause.

18

After supper Paolo decides to go with Miele. I take Lamberto back home. Nico and Ada go off together. Cesare tries vainly to infiltrate into the car with them. He goes off grumbling to himself that they are all 'shits turds and bastards.'

Dida walks lightly by my side. Her white skirt flaps round her legs.

'I'm sorry about the other evening. You know I can't think why I did it. Cesare was driving me mad. Perhaps it was resentment. No – it was more like desperation.'

'Are you still attracted to Paolo?'

'No . . . Maybe yes. But I don't love him. I don't give a damn about him really you know. Perhaps that's the ideal situation for making love. If one's too much in love one gets paralysed.'

'Don't you and Cesare ever make love?'

'No. I think he hates me. What do you think?'

'I don't believe he hates you. You do mean something to him.'

'I'm afraid he's repelled by me. Haven't you noticed the way he looks at me?'

'Cesare's cantankerous with everyone.'

'He never says a word to me. He stares right through me with such crazy indifference that I get scared. Have you noticed how he screws up his eyes whenever he looks at me? As if he were overcome by a desperate desire to go to sleep every time he sees me. He can't bear me. Do you know the only time he comes to life? When he talks to me about Ada – how intelligent and courageous and extraordinary she is . . .'

'If he doesn't love you why don't you just tell him to get lost?'

'I can't. I love him. Haven't you ever been in love? Felt you'd do anything to see him. Just to be near him however stupid it may be? Even if Cesare can't bear the sight of me it doesn't make any difference. And I'm not even jealous of Ada. In fact I like her. Besides I know that love is quite beyond reason. It's not his fault if he loves her and not me. Anyway she can't stand him. It's Nico she's after. And Nico wants me. A real mess isn't it?'

'Do you remember: Helena loves Demetrius who loves Hermia who loves Lysander who loves Helena . . .'

'It only needs a few drops of juice from Puck's love-in-idleness to

19

shift the object of one's desire. I know that. But knowing it isn't going to change anything.'

'Could you fall in love with an ass's head?'

'It's enough to see him and hear him close to me even if he's thinking of someone else. It's enough to know he's in the same room...'

'And if he loved you would you still love him so much?'

'I'd die of happiness.'

'And if the malicious Puck sprinkled some of his fateful juice into your eyes and you woke up in love with someone else?'

'It's only on the stage things like that happen Armida. I shall always love him.'

'You know what they say: The herb 'always' doesn't ever grow in the garden of the king.'

'Every morning I wake up with my stomach churning. I think – I must have eaten something bad. No – it's him I've eaten. And I can't digest him. He sticks in my guts. He makes me choke. I get up. I make coffee. I realise I'm not even conscious of what I'm doing. I'm just behaving mechanically from force of habit. My thoughts are all fixed on him. I have images of him stamped permanently on my retina. I bring them to mind: him going downstairs with that sailor's waddle of his – slightly unsteady on his legs as if the world were dancing under his feet. How he narrows his eyelids when he looks into the distance and his eyes become so clear and phosphorescent. Such purity. Such purity Armida that I fall in love every time I think about it. Him pouring wine into a glass, how he holds his arms folded with his elbows at right angles like a spade. Have you noticed how he walks? He sort of staggers. He keeps knocking into things. He's afraid of letting himself go yet at the same time he's always shedding bits of his body. He stops to pick them up but he's never quite certain that they really are part of him. Isn't that odd? And have you noticed how when he waves to someone from a distance he opens and closes his fingers like children do? How could I love anyone else when every little thing about him fills me with emotion?'

Lamberto is bored by our talk. He doesn't like our being so intimate together. It makes him feel excluded. He sneezes. He gives me a scared look. His nose starts to bleed. I take out my handkerchief. But the blood has already reached his shirt and his shoes. We make the last hundred yards of the way home with Dida holding him up under one arm and me under the other.

SITTING on the pavement outside the American Embassy. Paolo beating his drum with such exaltation that he's oblivious of being in the middle of the street with the police drawn up behind his back.

Embassy clerks pressed against the windows intrigued by this fine display of Italian youth in turmoil. Who are they to demonstrate for Vietnam? What do they know about such a far-off place? What business is it of theirs? These and other eminently reasonable questions are stamped on the white faces mildly astonished mildly amused that stand out against the snowy whiteness of the Embassy ceilings.

To them we all look identical all fanatics all equally incomprehensible. Yet in their own country exactly the same thing is taking place: other bureaucrats with white faces pressed against other windows watch other young people who will not work and will not make war and will not even agree to other people making war. Who sit on pavements and talk about things they'd know nothing about if they hadn't seen it all on television.

We bend over a photograph. Dida's cheeks are streaked with tears. To break the tension she throws out a few wisecracks about American soldiers being drugged up to the eyeballs. Cesare frowns. He is moved and perhaps for the first time it occurs to him that his persistent grousing doesn't make much sense. Nico holds his hand against the pit of his stomach. Lamberto doesn't understand and keeps on asking:

'But who are all these dead people? Why have they been cut down like this? Show me Armida. Let me see too.'

'Mai Lai Lamberto is a Vietnamese village where there was a massacre.'

'And these children have no heads?'

'No they've been burned.'

'Burned because someone set alight to them with matches?'

'No. Burned with bombs.'

Mai Lai a lullaby a lick of candy floss. Between the bleached colour of the ripe grain and the overcast clouded sky a naked woman her skin shrivelled by a thousand furrows her face contorted in a grimace of horror her pagoda-shaped straw hat hanging askew over her forehead.

On the ground lying in a confused mass the bodies of disembowelled women girls with broken legs men with blackened heads. Between the straddled legs of a young girl a baby of only a few months old. Head twisted obscenely on its neck. Tummy like a balloon deformed by parasites. Struggling on its bent matchstick legs to return to the sanctuary it had so recently left. In a desperate rush before the soldiers arrive with their flame-throwers before the planes arrive with their napalm bombs before the armoured tanks arrive with the angry roar of dragons.

Five hundred people encamped in front of the American Embassy sitting resolutely on the pavement in the middle of the street. A wing of uniformed police clean-shaven faces veiled behind transparent plastic visors arms closed on shining rifles sleepy eyes staring blankly into space. They wait for the order to attack. Balancing themselves on their toes they brood over fag-ends and coffee grounds and American comics:

Nembo the Kid raises his arms. His chest expands like a balloon. A yellow buckle on a red background scintillates on his space-suit. Red and blue boots with rusty spurs on his ankles like Mercury the cunning messenger of the Gods.

Nembo the Kid bends his knee. A feeling of power and defiance rises in his throat. He quivers for just long enough to focus his eyes on the goal of his flight and then he throws himself into the air and arrives like a meteor where some square-jawed individual is thrusting his knife into the back of another desperate character with slit eyes.

Next frame: A snake-like pigtail pops out from the corner of the picture to reveal that this incarnation of the devil is really a Chinaman with a benevolent appearance. Nembo the Kid his eyes emitting showers of red-hot sparks comes diving down and with a *splash plop ugh* snatches the knife from the hands of the assassin frees the beautiful half-naked girl who lies bound to a post and throws the Chinese impostor with the pig-tail to the ground. Summoning all his wisdom and strength and dedication to heroic deeds he slips through the window without delay to seek for other abuses and injustices to

23

settle and punish.

Between the *tom tom tom* of the drum and the hoarse shouts of the others I recognise the resonant voice of Miele. He is facing the red and blue striped flag which flaps wearily in the wind against the tall flagstaff. With his mouth wide open and the veins standing out in his neck he is shouting at the top of his voice.

He shouts out his hatred of fathers the disgust he feels towards old people with their impassive faces who for twenty years have thwarted his destiny towards their self-satisfied and triumphant expressions towards their greed that has made a clean sweep of his life. He shouts against his powerlessness as a university student against the abuses of professors full of arrogance who offer nothing but the dole-queue and corruption against tutors of all kinds who want to deprive him of his freedom to come to his own decisions against the fear that makes a coward of him before he has had a chance to live against the generals who send people to die for causes in which they themselves do not believe against all those who want to grab his soul in exchange for peanuts and a scrap of security against America who in the name of peace has strewn death-dealing devices all over Italy against himself and the temptation to resign himself and just let everything go. . . .

The shouting has something reminiscent about it: a rumbling of resentment against our real fathers so respected so much loved – our fathers with their Mediterranean faces their mouths cram-full of lies their stiff stand-offish noses and astute mafioso eyes those fathers whose images we see day after day at home and in the newpapers on television in trams in bars at work to remind us every minute of every day of the obscenity of the great media dream that we are a comma a zero a worthless trinket of gold and silver.

We have been sitting here for hours but no one gives the signal to move. Every so often the windows of the Embassy open and an apprehensive face appears. The police lean first on one leg and then on the other. And as we sit we sing with a determined self-confident belief in our protest for the children of poor peasants and slum-dwellers. The photograph of Mai Lai helps us to keep up the temperature of our indignation.

I can't manage to shout like everyone else. I don't know what it is

24

that holds me back what mixture of timidity what sense of the ridiculous like a blue sucking-fish that is always submerged in the deep waters of my conscience. I join in but without that commitment that makes you forget yourself and forget danger. I see myself from inside and from the outside: embarrassed awkward all ready to gesticulate and saw the air with my fists – and then overwhelmed by the stupidity of it all.

I feel the breath of the youths in uniform on my neck. The circle is closing in. I wait for the attack. I calculate the distance between the gates of the Embassy and the first alleyway to the left between the traffic lights and the bank. I think of Marilu who had her fingers broken under a soldier's hobnail boots. I think of Mirella who had an eye pierced by a stray projectile. I fear for my own eyes and hands.

Miele is oblivious to everything. He pours out his rage against that gray facade against that flag which every so often billows up revealing a belly of white stars on blue as if he had somehow brought together all the gods and assembled them to drive home just what was going on in this shitty world that was originally their creation.

Paolo has by now really become his drum. He is inside it. From his prison he drums and drums out to all his friends to all caring people all decent people all dissatisfied people all angry people all honest people. He calls on them all to come urgently to demand justice.

TOM tom TOM tom... the beat has an obsessive majestic rhythm. It smashes the tarmac to smithereens and the old world with it. It grinds down the hateful Americans who are devouring bit by bit the bare bones of the Vietnamese peasants callously scattering their cooking pots their garments their shoes their pigs their dogs their ricefields their forests their rivers.

Dida begins to sing at the top of her voice. *We shall overcome we shall overcoooome one daaaay* dragging out the vowels like harsh blows full of torment and resentment. Her eyes moist with tears her chubby arms raised upwards her great breasts barely contained by the rows of little mother-of-pearl buttons she offers her opulent body to the martyrdom of Vietnam. The more she sings the more emotional she becomes. Everyone is looking at her with admiration as the emblem of revolutionary womanhood.

Ada watches her. She too is singing as she sits on the edge of the pavement her little brown body all ready to leap into action. She too is divided between her anger and the need for a calculated strategy for a get-away. We exchange a covert smile while we concentrate our attention on the slightest movement of the armed men behind us.

Suddenly I realise from a few small hints that the time has come. The door of the Embassy opens a little to let out a plump individual in a dark suit who disappears rapidly into the crowd. The policemen stiffen behind us. There is an outburst of shouting – a sound quite different from the shouts of the demonstrators – followed by the noise of guns being loaded with tear gas bullets. The alarm is sounded among the demonstrators who suddenly raise their voices and quicken the rhythm of their slogans.

A moment later we are surrounded and attacked. A violent prod makes me jump to one side. I am conscious of the greasy smell of a gun right alongside my nose. I am all ears and eyes. I try to guess which direction the attack is coming from and where it is building up.

Lots of people are lying on the ground. They shield their heads in their arms. They cross their hands on the back of their necks to protect them from the blows of the truncheons. They don't resist when four policemen pick them up and carry them off.

Another violent shove against my back. I don't know whether it's from a truncheon or somebody's elbow. I swerve to the right and spot a gap between bodies and slip through it. Wail of sirens in my ears. Rancid smell of battle: sweat grease gym-shoes army food smoke tarmac cigarette-ends peppermint dirt.

I find myself face to face with a head covered in blood. The boy holds his forehead between his hands. He is screaming. No one pays any attention. A chair suddenly flies down out of the blue. Heaven knows where it came from. It falls amongst the crowd knocking over two young kids who clutch at each other as they tumble.

I dodge a truncheon. It comes down on the shoulders of a young man stripped to the waist. I thrust myself forward but I am pushed back by a hundred heaving bodies. A girl throws her arms round me shrieking. A piece of her scalp hangs down over her cheekbone.

I look for Miele but I can't see him any more. I catch sight of Paolo

26

trying to protect his drum. But a policeman smashes into it with the butt of his rifle while two others hit Paolo on the head.

I rush towards him. By the time I reach the centre of the mêlée he's gone. I turn back and thread my way between bleeding bodies. Finally I manage to elbow through the crowd. I take a deep breath and rush in the direction of the via San Basilio. There standing beside the fountain with the cupid I find Paolo with blood streaming down his face. Dida is beside him washing his wounds with the edge of her skirt. Cesare is leaning against the little wall sobbing. Ada precise and controlled as an army nurse tears strips off her blouse to make bandages. She staunches the bleeding and pours water from the fountain to wash the wounds. She wrings out the bandages.

I barely have time to regain my breath when we all move on to Ada's place in the via Dei Serpenti. She lives on the top floor of an old house without a lift.

She makes us tea laced with rum and produces bread and butter and ham. Paolo continues to lament his broken drum. He doesn't seem to be a bit bothered by the wounds on his head and forehead even though they are still bleeding.

'I don't feel a thing' he says. 'You know one never does feel pain in the head. Anyway my head will mend itself but not the drum.'

'We'll get you another.'

'Drums have a character of their own. I'll never find one as lively and mellow as that one.'

Suddenly Miele arrives. His trousers are all torn and there's a big bruise on his cheek. He is in a good mood and brandishes a bottle of wine.

'Let's celebrate! It all went very well. Tomorrow the papers will be full of it. It went more than well. Did you see the crowds? Aren't you pleased?'

No one wants to think about the papers. We are stuffing down bread and butter like children coming home starved from a school expedition that has ended badly. Miele uncorks the bottle and pours out wine for us all.

Ada's place is bare and white as if it had just been whitewashed. A big window with small luminous panes looking out over rooftops.

Wooden shelves painted white. Wicker divan of her own design. White cushions. Table of glass and iron that she made herself. Two large lamps made out of five-litre wine bottles. Chinese mats. Indian cushions.

It is past eight when we sit down to eat. Dida has pains in her chest where she was hit by a rifle-butt. Paolo offers to go with her to see the doctor but he is still losing blood so Ada and Nico go. They come back at two in the morning with the stirring news that Dida has a broken rib. We go home with her. We stop at a chemist to get sticking plaster and gauze for Paolo. Miele stays close to him carrying what is left of the drum. They've said they will bury it tomorrow morning in the garden of the Villa Strolfen.

Miele leaves without saying good-bye to me. I am getting used to his indifference. I decide I too will bury all that remains of my past longings in the garden of the Villa Strolfen.

'F ILIPPO telephoned. He's having a party to celebrate the death of his father. He's asked us out to that horrible little fake mediaeval castle near Lake Bolsena.'

'When?'

'Tomorrow.'

'The others as well?'

'Of course. He's invited us all. Only tomorrow there's something I've got to do with Miele. You go first and I'll join you later.'

'What have you got to do?' I bite my tongue as soon as I've said it – I don't like to seem inquisitive. Inquisitiveness and jealousy go hand in hand. Once they start marching together they never let go of each other.

'That's our business.'

'What about Lamberto?'

'He can stay at home. After all it's only for one evening.'

'Will you take Testone?'

'Testone can stay with Lamberto.'

The next afternoon Ada and I are spinning along the via Cassia in Dida's yellow Morris. Dida is going to meet up with us later with Nico and Cesare.

'Have you ever seen Galeria?'

'No.'

'A village completely abandoned overnight with all its houses left intact. No one knows the reason. Was it the plague? Or war? Or an earthquake? No one knows. I'd like to see it again – will you come?'

She presses her small brown hands down on the steering-wheel and turns to look at me frowning. I nod yes.

'Are you sure? You aren't agreeing just to please me?'

'No. I'd really like to.'

Her habitual attitude of mistrust really dismays me. Her conviction that she's boring that people don't like her because she's unloved and unlovable. That the world is rushing smoothly on while she is there watching it from a corner as if she doesn't really understand the rules and is always on the point of having to start again from scratch. Her clear eyes open wide to the world. Her

29

straight neck her finely chiselled nose her luminous smile . . . but then she doesn't smile that often. It's as if she were set apart watching people from the sidelines always in love with someone who doesn't even notice.

We take the road to Cesano. It winds downhill between fields of maize and orchards. We reach the Church of Santa Maria in Galeria. The path leading up to the ruins is signposted – straight ahead and turn left at the red gate. We follow the dusty white road beyond the gate. The car limps up a steep track full of potholes. It ends up below a sheer cliff alongside a field scorched by the sun. We go the rest of the way on foot between overhanging rocks withered grasses mulberry bushes swollen figs dried-up leaves.

We come to a stone arch. Through it we can glimpse the outlines of ruined houses. Eye sockets without eyes. Roofs like decayed teeth opening into empty space. Floors ripped up by huge twisted roots.

'Be careful of adders!'

Me with my leather sandals! I stop irresolute looking down at my bare toes. Ada overtakes me and walks ahead lightly and quickly. I plod behind her sinking up to my knees in the coarse grass stumbling through brambles my ankles scratched my feet dusty. An empty well. One house all lopsided its door swept away. Another with windows literally threaded onto a tree-trunk which has forced its way right inside the building. In a corner steps going down into a black hole.

'Do you want to go down?'

'No! I wouldn't dare!'

Ada pulls me down by the hand laughing. It was as if she had always lived in this village among the ruins and the jungle. At the bottom we are met by the sound of a fast-flowing stream. We jump over stone doorsteps we skirt round crumbling masonry we thread our way along narrow passages between broken-down walls.

Smell of mint. Smell of grass steeped in the sun. We push forward. The vegetation gets denser. The sun disappears. Roots of trees emerge out of the ground like sinister tentacles stretching up to grasp hold of us. Above our heads the branches of oaks myrtles and acacias arch together to form a dome. We stop suddenly in front of a wall standing upright against a gap in the slope. Some climbing plant has invaded it like a tangle of snakes slithering blindly in search of refuge. Thousands of ants bustle to and fro making the matted vegetation appear to be moving: a tangle of snakes wriggling with little electric shocks.

We sit on a piece of tiled floor inside a house that has lost its roof. Ada draws her knees up under her chin. Her eyes are half-closed.

'It's lovely here isn't it?'

'It's full of ghosts.'

'When I was ten I ran away from home and ended up here. I slept here for three nights.'

'Weren't you scared?'

She laughs. She has small regular white teeth. Her eye-teeth are stained slightly with nicotine.

'Yes perhaps I was. But it was the ghosts I'd come to see.'

'And did you see any?'

'Yes I think I did. A nun... I'm not sure. A woman with her head veiled. She squatted down over there by the church. She did a pee and then went away.'

She gazes straight in front of her at the crumbling wall shimmering with ants. Her eyes are determined. A determination that gives no sense of security. It is more the child of despair. She lies down on the fallen leaves her face turned upwards towards the dilapidated roof.

'Look!'

I lie back too and focus my eyes on the ceiling. Beyond the hole in the roof the sky opens out between broken tiles and tufts of couch-grass. A window into the mysterious softness of the world. Our eyes wander upwards and are lost in the watery lightness of the misty sky.

A long silence separates us. I think she must have fallen asleep. But her breathing has the irregular rhythm of wakefulness. I don't dare to look at her. Then all of a sudden I hear her low voice dark as the darkness of her hair.

'There's something cruel in my love for Dida.'

I don't answer. I turn a little on my side so that I can hear her better.

'I keep imagining I'm undressing her by force. I imagine forcing open her legs. The thought of it fills me with bliss. I grasp her by the knees and prise open that ghostly whiteness... It's the nun I saw there when I was ten. She looks strangely like her – that hair. That moonlike beauty. That pallor that's not of this world. I've fallen in love with that pallor... for ever...'

She sniffs. Her dark profile against the wall teeming with ants creates a sense of unreality. A mirage of vegetation.

'Armida I long to do terrible forbidden things. I long to tie her up to wound her to penetrate her with my clenched fist. There's a story in the Arabian Nights about a woman who's round and white and opulent. She walks barefooted over tiger-skins a hundred bracelets tinkling on her wrists and ankles. She walks without a sound – only the slightest rustle of silk and golden coins. I know that Dida is like that story in the Arabian Nights. It's Death who is asking for my love...'

'Aren't you being a bit too literary?'

'Perhaps. But that's the image I have from when I was a child. I ran away to come here so that I could see her spring out from among the ruins.'

'It's the image of a slave.'

'I do want to be her slave. The slave of a slave. I imagine feeling her walking all over me with her sensuous perfumed feet.'

'Why haven't you talked about all this to Dida?'

'You and your common sense Armida.' She jumps up. She stretches her legs. Then she lies down again. She puts a blade of grass between her lips.

'Are you offended?'

'No. You're quite right. I'm eaten up by common sense.'

'It's impossible to feel badly towards you Armida. You're so easily hurt. I don't know if you're good. You're too scared to be really good. But you're open-hearted. I want to kiss you. May I?'

We turn on our sides. She stares into my eyes. The shadows of her eyelashes soften her sombre look. I shut my eyes. I feel her thin cold lips on mine. The weight of her narrow chest and of her brittle bones against my body. Like clasping a bird of prey and feeling its feathers in my ears its luke-warm beak on my neck and being assailed by its delicate proud breath.

But the kiss doesn't last long. She soon moves away from me tossing her small dark head.

'I'm sorry Armida. I made a mistake. Kissing you made me think of her. Forgive me. It was an impulse of simple tenderness. But not directed at you...'

'Don't worry. I know it's Dida you're in love with.'

'I made use of you to steal something that isn't yours. Forgive me.'

'And if she hadn't made up her mind never to love you? You'd love her just the same?'

'For me love is a one-sided event. Sometimes for some unknown reason it provokes a similar feeling in return. But even when it works we all love according to our own needs and obsessions and fantasies.'

'That's a very cynical and fatalistic idea of love.'

'One of these days you'll come to agree with me. Yes even you.'

She speaks as if she were twenty years older than me. She takes my hand caresses it as if it were some precious object stroking it finger by finger blowing on each nail each finger tip like a mother tenderly reassuring herself that her child is alive and growing.

We make our way back in the gathering darkness jumping between the brambles and the crumbling stones startling the glowworms and the crows as we go. The car stinks of stale cigarette smoke. Ada sits silhouetted against the car window immobilised like a royal falcon. She lights a cigarette with slow deliberate gestures. We head down the track on the clammy grey road.

FILIPPO stands at the front entrance to the castle. He waves his hand to us. Dressed in shorts and a blue-striped jersey. Short bristly light red beard. Teeth like a horse.

'I was getting worried. They told me you'd left at four.'

'We stopped off at Galeria.'

'Did you meet any ghosts?'

'Dracula and his slave' replies Ada giggling.

'Did he bite you on the neck?'

'No. It wasn't dinner-time.'

It is the first time I've seen Filippo's castle which Cesare talks of so admiringly. I think it looks horrible. A fake 12th-century round tower built of cement painted to look like large irregular stones. An unsightly terrace out of all proportion. A circular fortress. A massive structure studded with gloomy slits.

'Dracula lives here not at Galeria' comments Ada looking round her.

'I am only his humble slave!' Filippo continues with the game. He bows low and goes towards a small cupboard. He returns with a dark round-bellied bottle.

'A little iced blood madame?'

The wine flows out of the bottle gleaming dark and thick. But Filippo has nothing wicked about him. On the contrary he is filled with a sad pitiful innocence.

The interior of the castle is sumptuous. Disquietingly so. Mainly the obsessiveness of the pastiche – perfect imitations of cuirasses helmets spears cudgels tabards ancestral portraits with threatening eyes black floors rooms panelled in dark oak gigantic standard lamps with fake candles of twisted plastic spiral staircases high ceilings walls stained with damp.

'It's all fake?'

'The lot. My grandfather built it in 1895. It's based on the plan of a 12th-century English castle. Apparently he dressed like the lord of a castle of that period and expected his wife to bake the bread and his servants to make wax polish in the cellars and shoes in the attics.'

At nine o'clock Dida arrives with Cesare and Nico. A little later

Miele and Paolo. Filippo runs up and down full of excitement opening vintage bottles of wine. A variety of glasses are lined up on the table: crystal chalices bordered with gold pewter goblets opaque glasses with little white flowers embossed on white enamel beer-mugs shaped like funnels or flowers or boots. Each time he brings out a new one his face is more flushed. We amuse ourselves by drinking each wine from a different glass: blood-red wine from Sardinia white wine from Puglia rosé from Valtellina sparkling wine from Friuli wine with an aroma of strawberries from Capri milky wine from the North full dark heavy wine from Sicily.

Dida and I cook helped by Filippo's sister Smeralda. She too is red-haired and sharp-featured. She is also very pale and as melancholy as wax.

Filippo has bought an abundance of food of all sorts: fresh mullet prawns snails smoked wild boar trout fresh country saladings bunches of basil great chunks of Parmesan cheese peaches grapes water-melons and ice-cream made with Morello cherries.

Dida her hair pinned up with a red and violet plastic comb slices butters and fries. Nico chops the basil and grates the cheese. Cesare sits on a stool in the kitchen and reads a two-weeks-old newspaper. Filippo Miele and Paolo come in and out carrying plates and knives and forks.

Filippo is in a state of euphoria. 'Now that the old tyrant is dead' he shouts 'I want to swim in good wine. I want to fill my belly till it bursts. I want to shout as much as I want. I want to screw as much as I want. I want I want I want. I want frenzy I want excess I want ecstacy. Let's celebrate. Let's drink. Come on Armida drink!'

Threading my way between the saucepans with one eye on the boiling water I swallow down a glass of ice-cold wine. Dida bustles about between the hot plates looking like a bacchanalian goddess: shining with sweat her ample breasts overflowing the opening of her dress her round arms full of dimples her stomach bulging beneath her transparent skirt her bare feet smooth and unblemished her toes as plump as a child's. She dips the ladle into the bubbling oil pulls it out sniffs it takes a sprig of parsley between her fingers and plunges it into the sauce. Every so often Nico hands her a gold-rimmed wine glass

35

full of red wine and she downs it in one gulp.

We dine late towards eleven o'clock. In the circular room lit by smoky tapers. Under the forbidding eyes of the real or fictitious ancestors who look down on the white embroidered tablecloth and the dozens of shining glasses that reflect the flickering lights.

Nico gobbles up everything at top speed. No sooner has he swallowed one mouthful than his lips part and his hand reaches out for a second. Ada keeps a methodical check on each course – so much for the first course so much for the second so much for the sweet without ever being greedy or over-eating.

Miele sits next to Paolo. They laugh together. They share each other's helpings. They exchange mouthfuls and drink out of the same pewter mug. I am sitting opposite but I don't succeed in extracting a single look from him. Why do I persist? Have I also succumbed to the masochistic game of unrequited love – like Dida and Ada and Cesare and Nico? Have my eyes also been spiked with the fatal juice of love-in-idleness in the wood not far from Athens.

Filippo looks lovingly at everyone. He insists on serving himself brandishing the big silver ladle as he fills up our empty plates.

Dida looks as if she were about to explode with the intoxication of being loved. Ada gazes at her tenderly. Nico takes every opportunity to fill her plate with tit-bits. Filippo blows her kisses across the table – a Junoesque figure by Rubens disporting herself naked among sleeping tigers and lascivious pythons. Her elbows glued to the table her mouth greasy with olive oil and her huge radiant eyes resting every now and then on Cesare who is the only one openly to ignore her. Even Smeralda watches her spellbound. Even the ancestors with their disdainful mouths transfix her with covetous looks from the walls.

After supper Dida and I go to clear away but Filippo pushes us out on to the terrace: 'I'll worry about that tomorrow. Just leave it for now. Now let's think only of ourselves. Come on let's go. The moon's shining out there on the terrace.'

A clear moon gleams as if it had just emerged from a bath of oil. Round and yellow it hangs over our heads and spreads shimmering pools of liquid like a golden fringe. We lie down on foam mattresses. We are gorged with food and restless and dazed with drink.

At Filippo's request Dida starts to sing a sweet love song. Filippo clicks his tongue with pleasure. Somebody's feet tap in time with the music. We are bathed in the benign light of the moon separated from the world by a dense curtain of darkness.

'I have a distinct impression that my father is watching us' says Filippo turning towards me. He is lying on his side his head propped up on his hand. His resonant voice rises up from the depth of his distended stomach. 'Anything that was round went rotten inside him – his eyes his glands his tonsils his balls. By sheer good luck his heart wasn't round. Is one's heart round?'

He is trying to capture a spark of gaiety to lighten what he is saying but it strikes a false note. His voice reverberates with emotion. As we lie bathed in the moon's radiance we listen to him spellbound as if he were a voice from history's past.

'My grandfather died in this house as well as my father. On account of his debts. He cut his throat to avoid having to sell his castle. But half way through he changed his mind and tore through the house crying for help. That was how I saw him: with his throat hanging open and dripping blood. Have you noticed that sword hanging in the dining-room? The one with the hilt embossed with gold? That's the one he cut his throat with. My father kept it for years bloodstains and all. Then somebody cleaned it – probably my grandmother.'

Not far away a tawny owl begins to hoot. It breaks the still air with its small sad cry. Filippo stops for a moment to listen to it. He smiles. Then he begins again.

'Mine's a family of men. Women don't exist in it. My grandfather married a country girl and then banished her into the kitchen. She wasn't even allowed to kiss her own son. My father was even worse. He grabbed a beautiful girl from the village and shut her up in a convent to be educated by the nuns and when she reached the age of sixteen he married her. He gave her two children and then sent her back to the nunnery. She's still there as ill-tempered as she is chaste. Every so often I go and see her but she doesn't like me. We're too different. Yes – a family of males. In love only with themselves. Always ready to make a pass at a woman but not society women or women of their own class. No. They only fancy dancing girls

37

prostitutes foreigners women with no fathers the homeless the nameless. To fall in love was seen as a vice. My Uncle Aroldo fell in love with a prostitute and was disinherited by my grandfather. Not because she was a prostitute but because he lost his head. He was no longer in his right mind and so in a fit of rage his father turned him out.

'It's strange how the children were always male. Perhaps any female would have been strangled in her cradle. My sister Smeralda is the first woman in four generations. I think my father would have willingly strangled her. But she isn't the sort to let herself be strangled. She resisted. She won too. It was the presence of a grown-up woman in the house that destroyed his health. As if all the round parts of his body could no longer develop and ended up mummified: his eyes his balls his glands. Through a deep despairing envy of feminine rotundity. In this house as you can see everything's geared to the male. Its style its furnishings its colours its smell. Everything relates to hunting to bodies confronting bodies to duels to philandering to solitude to companionship. Women were only admitted in the kitchen and were never allowed to trespass beyond its confines. Not for them to venture into the master's household – but he could pay furtive visits at night into their pokey little servants' bedrooms. The men snatched their bit of pleasure and then made off as fast as they could so as not 'to become infected' as my grandfather put it. 'Love my boy is a terrible disease.' Without realising that in attempting to avoid the terrible disease of love he'd become infected with other terrible diseases such as syphilis and gonorrhoea ten times and thrush more often than I can remember. They were always talking about thrush and referred to it as 'candida'. Candida became the companion of my infancy. I imagined her as a tall white-faced woman. I thought she was my mother. I pined for her. Over the smell of mild tobacco eau de Cologne lavender dusty books clove-scented brilliantine shaving soap whisky and soda Candida reigned in my childhood dreams. I'd imagine I heard the front-doorbell ringing. I ran to see. The door opened and a beautiful woman all dressed in white entered saying 'I am Candida. Take me in your arms.'

THE terrace gleams white under the moonshine. Everyone appears to be asleep. Ada curled up in a corner her knees up to her chin her bent head very dark barely lapped by the light. Cesare stretched out next to her his eyes shut his face turned to the sky. Nico on his stomach with his arms crossed under his forehead lying next to Dida who seems to be the only person awake and alert. Her full red skirt bunched over her white knees her back leaning against the low wall that borders the terrace her fair face turned towards Filippo. Smeralda lying quite still stretched out along the top of the wall.

'The local people say there's a mystery about this castle' Filippo starts again his voice hoarse and vibrant. 'A curse that makes it fatal for anyone to live here. But I know the real reason. There's no curse. The mystery of this house is the mystery of the family. And the mystery of the family is this belief in their own divinity. The fatal sin of pride. There was God the Father. Then there was Christ the Son. Weren't the Trinity all men? Father Son and Holy Ghost? My father's family had this divine presumptuousness: to do without the feminine. To become simultaneously both fathers and mothers. To give life to sons bypassing the maternal womb. To nourish them. To educate them. To create them in their own likeness. To perpetrate for all time this defiance of nature. And they almost succeeded. I am the last of four generations of patriarchs. I grew up with the conviction that woman is a shadowy unknowable entity. I only knew the father: his body his smell his nourishment his comfort. And what's the result?'

His laugh freezes us. A laugh that transforms itself into a despairing hatred and denial of himself.

'The result is that my heart is as deaf as a stone. I love no one except the great goddess Candida. I don't know whether I'm attracted by women or by men. I can only make love with myself. Complicated rituals that begin and end in my grandfather's vast mahogany bed. I'd like to suck a woman's breast. But I feel that the moment I do I'll die of fear. I've stayed imprisoned in this place for too long. Now I'm free and I'm all alone. My father is dead. I asked you here to break a spell. The woman transformed into a fox. Do you remember? Only if a man loves her as a fox can she return into her own skin and flesh. I'm looking for that man. Or that woman. I don't know which . . .

'What did you think of the wine? We've got a full cellar. But I'd like to smash every single bottle. I'd like to go and live in Rome in a little flat in the suburbs in some anonymous district with my enchantress. My sister Smeralda. But I already know I shall never do it. If I go away from this place even for a night I feel myself suffocating. I need its ugliness and its smells and for that matter its ghosts too.'

'Dida please may I kiss your breast? Don't refuse me. I'm asking for it as an act of grace. Let your breast be kissed by the most humble and most perverted of men.'

Dida looks at him for a minute without comprehending. Then she smiles. Her generosity overcomes her trepidation. Without moving she unbuttons her red blouse and brings out a heavy swollen breast. Filippo crawls up to her on all fours. He curls up between her legs like a month-old baby and opening his large bearded mouth attaches himself to her breast.

Ada makes a sudden movement as if she wants to interrupt this wicked game. But then she changes her mind. She curls up even more impenetrably into the dark corner of the terrace. Cesare sits up bewildered. Nico pokes his head out like a glow-worm startled in its sleep. Smeralda seems to have remained unconscious but something in her breathing shows that she is awake and alert.

I feel affected by that scene. An event both tender and spectral at the same time. A bearded man in the depths of despair in the arms of a plump Junoesque woman with white flesh. Trapped in the glassy light of the moon. Chaste and distanced like a tender religious sculpture. It is Candida embracing her son. There amongst us. In the castle with its curse. In the middle of a scorched and decaying countryside with no accompaniment except the eerie cry of a night owl.

I AM asleep in Paolo's arms. A bitter taste in my mouth from having drunk too much wine. My stomach blown out. My eyelids heavy. I dream I'm going to be sick. All I want is to run away. I raise myself on tiptoe I force my arms apart I kick my legs and I sail upwards. I am flying.

I wake up freezing cold. Paolo is no longer in the bed. For a moment my glance wanders over the walls which are lined with black and yellow striped paper. From behind a massive cornice an old man fixes me with a smouldering look as if he were consumed by a lust that has somehow lived on after his death.

I get up and guided only by the blue light of the moon grope my way slowly towards the door. The corridor is pitch dark. I feel as if I were in a third-rate horror movie: you turn a corner and find yourself face to face with a mediaeval warrior his legs and arms encased in shining metal his face hidden behind a helmet with dark fissures in it. Further on the head of a stag springs from the wall. Antlers as sharp as knives. Dead eyes exuding melancholy.

I turn the handle of the door that opens on to the stairs. Ada is sitting by the window. She watches me as I come through. She is holding a lighted cigarette in her hand.

'Can't you sleep?'

'No.'

'Wasn't Dida sleeping in the same room as you?'

'Yes.'

'Where is she now?'

'I don't know.'

'Is she with Paolo?'

'I don't know.'

She is lost in sorrowful contemplation. Her small amber eyes look out into empty space. She trembles ever so slightly.

'Are you feeling bad?'

'No. I'm going to bed now. You go to bed too.'

'Have you seen Paolo?'

'Ah! You're jealous.'

'I don't know. I woke up and found the space beside me empty. I

41

want to know where he is.'

'Let him be. Go back to sleep.'

I brush her cheek with my lips. I close the door. But I don't go back to my room. I continue down the corridor. I stop in front of closed doors. I try another door-handle. It gives easily. Inside the room Nico is sleeping naked stretched across an enormous four-poster bed.

I close the door. I proceed along the corridor. I descend a few steps and enter another passage narrower than the first. I go down some thickly carpeted stairs. I am again in front of a dark door carved with a fake bas relief: men carrying guns a pack of dogs with upright tails dead hares hanging head downwards ducks lying on their backs with broken legs. I lean slowly on the doorhandle. I push it downwards. The heavy door swings open by itself. The room is cut by a ray of light coming through a broken shutter. On the bed are two male bodies intertwined.

I stand transfixed watching this marble composition that moves imperceptibly with a slow contraction of muscles. Could one of them be Paolo? In that case who is the other? Miele? Filippo? Cesare? While I am hesitating they become aware of me and I am forced to beat a hasty retreat muttering excuses.

While I lean panting against the door I feel a hot breath on my neck. I turn round. It is Miele. Washed combed and dressed. A sly look. Happy. Only his flushed cheeks evidence of the wine he has drunk.

'At last I've found you.'

'I was looking for Paolo.'

'Come.' He pulls me by the wrist. We go down a flight of stairs. We open two doors and go through two rooms full of armour. We emerge into a dense overgrown garden. Miele pushes me up against a big pear tree and kisses me. I can't see his eyes. I'm aware of the smell of his aroused body. But I don't feel a thing. I am stiff and silent. He loosens his hold. He looks at me surprised.

'What's the matter?'

'I've been stuck in that garden at the tennis club. I watched you disappear so I gave you up. Now I don't understand what's going on.'

'I'm sure you love me.'

'How come you're so sure?'

'Because I love you. And I feel that you want me too.'

'But why haven't you said anything all these months?'

'Don't you like surprises?'

'No I don't.'

He throws his head back and laughs. I take his hand. I feel it soft and warm between my fingers.

'I love you so much Armida. So much that I'm afraid. I've been running away from you as fast as I can. I've got into a real mess because I didn't want to admit to myself that I loved you. The more I denied loving you the more I loved you. Now I know it. You can drive me away. I shan't force you. I only want you to know. I love you Armida. It's a stale word. I know it's stupid and old-hat. Something out of a pop-song. But who cares? I've got to tell you because I've got to. I've got to fill my mouth with it: I love you!'

'And Paolo?'

'What's Paolo got to do with it? In any case he's intelligent enough to understand love isn't concerned with friendship or with loyalty or that sort of rubbish.'

'Let me think about it Miele.'

'I'll give you all the time you want. You don't know how much lighter I feel from having told you I love you. I've been playing a game for far too long. Now you know it. Do what you want but love me Armida. Love me!'

'Do you remember – Traviata? "Love me Alfredo like I love you."'

We both laugh. Miele holds my face between his open palms. He looks at me with a frenzied intensity I hardly recognise in him. But I am in a hurry to escape. I free myself from his arms and rush back to my room like a robot.

WHEN Paolo gets up in the morning he has the wise melancholy face of an old shepherd living in the mountains – someone who spends his time talking to the sheep and the stars and who can distinguish edible plants from poisonous ones at a glance who can find a bird's nest in the middle of a thorn bush yet who's incapable of crossing a street in the city traffic. Incapable of understanding what's going on inside his own dark imperturbable soul.

He stands in front of me in the kitchen. His face looks as if it has spent twenty years being carved by the wind. His hands grasp for the bread. He fingers it greedily. He cuts it with painstaking precision.

'How would you like it if we had a child?'

He looks up. His face shrunken. Blind. He puts his hand to his ear as if he hadn't heard properly. I repeat the question.

'What's got into your head?'

'I'm pregnant Paolo.'

He smiles. He hands me a slice of buttered bread. Mechanical meaningless gestures. His eyes open a little wider. He stops smiling.

'Since when?'

'Two months.'

'Are you certain?'

'Yes. I've been for a check-up.'

A long silence. He puts his head in his hands.

'It's really true?'

'Yes it is.'

He puts his arms round me. Hesitantly. Moved. Cold. Matrimonial reserve has left him tongue-tied. A reserve that makes us behave like strangers when we are closest. 'What should I do?' He looks lost. Suddenly scared.

'Nothing.'

'How do you mean – nothing?'

'Nothing. It's my belly the child is growing in.'

'I'll help you.'

'Good.'

'I want to be with you when it's born. It's mine too...'

'I know that.'

'I want to be there to see it come out of you.'

'Good.'

He is seized by the fascination of fatherhood. He leapfrogs through all the stages of pregnancy. Already he sees his son growing up. Little legs encased in woollen trousers. Intent on following life's long difficult road hand in hand with his daddy.

Lamberto comes in. All dressed up in blue. A knotted scarf encircling his throat doing duty for a tie.

'Where are you off to?'

'Going for a ride on the bus.'

'Is that why you're dolled up to the nines?'

He takes a large slice of bread and butter from his brother and goes over to eat it by the window.

'Do you know that you're soon going to have a nephew?'

'How's that?'

'Armida is pregnant.'

'Well well.'

'Don't say that. You sound just like my grandfather.'

He is holding the half-eaten slice of bread between two fingers. He stops chewing. He looks at us suspiciously from behind his thick lenses. His lips tremble. He swallows painfully.

'I do declare you're jealous!'

Paolo smiles at him with benevolent complicity. Lamberto shakes his head. Big drops of blood run from his nose slide along his lips course down his chin and drop one by one on to the buttered bread.

'Get the ice Armida. No wait – I'll get it. From now on I don't want you to lift a finger. Can I tell Elizabetta?'

'Of course. Tell her.'

He rushes into the bedroom to telephone his mother. I hear him talking excitedly on the phone punctuating every sentence with giant exclamation marks. Testone comes in and lays his nose on my knee. He wants me to take him out. I pour some milk into his bowl. He laps it up with his tongue splashing milk all over the floor. I put newspaper under his bowl – but he has already finished. I get Testone's lead and go towards the front door. Paolo's excited voice reaches me:

'Where are you going to you idiot? I'll take Testone out.'

45

'When?'

'As soon as I've finished talking to my mother.'

I put down the lead. I sit in front of my writing desk. Maybe I shall be able to start re-writing that play I was working on some time ago. But I hear Paolo's voice still booming with excitement:

'I'll do the shopping today. Where's the lead? You clean the house and I'll do everything else. Bye bye Armida!'

I PARK in front of a rusty gate in the via Properzio. I turn the corner and slip through the entrance to number 15. I go up the staircase I ring the bell. No response. I am about to leave when I see a note poking out from under the door. 'For Armida.' A small envelope stuck down with glue. Fine handwriting. Delicate and rounded. I open it and read: 'Back late. Keys are with the porter. Wait for me. I love you. Miele.'

'The most compromising verb in the world' Cesare would say. 'A verb that sounds a note so absolutely false and out of fashion that no one can pronounce "I love you" without feeling ridiculous.'

I remain standing in front of the closed door with the note in my hand. 'I love you. Miele.' He's not afraid of feeling ridiculous. A sentence so looked down on and so unfashionable doesn't disconcert him at all. I am not put off by his fearless self-confidence. On the contrary all I think of is how I shall kiss him when I see him.

I leap down the three hundred stairs that separate the fourth floor from the porter's room. I collect the keys. I climb the stairs again two at a time. I open the door. I throw myself down on the bed seized by an irresistible happiness.

I get up and go into the kitchen. I fill a glass with water. I gulp it down. I go into the sitting-room. I turn on the radio. The deep harsh voice of Ida Cox. I start dancing bare-foot alone in the middle of the room. 'Oh baby baby I am all alone and you are gone . . . Baby baby I am alone . . .'

Suddenly I collapse on the floor. I am worn out and I lie there flat out waiting. Every time I hear a footstep outside the door I lift my head. But it's never him. Someone on the floor above is doing exercises on the piano. Do re sol do re sol do re sol. I look at my watch. It's eight o'clock. Miele hasn't come back. Paolo will be waiting for me. Lamberto has to eat. I must go home. I scribble a note telling him that I waited for him. I leave.

While we are having supper the phone rings. I know it's him. I rush to the phone. Yes it is his tender voice at the other end of the line.

'I'm sorry about today.'

'It doesn't matter.'

47

'I'm in love with you Armida. I'm crazy about you. I can't think of anything else. You're always there in front of me. Tell me that you want me. Just tell me that if you don't want me to die.'

'I came to you to say exactly that.'

'That you love me?'

'Yes.'

Silence at the other end. I think the line must have been cut off.

'Are you there?'

'I'm here.'

'You aren't speaking.'

'I've got no breath. I've got cramp in my stomach. God how I love you Armida. But don't be scared. I won't push you I won't put pressure on you. I love you for what you are and for how you are. I love you and that's that! Even if you betray me even if you don't care a damn about me don't ever forget that I love you...'

Now it's me who can't eat. I go back to the dining table. I try to nibble something. But my stomach is closed and barred. Paolo is so taken up by new thoughts of fatherhood that he's oblivious of my change of mood. Lamberto guzzles away at the potato pie I made for him.

'Have you thought where we'll put him?'

'Who?'

'The baby Armida my silly love the baby.'

'No I haven't.'

'I've been thinking. He can be in our bedroom for a few months while you're feeding him. But after that it would be a nuisance and anyway it would be better for him to sleep on his own. Lamberto's room wouldn't be suitable. Nor the sitting room. I've been thinking of your study. What do you think about that? We could put the table on one side and have the bed in the middle. We could have new curtains and some white-lacquered furniture.'

The doorbell rings. I go to open it. Dida rushes in throwing her arms round my neck. Behind her come Ada and Cesare and Nico.

'Congratulations Armida congratulations.' They all kiss me shake my hands and dance round me.

'Have you decided what you'll call it yet?'

48

'I haven't given it a thought.'
'Call it Narcisso.'
'Why?'
'Because he'll be male and blond and handsome. He couldn't be anything but a Narcisso.'
'No call him Giorgio Leone.'
'Call him Nelson.'
'What if it's a girl?'
'What about Giocasta?'
'Iolanda.'
'Why not Petunia?'
'For heavens sake leave her in peace. Can't you see she's tired?'
Paolo puts his arm round my waist and escorts me to the armchair. He gives me a gentle push to make me sit down. He brings me a glass of lemon and water.

I GET into the car. Awkwardly. My belly already quite large. I am short of breath. I start the engine. I drive off down the via Cassia. It is hot. The wheels glide softly over the tarmac. Along the road the grass is burnt and the trees swell with shadow.

I arrive at the castle soaking with sweat my eyes dazzled by the sun. It seems uglier and more spectral than ever. I leave the car open with my bag inside and walk clumsily up the steps. Before ringing the bell I tidy my hair and try to get my breath under control. Filippo opens the door. His sallow face sliced vertically by the light through the opening. He says 'Oh' with his eyes his mouth his nose. His moustache is dripping with milk.

'It's you Armida? How are you doing? I wasn't expecting you. How nice! Come in come in.'

Inside it is dark and cool. There's a smell of tobacco and boiled cabbage. I sit down on a hard chair with a back of tooled leather. I ask him for a glass of water.

'Here's water for you. Now tell me – what are you doing here?'

'I'm looking for Miele.'

'But why here?'

'I don't know. Paolo told me he often comes to see you.'

'I haven't seen him for three months. Where is he?'

'I don't know.'

'He could be away on his travels. Miele can't stay in the same place for more than a couple of months. He's got friends here there and everywhere. Why don't you telephone his friend Gunther in Zurich. He could be there.'

'Do you have the number?'

'No I haven't. But Dida would be sure to have it.'

'Why Dida? What's Dida got to do with it?'

'Didn't you know that she and Miele have been involved with each other?'

'When?'

'A few months ago.'

'How do you mean – a few months?' I look at him in bewilderment.

'Why are you in such a state about where he is?'

50

'He's disappeared for over a month.'

'Ah . . . So you're in love with him too?' He fixes me with a sly look. His moustache is still soaked with milk. His eyes soft. Malicious. I want to tell him to mind his own business. But I don't.

'Where's Smeralda?'

'I don't know. Yesterday Paolo phoned to ask her to go to the seaside with him. Haven't you seen her?'

Filippo is in his element. Trapped in his baleful castle we play a game of cat and mouse with each other. A game of licking one's whiskers that has come at just the right moment to interrupt the monotony of his solitary life.

'Is it true you're expecting a baby?'

'Isn't that a bit obvious?'

He looks down at my belly. He stretches his mouth into a smile that is almost a grimace. I don't know if it's out of fear or disappointment or envy or pain. Now he is no longer playing. His face becomes bloodless. His kindly grey eyes take on a sad humble look.

'Are you pleased?'

'Yes and no.'

'Why yes and no?'

'Because I see the future as something very confused and I'm not very interested in it. A mother should be worrying about the future shouldn't she? But I'm not really given to thinking about it. Right now all I can think about is Miele and the fact that I can't find him.'

'Did you know I can see into the future like an ancient sorcerer?'

'You Filippo?'

'Yes. I see because I am blind. The present has no interest for me. I'm only interested in the past and its involuntary transformation into the future.'

'What do you see there?'

'I see . . . I see a black baby. Now . . . I see a window. You're leaning out of it dangerously far. Perhaps you're going to throw yourself out. But I don't think so because you're still wearing shoes. Your feet are ever so pink.'

'What's the meaning of a black baby?'

'I don't know. Perhaps it means death. Perhaps it means

51

something else – unhappiness.'

'You're a very obscure sibyl. Also a rather ill-intentioned one.'

'Don't interrupt me Armida. I'm experiencing a moment of grace... I see you in a railway carriage. There's a man sitting by himself drinking. He's crumbling your heart to pieces between his fingers.'

'Miele?'

'I see you in hospital. You're in bed eating pork...'

'How dreary you're being Filippo. You're talking like a bogeyman. Stop telling me all these horrible things. Tell me I'm going to have a lovely baby and that I'll be happy with Miele and that my plays will be staged.'

'The fox will succeed in crossing the lake but it will come out of the water with its tail soaking wet. Perhaps without a tail at all. And what is a fox without its tail?'

'It's this house that fills you with these sickening thoughts. Why don't you sell it and come to live in town?'

'Yes I'll sell it. I can't go on living here. But I'm not sure I'll be able to live anywhere else either.' He rests his transparent yellowish hands on a marble table-top and looks at me with widening eyes. 'I'd lose my past. Then what would I have to sustain myself with?'

'You're talking like an old man.'

'Do you know the other day I found I was calling the dogs in just the same voice as my father used to. And last night I dreamed I was dressed up like my grandfather and going out to hunt with his dog Babo that died years ago.'

I kiss his cheeks and drive home hell for leather in a stream of cars along the Cassia motorway.

I wake up. It is the middle of the night. I feel as if I am fainting. Drenched in sweat. A sense of utter exhaustion. All my strength gone. I open one eye. I see myself. I am lying prostrate on the bed. I put my hand between my legs. I withdraw it. It is wet. I lift my fingers up in front of my eyes. They are red with blood.

I get out of bed. I can't stand up. I shout 'Paolo'. He wakes with a start. He looks at me anxiously. I ask him to get me a towel. And some cotton wool. I stuff my pants with cotton wool. I try to get back to

52

sleep. Paolo is already asleep again with his mouth pressed against my naked shoulder. Damp warmth of his saliva on my chest. My eye settling on the carved window frame as it watches me opening my mouth breathlessly like a fish. Blood still gushing out. I press my belly with my hands. I am scared that the child will slip away lost in this violent flood. I wake up Paolo again. He gazes at me in a fright. Incredulous. He kisses my shoulder not knowing what to do.

'It's my child too. I don't want to lose him like this.'

'Go and fetch a doctor quick!'

'And leave you here all alone?'

'Ask Lamberto to bring me a glass of water.'

I try to raise myself into a sitting position but my legs won't respond. The blood has already soaked through all the cotton wool and is flooding through the towel on to the bed. Paolo looks at me. He can't make up his mind to get dressed. He picks up a shoe and throws it down again. He runs into the bathroom and comes back immediately with the soap in his hand. He puts it down on the bed while he goes to look for his shoe.

'What the fuck has happened to you Armida? If only I knew what's wrong. If only I could understand...'

'Go Paolo. Run.'

'I'm going. I'm going. But where the hell have my socks disappeared to?'

'Go without socks. There isn't time....'

But he can't get himself dressed. He returns to the bed. Kisses my forehead. Grabs hold of my hand. Runs into the kitchen. Brings me water. Puts on one shoe. Finds he still has his pyjamas on. Takes off the shoe to get out of the pyjamas. And then can't find the shoe any more. My eye is still there on the window frame and I watch myself fading away. I press both hands against my stomach deluding myself that I can stop this torrent. But the blood goes on gushing out in leaps and bounds flooding spontaneously into rivulets and streams.

'Paolo call the ambulance. Tell them I'm dying. Call the ambulance!'

'Yes yes I'll call them immediately. But why didn't we think of that before? How are you? How are you feeling?'

53

'Call the ambulance.'

'The number? Do you know the number?'

'Paolo...' I begin. Then I fall head first on to the floor. When I come to I am in bed in hospital. Bed number 55. In a room with eight other women two needles stuck into my veins sticking plaster on my wrists and Paolo's eyes fixed on me.

A tall woman with a Venetian accent is comforting me with reassurances. Her face two inches away from my nose. 'We've managed to keep the baby! Isn't that good?'

I look past her at Paolo who smiles at me. Exultantly.

'The baby's alive! Do you understand Armida? It's alive!'

He seizes my hands and presses them tight. He kisses my cheek passionately. I'd like to say something to him but my tongue is stuck to the roof of my mouth. All I want is to go to sleep.

A<small>T</small> two o'clock Paolo arrives with a well wrapped parcel. Inside it are clean nightdresses books mineral water sleeping pills coloured handkerchiefs eau-de-Cologne. He places them all gently on top of the metal bedside table. He gives me a kiss. He looks round. He has already made friends with my neighbours in the surrounding beds: Maria the country girl from Maccarese. Pina who has a fruit stall at Vigna Clara. Teresa the shop assistant from the via del Gambero. Gesuina the elderly countess from the Parioli district. Velia who is a student at the high school.

At four o'clock Paolo leaves. He comes back in the evening at seven even though it is outside visiting hours. He gives the porter a tip to let him through. The ward is still full of mothers aunts nieces daughters cousins who come mostly at night to help those patients who are more seriously ill.

Sometimes Lamberto comes with him. Or Dida. Or Cesare with Ada and Nico. They bring me red wine. 'It'll give you a lot of good red blood Armida. Drink it!' But I give it to Pina in exchange for some fresh fruit. They laugh and joke and sit on my bed and tell me about all the latest political manoeuvrings. Every time I see them arriving I long to catch sight of Miele's chestnut hair amongst their heads. But I never do. And no one knows where he is.

I read one book after another. I amuse myself talking to my neighbours. So long as they don't start talking about their illnesses. Then I give up. I turn round and face the wall. Luckily I have a bed next to it and I can read in peace. They are understanding and don't take offence if I suddenly shut up like a clam.

My story affects them: they have taken me under their wing. Particularly the Countess Gesuina and the fruit-seller Pina. In their eyes I am a young woman in danger of losing her baby but whose haemorrhage has been arrested by the magical art of the gynaecologist. 'He's got the hands of an angel.' A young wife adored by her husband who is for ever bringing her cakes and flowers and who sits on the bed holding her hands in his and who stays for hours on end without getting weary.

Most of the women are there because of botched abortions: gashed foetuses perforated through clumsiness poisoning from concoctions of parsley and bleach. Even old Gesuina who looks sixty but is actually only forty has had an abortion that went wrong.

In the evening they gather round Pina's bed and play cards. In silence. Tense and concentrated. They play for money and anyone who interrupts them had better look out. Only occasionally is a voice raised when someone gets angry. But the others give her a pinch to make her shut up. When the nurse arrives she tries to stop them but there's no way they are going to take any notice of her.

One day Paolo brings Smeralda. She is nervous and bites her nails. She looks at me as if she doesn't see me. Flames of red hair envelop half her face. A spectral look which reminds me of her brother. Only brought to life by a handful of scattered freckles.

Paolo behaves towards her like a father. He is solicitous and yet uneasy. She puts a tin of biscuits on the bedside table. He hands me a bottle of Spanish brandy. As soon as they've gone I give them away in return for some figs picked fresh from the tree.

'Are you in love with her?' I ask him when he comes back in the evening.

'She attracts me. But it's you I love Armida. And this baby who'll soon be born. I love him too.'

'Why don't you tell me the truth? Everyone treats me as if I were dumb.'

'I've told you she attracts me. Yes we make love sometimes. But I don't love her. Do you understand? Anyway I've no intention of losing you or of losing my child.'

'Nice of you to tell me.'

'It's you I love Armida. No one but you.'

He said it with absolute sincerity. With the complete conviction that things which are only partially true have when they are underpinned by a vision of the future.

Every so often the nurse appears. She uncovers my belly and places a very small plastic funnel on my skin next to my navel. She presses it against her ear and listens with her eyes shut. Then she gets up smiling triumphantly.

'Baby's all right Armida. Well done. Well done.' And off she goes

56

tap-tap-tapping the high heels of her white shoes.

Now I can feel the baby beneath my open palm. A projection that could be a knee. A roundness that is possibly a head. An occasional half-hearted kick. It comes alive most of all when I am sleeping with my belly as motionless as possible on account of that unstoppable river of blood that still flows day after day from between my legs in spite of the huge quantities of vitamin K I am taking.

'But the baby will make it' the doctor says swallowing a mouthful of saliva that I imagine must taste ever so sweet judging by the way he rolls it round his tongue savouring it and sometimes spits it into a small mauve handkerchief and looks at it lovingly.

His orders are: 'Lie completely still. Keep eating. Rest. Sleep. Drink a lot. Don't think about anything.'

I remain nailed to the mattress without daring to move a millimetre. I eat like a horse: rare steaks pasta cream cheese cakes. Everything tastes of egg-yolk and unwashed saucepans. Like when I was at boarding-school. I gobble it all up without tasting it without giving it a thought forcing it down the funnel of my throat. I drink pints and pints of milk. I've become enormous: my arms have doubled in size. My breasts are a dead weight brimming over on to my chest.

'It'll be a boy' Gesuina tells me one day as she dangles over my belly a ring suspended by one of my hairs. 'If it swings to and fro it's a girl and if it goes round and round it's a boy.'

The ring starts to go round and round in a frenzy. Satisfied she stops it with an elegant gesture.

'It'll be a boy. I guarantee that.' And she kisses me on the mouth.

'Supposing I want a girl?'

'But it isn't for you to decide. It's fate.'

'Not God?'

'What do you think such trivialities matter to God? Our Lady can decide such women's things. But our Lady never says a word because she's afraid of God. She stays silent and when He gets back home in the evening and says "Madonna have you been good today?" She tells Him "Yes" and if it's not true He gives her a kick – '

'So who's Fate?'

57

'A woman with a hat. . . . If you ever meet her on the street she smiles at you as if to say "I haven't time I haven't got time –" She's forever running from one house to another from one bed to another. She thinks of everything – all the little things that God doesn't see: love affairs intrigues jealousies gossip births abortions. Etcetera etcetera.'

'God doesn't see abortions?'

'What do you expect Him to see? His mind is on the infinity of the universe. Abortions are women's trifles . . . small inconveniences . . . That's what she thinks with her hat always askew always in a rush when she's needed and as often as not arriving too late because like all women she's got too much to do.'

H E'S mischievous this son of mine! Whenever I'm asleep he wakes me up by giving me a kick in the side. I turn my head on the pillow. I take a deep breath. There he is curled up in a ball. Watchful as ever. A bit browned off that I'm no longer asleep so that he can wake me up with one of his little loving thumps.

Towards five in the morning I doze off and then hey presto he gives me a cheerful little kick – Mummy wake up it's morning and I'm here and you're an old silly hiding yourself away. Why don't you get up why don't you fly away carrying me with you over the rooftops?

I call the nurse and ask her to put me on the bedpan. He sniggers. My perpetual need to pass water amuses him and he breaks into little bursts of laughter. Sometimes I echo him without thinking and the nurse looks at me in alarm her rigid eyebrows like bar-lines above her severe eyes.

Paolo is very excited by these internal movements which reveal the personality of his son.

'He really makes himself felt. You can see it. He's like me when I get angry.' He laughs. He presses his ear against my belly and listens avidly.

'He's kicking he's really kicking. Can you feel his feet his little feet Armida?'

Filled with enthusiasm and euphoria he longs to snatch him out of my womb without a second's delay and take him for a walk. Not that my womb is a very secure place for him its door bolted and barred against him for ever threatened by haemorrhages and by drowning in its slimy waters. To be safe and sound in his bamboo cot on a woollen mattress covered by a blue sheet decorated with little chickens would certainly be safer. Paolo would watch over him better than I do. I am too distracted too full of aches and pains and perhaps not very maternal anyway. Paolo would bring him up scientifically according to all the latest paediatric research lifting him gently on his back and placing him on silver scales warming the milk to just the right temperature wrapping him in the white hand-made shawl that used to belong to his mother.

Paolo looks at me with a mixture of tenderness and reproof. How is it possible that I am incapable of achieving the simplest thing in the world – something that even the most primitive woman knows how to do?

One morning he arrives with his mother the beautiful Elizabetta laden with presents and money. She sits on the bed and covers my face with kisses. The sweet vivacious Elizabetta . . . who lives in Milan and owns a chain of shirt manufacturers. She's had three husbands and supports two of them as well as the three of us Paolo Lamberto and me. And now she will have the little grandchild to keep as well. She has the sort of impetuous and slightly brusque openhandedness of someone who is used to being in command.

'You can't stay in this awful place Armida. We'll pack up everything and go to Milan. My dear child as far as I can see the doctors here in Rome are a lazy irresponsible bunch and the hospitals are absolute rubbish-tips. I'd like to see you in a nice room with lots and lots of flowers and a nurse all to yourself.'

'But mother I can't move!'

Her laughter is infectious. She seizes my wrist and pulls off my blanket. She looks between my legs. I try to hold back that trickling stream that flows inexorably towards my damnation. But I don't succeed. Just as her head draws close a huge black clot slips out. I give it a quick sideways glance of shame.

'It's madness my love. Do you want to lose the child? I shall get you out of here as soon as I possibly can. Let's go let's go.'

I insist that I can't move. She shakes her head as if to say 'leave it all to me.'

Two hours later she arrives with four nurses and a light folding stretcher. They shift me and all my bedclothes straight on to it without me even having to get out of bed. They carry me out to an ambulance which takes me to Milan in five hours flat with its siren going full blast all the way.

The Villa Santa Chiara Clinic. Sparkling clean. Very quiet. Swimming in the scent of fresh flowers. A room all to myself with a television set in front of the bed a big window veiled by pale yellow curtains a glass light globe above my head. A green-tiled bathroom which I am not allowed to use. I am forced into total immobility.

Even more so than before. Now I can't even turn over on to my side.

I am looked after by two doctors. One comes in the morning: he is short thin bald elderly formal. The other visits in the evening: he is a brusque young man a bit on the plump side with tufts of hair sprouting out of his ears and nostrils.

Paolo sleeps on the bed next to mine. When he can't be there my mother-in-law Elizabetta sleeps there. She's very sure of herself. Reasonable yet masterful. She gets exactly what she wants from people without ever having to resort to compulsion. She uses gentle persuasion and infects them with her enthusiasms. She's generous her arms are always filled with presents. She's never heavy-handed and never expects anything in return. Her only aim is to overwhelm people with her passionate faith that in the end anything and everything is possible if only one wants it enough.

My belly however refuses to become involved. It's full of ill-will towards this over-demanding child. It can't resist this stream of fresh blood as red as Chinese lacquer gushing from my womb. However vexed Elizabetta gets and however much I am seduced by her optimism the malevolent stream continues to flow. However much my veins are lacerated by the hundreds of injections they give me at all hours of the day and night there are ever more massive blood-clots. And I'm only too aware of the risk that clots forming in the arteries can cause paralysis and death.

My mind is a blank. I've put my trust entirely in the doctors. I've surrendered myself to them: to the formal one in the morning who feels my belly and takes my pulse and looks into my eyes and then bows and departs. And to the one in the afternoon whose cheeks always bear the imprint of a pillow and a watchstrap as if to proclaim that he's had a good afternoon nap. They can no longer find anywhere to insert their needles for the blood transfusions. Sometimes they stick them in my ankles sometimes in my wrists and sometimes in my neck. The search for a vein can last anything up to half an hour. The doctor gets impatient and tells me to be a good girl and not to get agitated though actually he is the one who's agitated and sweating as he pushes in the needle hits a vein loses it tries again loses it gets discouraged and takes offence as if the vein had a personal grudge against him.

I slip into a state of defenceless passivity that is my only resource. As I face the struggle to survive I let myself go totally inert. All I want is to be left in peace. I surrender myself into their hands because resisting them only brings pain. I am reduced to a dead weight: a slob who is crumbling to pieces my eye-sockets eating me to death my face and my back aching all over incapable of wishing for anything except to put an end to it all.

Y ET there is a kind of understanding between me and my son that reaches beyond the needles the blankets my aching flesh and the viscous water that imprisons him. An unwritten and unspoken pact that whatever else may happen we shall always stay together. Sometimes I find myself watching the nurse with a derisive ironical smile. No one not even the top doctors in Milan not even my fantastic mother-in-law Elizabetta seems to understand the cause of this haemorrhage. No one has a clue how to stop it.

Only my son and I know what it's all about: a carefree silent determination to challenge the natural laws of pregnancy. This child cherished longed for and loved even before he is born is cocking a snook at anyone who treats him as already theirs. He is involving himself in a risky yet intoxicating game: to perform the most incredible acrobatics inside my swollen belly without for a moment entertaining the possibility that he might break his collar-bone. He is safe with me and I with him. Together we'll make it in spite of the whole world.

Every so often the thought of Miele drifts disquietingly to the surface of my mind. It fills my head. I imagine him walking somewhere in some part of an unknown world full of blue and red parrots with a pocket edition of Marx in his hand.

But that other one inside my belly is jealous. He can't stand the thought or even a hint of anyone except himself. He suddenly turns a somersault angrily pulling at the ropes of my belly and making me snatch my breath.

'Mama how can you wander so far away when I'm risking my life for you?' And he laughs gleefully at having given me a fright. What he wants is for all my attention all my thoughts all my pleasure all my desires to centre on him and on him alone.

The days pass calmly and monotonously. At fixed intervals I am lacerated by needles. Everyone treats me more and more as if I were a house inhabited by an unpredictable and tyrannical lunatic.

Paolo and his mother arrive laden with flowers. They uncover my stomach and bend down with their ears glued to my taut flesh. They laugh together. They exchange signals. They follow the movements of 'their' baby. Then Elizabetta delicately pushes to one side the outsize baby's nappy I wear between my legs. She sees the fresh red stains and purses her mouth.

'You've got to keep going Armida. The baby's fine. You've only got to hold out for one more month.'

The bedside table is laden with almond cakes chocolates orange-flavoured biscuits candied fruit choux pastries none of which I eat. Enormous white lilies splotched with pink watch me tremulous in their vase.

Paolo's cousins come to see me wrapped in pink chiffon jackets with little straw hats which they've bought for the occasion. His father comes with his new wife. He holds my hand between his warm dry ones. He gives me a brief moment of pleasure. I've always had a weakness for Paolo's father who is a bourgeois with a soft heart.

Old college friends of Paolo's – great hefty blond athletes – come with their wives decked in jewellery. Elizabetta chases them all away using my exhaustion and my weakness as a pretext.

Now I am unable to eat a thing. Everything I eat I throw up.

Elizabetta quickly and efficiently shakes up the pillows and sets the room to rights. Like Snow White while the seven dwarfs are out cutting wood in the forest. In the evening they find everything in order all nice and clean the table laid for everyone and the steaming soup-ladle in her hand.

Her encouragement makes me feel better. I keep going for her sake: in some way she has infected me with irrevocable determination to have this child whatever the cost.

LAST night strange to say I slept calmly without the usual mischievous kicks from my solitary acrobat. I wake up having had a good night's rest even though my body still feels tense. The muscles in my back have become rigid and my stomach is as tight as a drum. I feel hungry for the first time. I gulp down a cup of milk and a handful of biscuits shaped like medallions. I wait expecting to throw it all up. But my stomach holds out.

At nine o'clock the doctor arrives. He puts his ear to the funnel: the usual examination: tapping listening waiting outside the door of my house of ill-omen: the house of my capricious familiar.

The doctor's face clouds over. All at once I become aware that something is wrong. He calls the nurse. Together they spend half an hour feeling and listening. Their eyes glued to my stomach their faces inscrutable colluding with each other in an attempt not to alarm me. Tense with their comical efforts to conceal their complicity.

Soon afterwards I am in the labour room. My legs wrapped in a sort of handcuff of coarse cotton my breasts covered by a small sheet that smells of bleach. The morning doctor rummages in my belly with his plump white hands. The afternoon doctor helps him by pressing down on my stomach from outside. They are like Day and Night one white and bright and round the other dark prickly and murky. I watch them milling around in my belly as if it didn't belong to me. They make zany movements: Day puffing and panting Night pushing and sweating. At one moment Night sits on my belly as if it were a suitcase that refuses to shut. I think of giving him a bite on his hand when I hear a metallic voice saying 'There's nothing more to be done. She won't let go of the child and I'm afraid it's dead.'

My muscles go rigid in the last embrace with my lover son who has decided to make my dome into his tomb. We are both of us dying in a love pact that welds us together against the world. He possesses me. I surrender myself into his possession. He clings to me. He embraces me in the agony of death.

I hardly feel it when they tie my ankles to prevent me tossing about. I'd like to aim a good kick at their all-knowing heads. I'd like to send them to the devil. I've a savage desire to sink exhausted into the black waters of the void. Where my son and I lie together in an idyllic embrace.

But the needles are there to keep us apart. The anaesthetist finds a small piece of vein that is still intact somewhere in my left leg. I feel a sudden burning in my throat. My eyes cloud over. There is just time for me to catch a glimpse of Elizabetta who appears behind the glass screen giving me encouraging signals.

Then I collapse into sleep. My muscles relax so that my son can be snatched from me by expert hands. Without even a caress they throw him into the refuse bucket. Then they tell me he was a boy just as Gesuina had predicted that he had blue eyes and that he was smiling and sturdy. The little acrobat has broken his collar-bone and has fled from the family for ever.

They have to slap me to wake me up. I don't want to come back any more. I am in the shadow of an overwhelming grief that tears at my guts. I am numbed. I can't drink. I am not getting any better.

It is Elizabetta's strength that pulls me out of the quagmire of this devastating still-birth. 'I pulled you out by your hair' as she put it. 'You really were more dead than alive.'

The first face I see when I open my eyes is hers. Beautiful. Far far removed from any notion of surrender or defeat. 'We'll have another won't we Armida? Get some rest now and don't worry about anything.'

Paolo dries his tears with paint-smeared fingers. He's started to paint again and he's done some amazing desolate paintings in which the blue melts into the green of a sky without angels or gods. I let the days pass by like snatches of brief predictable dreams. Listlessly I start eating again without tasting anything I put in my mouth.

Every morning they bind my chest. My breasts are swollen with milk. 'And we must make it go back mustn't we dear?' says the nurse in a maternal tone of voice. While she says it she is conscientiously tightening the bandages. She leaves me alone in bed trussed up like an abandoned mummy. In the evening she comes to take them off. She nods her head with satisfaction. 'Now it's going back' she says as if she were speaking of some strange unpredictable animal. She takes a nipple in her fingers and squirts a few drops out of it. She seizes two

66

squares of gauze and lays them gently against my painful breasts. With the broad sweep of a scythe she bandages me up again.

One morning the first thing to catch my notice is an envelope standing on the bedside table. A letter. The writing is Miele's. I recognise it immediately. No one else curves his 'ms' in that way and twirls his 'ss' as if they were sea-serpents. 'Armida Bianchi' – that's me all right. Goodness knows how long that letter has been there and I never knew!

I don't dare to stretch out my arm. I am afraid of not being able to reach it. And then how will I find strength to open it? As usual I am nailed down with needles in my ankles and in my wrists and by the blood that drips slowly into my veins.

I start to laugh. It's a hundred years since I laughed. I thought I would never laugh again. It gives me a strange pleasure to laugh with my mouth and with my head and with my neck and with my chest and with my arms and with my belly. A laugh that fills me with hunger and a longing for action.

Finally they take out the needles. I get the letter put on to my chest. I tear it open clumsily but I'm unable to read it. I can only observe how the letters are formed leaning over as if they'd been hit by a raging wind. A few try to rise again and pull themselves up on their short legs. Others don't even try. At the top of each menacing sentence the rigid stroke of a 'T'. At the bottom of a sea of words the signature: an elegant and stylished M a ribald priapic I an E reclining languidly on its side a tall slim L a little vain in its baroque perfection a final E thrusting towards the future and then a full-stop as if to say: 'after me Nothing. Any other sign is irrelevant.'

'Dear Armida – I've only just heard you have been very ill' – a conventional letter without intimacy without passion. The sort of letter one has to write out of a sense of duty.

I put it to one side disappointed. But then I have second thoughts. I read it again. And I discover there is something I hadn't noticed before: a telephone number written upside down right at the bottom of the page. No explanation. Just a little six-figure number. A cabbalistic message for me alone. So that's the secret of the letter which he's probably thinking is bound to fall into the hands of

67

Elizabetta or Paolo. I wait for the night when I am by myself. Elizabetta is sleeping at home and Paolo has left for Rome. I am alone with my lion-headed lilies and my roses so stridently red my biscuits and my books.

I dial the number. But I make a mistake. I dial it again three times. Finally I hear the phone ringing at the other end of the line. Endless bleep-bleeps echoing in an empty room. Four five six rings. No reply. I am just about to give up when at the last minute I hear a 'Hullo?'. I try to answer but my voice won't come. The words stick in my throat. I clutch the phone unable to make a sound. Yes it is his voice: a little drowsy as he keeps on repeating 'Hullo? Hullo? Who is it?' Then abruptly puts down the receiver.

I dial the number again. At last I manage to get out a few words: 'It's Armida. I got your letter.' I stopped paralysed. It takes him a moment to regain his self-assurance.

'Armida? Where are you calling from? What are you doing? Do you know I keep dreaming about you? Fuck it all Armida I want to see you so much... But where are you? Is it true you very nearly died?'

'Do you really want to see me?'

'I'll come straight away if you want me to. Tell me where you are and I'll set off at once even if you're in Australia.'

'No you don't have to do that. Just tell me what you're up to.'

'I'm working on my thesis. I'm stuck permanently at home studying. I've lost five kilos. If you saw me now you wouldn't recognise me. God its seems unbelievable I haven't seen you for so long!'

'It's you who disappeared not me.'

'I had to make myself scarce for a bit... to do with politics... I'll explain it all to you one day. Do you still love me Armida? You're all I think about.'

By this time I'm falling out of bed with all my books the telephone the flowers and the biscuits on top of me.

'Tell me where you are and I'll come. I can't bear to be miles away from you any more.'

But if there's one thing I'm certain of it's that I don't want him to see me in my present state: swollen bandaged tottering shaky and as pale as a dried bean.

'We'll see each other when I'm better Miele.'

'Don't you want to see me now? Have you forgotten me?'

'Will you be in Rome Miele?'

'I've told you. I've got my exams.'

'I'll see you in a month's time then. Will you wait for me?'

'At least let me telephone you.'

'Ring me at two o'clock. I'm usually alone then.'

'Till tomorrow then... I'm so happy that you rang. I didn't dare... I was afraid it might be inopportune... Can I tell you that I'm in love with you?'

I pick up a mirror. I haven't touched it for months. I see a drawn transparent face small blue eyes lost in great eye-sockets encircled by dark haloes. A resigned wasted expression I hardly recognise. Black bruises in the hollows of my elbows like a hardened heroin addict bruises on my ankles bruises on my wrists. And I'm all puffy. Puffy with ill-digested food and stupid resignation and boredom.

I throw off the blankets and put my feet on the ground. I just have time to cling to the vase of fresh lilies. I bring it down after me together with a pile of books. My face between fragments of china. Water all down my chest. Rusty pollen from the stamens on my hands. The scent of those lilies will always remain with me like a song of thanksgiving.

At this moment Elizabetta arrives and pulls me up. She is quite scared. She wants me to start the drip-feed again but I absolutely refuse.

'No I'm all right. I only fell because I've become so weak and sloppy. I'm all right. I don't want any more needles or blood transfusions. Tomorrow I want to go home.'

WALLPAPER festooned with flowers. Outsize begonias red and mauve lilacs cherry-red cyclamen. A white porcelain lamp linen curtains that swell out at every breath of wind a chest of drawers smelling of lavender. The window looks out on a small wood of fir trees with fringed branches. Between the branches the country beyond shining in the sun swarming with houses factories schools barracks electricity pylons silos warehouses. All veiled by a curtain of smog like a pale blue mosquito-net which distances and softens the edges of things.

Bread and figs. Bread and smoked ham. I eat on my own. I have exactly what I want and when I want it. I get up for a few hours each day and sit in front of the window and read. I wait for Miele's telephone calls.

Elizabetta is delighted to have me in her house. Together with Paolo who has begun to paint again and Lamberto who buries himself in an armchair in the garden studying English.

As I get better I go for walks with Elizabetta among the fir trees. She makes me walk barefoot on the fresh grass. She fills my arms with gigantic and perfect dahlias that grow in her garden with the aid of potent chemical fertilizers.

Sometimes I manage to make it as far as the summer-house at the bottom of the garden where Paolo paints in the studio used by Elizabetta's young husband. They greet me without much enthusiasm.

Paolo paces up and down the studio with his sleeves rolled up and his eyes alight. He wears a pair of brief shorts stained with paint. Gerardo is friendly yet elusive. He titters bites his moustache and fidgets about making wisecracks and waiting for me to go away.

There is a half-eaten plate of grapes in the middle of the floor. Beside it sitting on a sheet of plastic is a young blonde girl with black eyebrows meeting in the middle which gives her a bad-tempered look. It is Gerardo's model Zaira. She is naked with a small rag for cleaning brushes thrown across her stomach. She watches me with empty eyes. I help myself to a few grapes. I lie on the divan panting in an effort to get my breath. I notice her bending double in an attempt to cover up her belly and breasts with that little paint-stained rag.

70

'Do you feel ashamed in front of me?'

'No.'

'But you are hiding yourself.'

'It's... it's because I'm pregnant.'

'Is that something to be ashamed of?'

'I don't mind them painting me when I'm like this. But in front of strangers I feel embarrassed.'

'Not so long ago my belly was even bigger than yours.'

'Well if it doesn't worry you I suppose it shouldn't worry me...' She smiles shyly. With a graceful gesture she throws the rag off her stomach and looks at me timidly. She is wary of me. She's been so much put down by other local women.

'When are you due?'

'In two weeks.'

'Are you pleased about it?'

'Yes... in a way... I'm not married. I'm not even engaged. My father beats me up pretty well every time I go home. I'm trying to make a bit of money to get away to Milan.'

'If you need any help let me know. I'm always at home here.'

'Oh... thank you...' she says in a whisper.

I rise and Paolo rushes to the door to see me back to the house. But I tell him that I'll make my own way back. He breathes a sigh of relief and closes the door gently but firmly behind me.

Along the path I meet up with Elizabetta. She has just got home from work and her dress is soaked through with perspiration. I talk to her about Zaira. I ask if it is possible to help her.

'Who pays for her to be a model Armida? It was me who arranged for her to come. I know Gerardo fancies her. For all I know they've been making love already. But that's of no consequence. I don't believe you can force people to love you. I don't believe you can force them to be faithful either. All I ask from him is affection and a bit of respect and consideration. Everything else... well that's life isn't it.' She says it with a laugh holding a carton of olives in one hand and a spare part for Gerardo's motor cycle in the other. But she says it to convince herself rather than me. The tone of her voice carries the bitter certainty of someone who knows everything has to be paid for in hard cash and that love never got anyone anywhere. Yet she looks so beautiful in her crystalline darkness. 'I'll find her work in Milan as soon as she's had the baby. But I don't know if she'll be able to leave the child. Her mother died last year. Her father is a peasant who's almost blind and drinks half a bottle of spirits first thing in the morning and keeps that up till night-time and who beats her up whenever he gets a chance. So I've got to find somewhere for the baby. I don't know... maybe I'll bring it up myself.'

Burning sensation of defeat. The child I've been unable to give her to be replaced by this small unknown creature who isn't even born yet. I have betrayed her confidence in me. She'll never let this weigh on me but it will always be a shadow to darken our relationship.

AT night in that room brimming with begonias strange things are happening: a naked man standing upright by the window. A woman lying down trembling. A man with legs wide apart knees pressing down on to the mattress pushing doggedly with feverish persistence against his wife's painful belly. A woman willing her atrophied senses back to life. A man investigating the tight cold lips of his wife. A woman refusing to recognise the taste of a loving tongue. A man lying on his side smoking. A man's thoughts coagulating in dense droplets on his forehead. A woman staring up at the ceiling with dark lifeless eyes.

A man and woman looking at each other in anguish not knowing how to recapture the smells and tastes that had made them fall in love four years before. In that room of the begonias are consummated the last death-throes of a marriage that has ossified. The death of the baby with blue eyes has bequeathed an ill-omened legacy – the death of all desire. It has broken the kernel of their passionate bond. It has transformed two loving accomplices with their familiar preoccupations into two dead bodies stretched out in the darkness two bodies struggling anxiously and stubbornly to stir in each other some new excitement in the memory of their long lost pleasures.

In the begonia room with its brilliant colours of raspberry pink cherry pink and flesh pink next door to the magnificent great room with walls covered in white silk where Elizabetta and Gerardo sleep our marriage has been torn apart just as my veins were tortured by the needles.

During the day Paolo shuts himself up in Gerardo's studio to paint. Out of his hazy canvases peer the round bellies of women surrounded by prehistoric monsters. Crocodiles with human heads. Snakes with a thousand forked tongues. Cats with toads' heads. Toads with rats' teeth. A menagerie of perturbing and threatening figures.

He doesn't come in for lunch. When Elizabetta is there I eat with her in the garden. When she stays at work I eat by myself and read. Lamberto has his own hours and prefers to eat in the kitchen where he can keep an eye on the saucepans and the oven.

I've started to write plays again. In the afternoon when it gets really hot I shut myself in my room and sit at a little table in front of the typewriter with a glass of iced tea beside me.

I've begun to do exercises. I eat nothing but fruit and salad so as to lose weight. Slowly slowly the colour in my cheeks is coming back. My muscles are getting less flabby. Towards evening I set off on a bicycle to go to the village. I stop at the newsagent and the greengrocer. I come back my basket laden with pears and grapes.

I feel quite relaxed on my own. With the image of Miele before my eyes. I don't want to know about the future. I don't want to make any decisions. I surrender myself to the ups and downs of each day as it comes. When I was in hospital every day was the same all equally predictable. Now they are diverse and unpredictable.

The wind has changed. October is here. It is already bringing dead leaves the smell of autumn soups damp rooms wet pavements grapes hung up to ripen foxes that come out at night to raid the chickens bicycles recently oiled.

One morning at five o'clock Elizabetta rushes in to the begonia room. Paolo and I are sleeping in each others' arms our legs intertwined and our breath mingling.

'Armida come and give me a hand.' I don't understand. I toss and turn to extricate my foot from the twisted sheet wound round me. Paolo looks at his mother open-mouthed.

'What time is it?'

'It's nothing to do with you. Go to sleep. It's Armida I need.'

'But what's happening?'

'She's having her baby.'

'Who?'

'Who do you think you half-wit? Zaira of course.'

She dashes out of the door with me close behind her. I am barefooted and have put on Paolo's dressing-gown inside out.

'But where's she having it?'

'In Gerardo's studio. Hurry!'

There among the paints and the bottles of turpentine. Stretched out full length on the floor. Alone. Her face composed and serious. Holding back her moans with that instinct of the poor to give as little trouble as possible.

'Zaira. The doctor's coming soon. Meanwhile we're here.'

'I don't want the doctor. I want Maria.'

Keeping calm so as not to contradict her Elizabetta tries to convince her in a friendly yet determined voice: 'You'll see Maria too. I've sent for her. But we must have the doctor as well.'

'No. The doctor embarrasses me. Don't let him come in. Please.'

'All right. We'll ask him to wait outside.'

Gasping for breath she nods agreement. She presses her large peasant hands on her stomach. Fascinated I gaze at her smooth polished belly with the fair curls that cluster round it. Everything seems so easy.

Maria the midwife arrives. I was expecting someone of huge proportions. Instead I find myself facing a tiny person less than four feet tall with piercing sharp eyes and the arms of a dwarf.

'Breathe in deeply Zaira. Then push the air out' she orders. Zaira breathes in filling her narrow little girl's chest.

'Now push. Push harder. Harder! Push harder still as if you were having a shit.'

Zaira opens her golden eyes very wide and pushes. Within a few minutes a sturdy baby girl covered with black hair comes out gasping. All ready to drink in its new element: air. Zaira has only screamed once when her daughter's shoulders pass through the narrow passage of the pelvis. But she at once bit her lips as if asking to be excused for the trouble she was giving. Grateful for the way we rush round her. Trusting. Confident. Open to whatever happens.

'It's a girl. She's lovely. She's so chubby and healthy. The only thing she needs now is to be baptised. What are you going to call her Zaira?'

With confident motherly gestures Maria holds up the new-born baby by her feet gives her a few slaps cuts the umbilical cord and washes her in luke-warm water.

'Are you happy now?' Elizabetta bends over Zaira attentively. Already she is making the child hers smothering her with nappies little shoes and bonnets and gold brooches. But Zaira is asleep her mouth wide open her hair stuck down on her forehead satiated and satisfied.

'How like Paolo the baby looks' I say in a low voice.

Elizabetta looks at me in astonishment. 'That can't be Armida. You weren't even around when she was conceived.'

But that wasn't what I meant. All I'd noticed was the resemblance and how it might have been our child. I had spoken without thinking and given Maria something to laugh at. She was already muttering between clenched teeth something about husbands who are all fly-by-nights and who as soon as they see 'a fine strapping woman lose what small amount of common sense they ever had.'

I am the one to be astonished. Astonishment at the ease of this birth at home. While I spent months festering in hospitals surrounded by drugs and doctors and in permanent danger of pegging out. For the first time I realised that my pregnancy was a stupid useless defiance of nature. The arrogance of the rich. If I had been poorer I would have miscarried in the first few months when I had the first haemorrhages. As the afternoon doctor said to me one day: 'It would have been more sensible to let you abort in the third month before the baby started to grow.'

For a moment I experience a feeling of hatred towards Paolo and Elizabetta with their unforgiveable greed of the rich. Who were quite willing out of habit out of greed out of haste to put my life in danger so as to assure themselves of an heir. The boy with the azure blue eyes who is lost in the empty spaces of my consciousness together with the memory of Paolo's tender kisses. . . .

THE start of winter. The air becomes thick and damp. Back in Rome we find the house has been invaded by fleas. Testone has been staying in the country with Filippo and his absence has set them loose. They jump over our ankles like ballerinas in a microscopic circus without even having the strength to cling to our flesh. However Testone although washed and disinfected takes them all back on board like a good Indian elephant and walks them around for days every so often sitting down patiently to scratch himself.

For the last ten days Lamberto has been staying with friends in the country near Geneva. He has got fatter. He has brought back a suitcase full of mayonnaise in tubes: the ultimate delicacy of his dreams. In the morning he spreads it on buttered bread and wolfs down eight or nine slices. The blackheads round his eyes and nose have grown bigger. They have become small extinguished volcanoes.

'Did you enjoy yourself?'

'I meditated.'

'You know I lost the child who would have been your nephew?'

'I know I know.'

'Are you sorry?'

'I've got my own ideas.'

His self-assurance always takes me by surprise. This child prematurely wrinkled with age doesn't seem to suffer from small everyday fears. Perhaps his disability really consists in this: he is incapable of imagining himself interacting with events. Instead he remains embalmed on a summit of certainties watching the insane chaotic world slide along beneath his absent-minded gaze.

'Why do you talk such nonsense Lamberto?' Paolo's face in the doorway sends me incomprehensible signals.

Lamberto gives me a condescending glance as if he were looking at somebody who had failed to make the grade. He takes off his glasses breathes on them polishes them with the edge of his shirt and replaces them and smiles at me good-naturedly.

Paolo gives me a wink. I am just about to fling my cup on the floor when Testone comes in wagging his tail. He jumps up pushing his front paws against Lamberto's chest and throws him off balance. The chair slides in one direction and Lamberto in another. Paolo rushes forward. I dive quickly to grab the chair and my cup leaps from my hand toward the wall. A loud thud. A cascade of broken china and spectacles. Lamberto bursts into piercing cries. Paolo shouts that it's my fault. I pick up the broken fragments just as the blood starts gushing from Lamberto's nose.

The next thing we hear is the neighbours banging their shutters. 'For Christ's sake keep it down. How the hell can anyone get any sleep?'

Just then the door-bell rings – it is Dida. Paolo propels Lamberto who is still losing blood across to her and hurls himself against Testone who is lying down in the corner beneath a table.

Dida greets Lamberto with her amply body always ready to console the depressed the thirsty the abandoned the sick the mad and the miserable.

After supper Ada arrives. She tells me that Miele is going to show up around ten o'clock. I start my long wait for him. I put Lamberto to bed. I cook a dish of pasta for all of us but in my thoughts I am standing there at the door with my hand on the door-handle and my ears focused on the landing waiting to hear the clatter of the lift.

Twenty past ten and he still hasn't come. We eat the pasta and discuss the latest in politics: Nixon has asked for peace talks with Vietnam. Meanwhile they've set free six 'green berets' who have killed a Vietnamese woman. 'Killing is their profession. That's what they've been trained for.'

'That's what Robin Moore says in his book. Have you read it?'

In Belfast they're flaying each other alive. They stuff bombs into people's mouths 'From mouth to mouth you know. They pass a bomb round as if it were a sweet and as soon as someone touches it with their teeth – wham! off it goes.' In Prague yet another human torch. A young man of 24 burns himself alive in front of Parliament. The Soviet Union sends seven men into space 'to walk slowly and leisurely among the downy plumes of the universe without a sound from their milk-white rubber boots.' Lt. William Calley is to be tried by court martial for the premeditated murder of civilians in South Vietnam.

... When it's too much it's too much and it collapses. Those who show off make fools of themselves. 'Lads – moderation is everything. Never exaggerate never give way never commit rape never break your word never cry for help never abandon ship never take the lid off the melting pot especially when it is sizzling at boiling point . . .'

'The lieutenant famous for his marksmanship. He can hit a ten cent piece at a distance of twenty paces. On March 16th 1968 he personally shot and killed one hundred and ninety civilians.'

At half past ten the door-bell rings. I rush to open it. It's Cesare with Nico. They hug and kiss me as if I've been raised from the dead. They take hold of my arms they touch my stomach my breasts they kiss my cheeks.

I fill more plates more glasses. I've never had to make such an effort to conceal the feeling of impatience that keeps me on the tip of my toes on the tip of my thoughts on the tip of my heart like an athlete ready for his most demanding high-jump.

At a quarter to eleven the bell rings again. Only I hear it in the confused din of voices. I distinguish it like a clarion call amidst the laughter and the chatter. I get up and dry my sweaty hands on my skirt. I walk slowly towards the front door.

I open it. It's him. For long seconds we remain on the threshold fixed on each other. He has got thinner with a long beard and hair plastered down over his ears. I have got fatter and paler. I've got circles under my eyes. Someone shouts from a distance 'Who is it?'

It's a signal for us to embrace. I shut the door behind me and there on the landing we seize each other by the waist by the neck by the shoulders with voracious delight. With that fierce delight that sometimes happens in love. The delight of eating and being eaten of being both predator and prey filling our mouths with the most passionately longed-for morsels: lips cheeks eyelids ears tongue neck.

We turn in a giddy dance our legs entwined our faces pressed together our tongues lost in the game of discovering each other again. We dance and dance on the icy landing lit by the glimmer from a glass cube of light. Everything is flying in a whirl of confused sensations: the begonia room explodes the hospital room jumps into the air and minute fragments of it hang in space. Elizabetta and Paolo are two unrecognisable shadows lost and far away Zaira with

79

her swollen belly the baby who looks like Paolo getting smaller and smaller until it becomes an ant the needles stuck into my flesh slipping away into the far edge of memory everything flying joyfully past on the landing while I drown in the smells of this unquiet love.

'**I**'VE decided to go and live on my own.'

'Are you unhappy with me then?'

'You know we don't get on.'

'That's not true. If there's something wrong it can be put right.'

'I don't think it can.'

'Let's make a pact to be freer. We'll arrange our marriage more simply. Don't let's destroy it. I need you.'

A light sad kiss. He bites my lip. And I let myself be carried away by his new energy. Let's try again. As Paolo says married life is something quite different from passion.

'However I must tell you that I'm in love with Miele.'

'I know that. It's quite normal. It's happened to me too. After years of living together it happens. But it doesn't mean everything has to break up. If you go to live with Miele the same thing will happen with him after a while and then what will you do? Have a chain of husbands for the rest of your life?'

He kisses me on my groin. His fingers drum on my thigh as if he were drawing forth a melody of reconciliation. 'And we'll have another child Armida – yes?'

I see myself nailed to the bed with needles in my ankles. I cry out 'No I'll never have another child!' He smiles unbelievingly. He plays with my curls. He pulls them and kisses them and rolls them round his fingers with an altogether new tenderness.

Even Lamberto becomes affectionate. He doesn't say 'I see I see' any more. He sits next to me with his history books and asks me to tell him about Herodotus.

One afternoon I see him coming towards me all dressed up in blue wearing a pale red tie with an artificial knot which squeezes his throat gold cuff-links and shiny shoes of black calf. I know how much he hates those shoes. The effort it costs him to do up the laces with fingers that won't obey his brain and jerk all over the place. He has put them on for me.

'Shall we go for a walk Armida?'

'Where do you want to go?'

I like it when he acts the gentleman in disguise: when he puts on a good-natured smile to hide how worked up he is at the thought of a simple journey in a bus.

With my arm in his we advance into Corso Umberto to do some shopping. We stop in front of an umbrella shop. He is taken by a red umbrella of waxed canvas with a big silver butterfly fixed on the handle. He wants to give it me as a present.

'But have you got the money?'

'Yes I've got a sackful of money set aside. Wait here till I come back.'

He goes into the shop. I see him confabulating with the sales girl. He pays and comes out holding the umbrella by the handle. He puts it into my hands beaming.

'Now let's go and have some tea. Would you like that?'

'Yes. That is a lovely idea.'

'We must seem just like husband and wife mustn't we?'

'Yes perhaps we do.'

We go into a tea-room whose walls are hung with mirrors.

'So you'd like tea?'

'Yes.'

'And some cakes?'

'No. Just tea.'

'With milk or lemon?'

'Milk.'

'Waiter. Two teas with milk and a dozen cakes.'

'Do you think you can eat that many cakes?'

'No. But I like grandiose gestures.'

What a perfect actor he is! A delightful impersonator of himself. He observes himself in front of a mirror. He likes himself. He congratulates himself. His enjoyment at playing and giving pleasure is irresistible.

The waiter arrives with the tea and cakes. Lamberto pulls out a big wallet bursting with money and pays with confident gestures. He leaves a hefty tip as well.

He pours out my tea spilling half of it on the table.

'I'll do it' I say. But he restrains me with two fingers on my arm.

'It's me who's invited you out Armida.'

82

For the first time I'm conscious of him giving me a look of real affection. Stirred by his enthusiasm I join in the game.

'How much sugar?'

'Two.'

Twice I watch him concentrate in a spasmodic effort to move his fingers from the sugar basin to the tea-cup. Such a long journey is very difficult for him. All the same he manages it and he is delighted with himself when he tips the sugar into the boiling liquid with a slight flick of his wrist.

He begins again. But half-way there the teaspoon overturns and the sugar spills on to the table. With a lordly air he clicks his tongue as if it were only a minor mishap. Patiently and meticulously he begins all over again. He wipes his perspiration away with a handkerchief. He touches his nose always terrified at the thought of the blood that can spurt from it. He reassures himself that the tea is sugared to taste and that the cakes are in their place in the centre of the lace doily.

At last he reaches out for a cream-filled cake. He brings it up to his mouth. But his lips stay closed. The message hasn't got through. The cake squashes against his clenched teeth. The cream spills over his clean shirt. His eyes fill with tears. He grinds his teeth. There is about to be a crisis.

I grasp his wrist. 'Don't worry Lamberto. It's nothing to blame yourself for. It's nothing serious.'

He calms down for a moment. He puts the squashed cake back on his plate. He helps himself to another. He is about to take it up to his mouth. But his nose starts to drip. The blood falls on to the cream. His hands don't know what to do: whether to clean up the cream or to try to push the cake against his clenched teeth or to carry on with tea as if nothing had happened or to hurriedly dab his bleeding nose. I pass him a clean handkerchief but by now he is lost. He doesn't look at me any more. He pulls his tie off with an angry gesture and flings it at a little girl who is sipping a cup of chocolate. She lifts her eyes up at him with astonishment. There are alarmed looks from neighbouring tables. The waiter is about to descend on us.

We get up. We go out. He is in front of me waving his arms with his shirt unbuttoned and splattered with cream and blood. I am behind trying ineffectively to calm him.

At home he shuts himself in the bathroom. I hear the water splashing in every direction. Then I see him emerge with his penis erect. He goes weeping towards his brother's studio. Paolo is painting. He comes out with his eyes clouded and suffused with pain. He paints with his belly wide open and his intestines in his hand – lacerating colours torn open by living flesh warm blues monstrous figures concealed in emptiness. Tormented paintings dripping carnality almost obscene in their lack of moderation.

We spend the night in each others' arms unable to make love. Snuggled together we recapture the old pleasures of feeling each other's skin against our own, each other's smell that mingles with our own taste secreted between tongue and palate.

SIGNORA Giovanni is waiting for me at the bar. We sit facing each other. Her blonde hair is shaped like a small helmet. Her mouth is twisted in a crooked smile. Her son is playing the pinball machine at the end of the bar. He is very fat and his bottom almost bursts out of his trousers.

'Would you care for a Daiquiri?'

'Yes' I say even though I don't like drinking alcohol at three in the afternoon. I wait for the appearance of the slender glass with its edge dipped in sugar. Then while she natters on about films I swallow the sticky white liquid with my eyes closed thinking of Miele.

'They always make me play the bad woman. A lesbian a shrew a spy a prison-warder a torturer . . . I'm branded with a hard face while I'm really a soft-hearted person and I hate everything that isn't above board. Do you approve of lesbianism?'

Now I remember having seen her in a film dressed as a Nazi in a black leather jacket her smooth hair a metallic blonde. She was leaning over a tortured partisan inhaling the smell of his blood and his tormented flesh breathing in the air through two very small cruelly-shaped nostrils.

I try to discuss the rent which seems to me too high. The flat is tiny the bathroom nothing but a hole and the stairs in a terrible state. She holds her hand with its mauve-painted nails above the lease and refuses to discuss it. There's nothing I can do. Anyway I'm no good at bargaining. Suddenly I'm weary of it all. I sign and say goodbye but she detains me. She is happier now. She puts two keys tied with string into my hand. She finishes drinking her Daiquiri. She tells me how hard life is being in films and how impossible it is to get out of a role that one is stuck with and can't get rid of. She has an indomitable quality about her that makes me feel quite warm towards her. We end up ordering another Daiquiri and we drink it chatting together like two old friends.

An hour later I am in my new flat. On the seventh floor of the via Andrea Sacchi. Two ugly shrivelled rooms a fillet of a bathroom a kitchen that has been scooped out of a hole in the wall.

I go out on to the balcony. In the distance to the left is the Tiber running hidden behind a high grey wall. In front of it a piece of derelict land strewn with rubbish. Further on new yellow houses cross horizontally bisected by a line of emerald green tiles. The Lungotevere like a thread disappearing in a dense fog that envelops the street lamps in thick white clouds.

Testone sniffs with curiosity in every corner. He is wagging his tail hesitantly a little nervous of the novelty. On the floor in the middle of the room are some violets that Paolo has sent me.

I throw myself on the bed. I close my eyes. Via Andrea Sacchi – how strange it is. 'It'll be your studio my child. Where you can work at your play without anyone disturbing you.' Elizabetta's voice in my ear. Kindly reassuring but also vaguely menacing. 'Don't take it into your head to destroy the family. I've entrusted you with both my sons and now you can't slide out of it – not on any pretext.'

I'm due to meet Dida and Cesare at 8 o'clock. I haven't yet unpacked my things from my suitcases. The sofa is still wrapped in plastic and has to be put up. The kitchen is a desert. In the bathroom there isn't even any soap.

My mother has given me a bed. An old large single bed with a soft mattress. The only thing I've brought with me is my work-table with its wide top that's covered in cuts and holes. It gives off a goodly smell of old pinewood. On it I've put my old typewriter and two pages of the play I've been working on a ream of extra strong paper and a pile of books on the theatre.

My other books are stacked on the floor along with shoes coats shirts and glasses. 'You'll only be on your own for a bit. It'll do you good. Then the two of you'll come back together and have another baby. Isn't that so little one?'

I don't say yes or no. I don't like to disappoint her. I'm fond of her. And I feel an absolute shit in my determination to live on my own and not to have any more children.

At seven Ada arrives. With a jar from Calabria filled with salt.

'Didn't you know that a new home should be christened with salt?'

She kisses me on the cheek. She goes through the flat and throws salt into each corner. She laughs. She spins round four times.

'What's happened to you? I've never seen you so happy.'

'Nico and I have decided to get married.'

'But surely – isn't Nico in love with Dida?'

'So am I.'

'So then?'

'That's why we're getting married.'

'And Dida?'

'She's in love with Cesare. You know that... more than ever in love. They might even end by getting married as well.'

'But Cesare? Isn't he in love with you?'

'You're being very naive Armida. What better reason is there for getting married than for both of you to be in love with the same person?'

'So where are you going for your honeymoon?'

'To Helsinki.'

Her sharp amber eyes. Her head held erect on her neck like a trophy. Two almost invisible wrinkles round her mouth which however much she smiles express above all her sense of desolation.

'And Paolo?'

'He's going to the States. He's got a scholarship to study in Boston.'

'Testone's staying with you?'

'Yes.'

'And Lamberto?'

'He's going back to be with his mother.'

'The group's falling apart.'

'On the contrary. It's consolidating. With two marriages...'

'Marriage only serves to shore up a building that's collapsing. Getting married may create the illusion that the group's staying on its feet. Actually it's in ruins.'

I can hear the door of the lift banging. I recognise Dida's light hurried fingers on the bell. I go to open the door. She's enveloped in a penetrating scent of jasmine. We embrace. Cesare is standing immediately behind her. He's seen Ada and he stops at the door to gaze at her ecstatically. Dida goes round the flat diffusing waves of jasmine. She's wearing a white skirt and a top made of pink organdie. She emanates softness and openness. A calm openness of enervating sweetness and yet unbroken strength. Immediately the flat is full of her voice her gestures her body rising like bread in the oven. Ada follows her with watchful eyes. Nico sits at her feet and is content just to look at her.

Cesare allows himself to be loved by her with a certain cantankerous pride. He's become accustomed to this love that takes the form of silent adoration and that asks for nothing in return. He glories in it. He regards it as being his most sensational conquest. And if he doesn't love her perhaps it is only so as to retain for as long as possible her absolute love for him.

Miele joins us in the pizzeria. He sits down next to me. He squeezes my hand underneath the table. 'When can I come to see you?' he asks in a whisper.

There is talk of a very big demonstration coming up soon. All the left will take part. They discuss leaflets and loud-hailers.

'Who's free to do a massive leafletting in front of the Sisma on Friday morning?' asks Miele impulsively. Dida raises her hand. The sleeve of her pink blouse slips down her bare arm. Everyone's eyes are fixed on this piece of luminous flesh.

'Good. So Dida can make it. Anyone else?' Nico raises his hand awkwardly. It's fully understood that he only does it to be with Dida. Cesare grumbles something between clenched teeth. He won't be going. To assert his independence. He'll probably stay at home and torment himself thinking how he ought to have been there.

I N the mornings Testone and I go for long walks along the Tiber. He in front very black and hairy with feathery whiskers that challenge the world. I follow swaying thoughtful plunging into the fresh air as if it were a new raincoat.

He stops at every plane tree lifts his hind leg and directs a spray of steaming urine against the trunk. I lean on top of the parapet looking down at the dull green water that flows with slow imperceptible movements carrying along pieces of wood weeds bottles and bits of plastic.

Every so often Testone runs twenty paces ahead and leans his paws against the window of a car parked alongside the pavement and scrutinises the interior attentively. He reassures himself that it has nothing to do with Paolo's car. He looks to make quite sure he isn't inside and then he comes trotting back to me. If I'm far behind he sits down on his bushy tail waiting for me his head a little bent on one side and his whiskers drooping over his wet muzzle.

At other times he picks up a piece of wood or a broken sandal or a small rubber ball left abandoned and brings it up to me. He places it delicately at my feet and waits for me to have a look at it. If I tell him 'no! Leave it alone! Dirty!' he bends his muzzle to the ground with a mortified look and runs off to search for something else. If I say to him 'Testone what a lovely thing you've brought!' he throws it up into the air with his nose and catches it in flight with his teeth wagging his tail cheerfully.

Now my days are entirely concentrated on my work. I get up at eight. I wake up with a feeling of emptiness. Mechanically I stretch my arm to the other side of the bed and each time I get a surprise. I'm still not used to sleeping on my own.

I eat breakfast in the kitchen: bread and butter and marmalade and jasmine tea. Sometimes I boil myself an egg because I won't eat again until the evening. I wash myself in the tiny bathroom splashing water all over the walls. The shower is powerful and is liable to flood the floor. When I've finished I go over it with a mop.

I go out for a walk with Testone. I buy a paper and a few provisions for the day. At half past nine I sit down at the table and write. My

89

fingers skim over the keys. My mouth is dry with the taste of power.

From time to time I raise my eyes towards the slip of sky that falls like a sparkling wave on the houses opposite. A feeling of exaltation holds me suspended between the ceiling and the floor in a state of happy levitation.

But the hurried zig-zag flight of a swallow or the sound of a car-horn or the sound of the lavatory flushing in the next-door flat or the crying of a child is enough to throw me into the blackest depths of discouragement. I feel completely worthless. I'm a dead loss at writing. My head is as empty as a newly-washed saucepan.

I am within a stone's-throw of the football stadium. On Sundays during the match I can hear the crowds shouting. Just round the corner is the bar of the tennis club. I sometimes meet Miele there to re-live the emotion of that first time when he talked about himself. I'm two minutes away from the Farnesina and the English Cemetery. Sometimes Testone and I walk as far as the pine-woods behind the Farnesina with its tree-lined hill leading up to the cemetery. We clamber up our feet sinking into the dry scented pine needles. We meet strange men in jackets and ties. Men who come and go restlessly looking nervously around them. Behind the oleander one can hear whispering. Other men with strong tattooed arms stand and wait smoking.

Testone and I walk straight ahead. We make it clear we are minding our own business. Commerce becomes brisker at seven o'clock in the evening. But even in the morning there is always someone in search of a body that can be bought.

While I am walking I think about the script of the play I am writing. Helena loves Demetrius who loves Hermia who loves Lysander who loves Helena on a midsummer morning around the Piazza Cavour.

'Cohabitation friendship love affairs enchantment betrayal fasci-nation faithfulness egotism fickleness sexuality violence desire. Tell me to what point to what point can I pursue and snatch at pleasure in spite of you and whoever else loves me or might love me? Isn't it this that controls the complicated neurotic system which we call morality?' Said by Helena to Demetrius in a flood of frustrated love.

90

At one o'clock I drink a glass of cold milk and then I lie down for an hour on the bed to read. Sometimes I fall asleep. At three o'clock I go back to work. My writing still limps along. I am dazzled by the sheet of white paper. Disappointed by the black hieroglyphs that cover the mysterious white page. The imagination sails all on its own out to the open sea – then you find you have to imprison everything within a sheet of 'extra strong' playing upon the twenty-six keys of an Olivetti 32.

At six o'clock Miele telephones. Within minutes of leaving the University. He announces in a rather out-of-breath voice that he's on his way. Testone is already out on the balcony to sniff the evening air that wafts down warm and milky.

Miele arrives out of breath. He brings a dish of cakes and we eat them together sitting on the balcony. We drink wine diluted with water. He always has a thousand things to tell me about his day at the University: the lecturers meetings rows sit-ins. And then he explains his plan for a seductively plausible speech to the Assembly as if changing this country was entirely his own affair and anyone lucky enough to have the privilege of following him would automatically be choosing the right path.

Later on we join the others in the pizzeria or in Ada's place. She is the oldest of us and she has already got a degree. She works with a group of architects and is starting to earn good money.

Sometimes Paolo comes with Smeralda. Sometimes by himself. He looks miserable. He doesn't say a word. He watches me with resentment. He is getting ready to go to America and utters comical sighs of resolution. We quarrel only when he says 'If you have a child by someone else don't foist it on me because I don't want it.'

'After I nearly died having the son you wanted at any cost . . .'

'But you might do it . . . with someone else. And we're still married. It would automatically have my name and I don't want that. That's why I'm asking for a divorce.'

'Do what you please. But you know I haven't any money.'

'My mother will pay for it.'

'What are you afraid of? Tell me.'

'If you had a child by Miele and then registered it in my name you could even sue me for maintenance.'

'You make me laugh Paolo.'

'I don't trust you any more. You could do anything.'

'What sort of thing?'

'You've broken up our marriage. You were determined to take off. You're continually asking me for money. You make love with someone else.'

'I only ask you for money because I haven't any. But I will have as soon as I get work. I've no intention of ruining you don't worry.'

'Before I go to America I want you to sign a paper promising that you won't saddle me with children that aren't mine.'

'You've got an obsession about it. I've no intention of having any more children anyway. I'll sign whatever you want... You're an untrusting pig-headed fool...'

'You're pig-headed. What about when I suggested we stayed together under conditions any other woman would have jumped at?'

So that's how things stand. Every time we meet we feel bitter and resentful towards each other. And Testone who is so happy to have us together and jumps up and puts his paws on both our chests has to make do with an absent-minded pat on his ears and a playful pull on his tail.

NICO steps forward bent and rigid. Thin as a rake. Eyes tender and dark. Ada is beside him wearing a severe blue dress and looking like an air-hostess.

'All you need is a cap' I whisper in her ear. She smiles. She is holding a bunch of cornflowers in her perspiring hands. She puts them under my nose.

'They're nice. Smell them. I'm no great shakes as a bride. I've got it all wrong. Give me a kiss.'

Cesare arrives in a brand new mustard-yellow car. He gets out carefully so as not to crease his newly-pressed trousers. His eyes are heavy-lidded and sombre. He waves his arms about. He kisses us all. It is almost as if he were the bridegroom.

Filippo is there too stuffed into a greatcoat of black and green herringbone tweed that must have belonged to his grandfather. He smiles under his moustache and looks more like a ghost than ever. His eyes search round for Dida who hasn't arrived yet.

Nico's parents have come up from Calabria for the wedding. And with them a little group of sisters brothers nephews and nieces all dressed in blue and white the men wearing shiny ties and the women with little gauze roses in their hair.

Ada's parents are not here. They live in London and didn't think a wedding was sufficient reason to uproot themselves. One of her aunts has come enveloped in a long grey coat. She greets everyone with an ecstatic expression on her face. She comes from a small Irish village and this wedding is for her an encounter with the heatladen and flowery South. The South of men like Rudolph Valentino with their passionate kisses the South of shadows and bloodthirsty mysteries the South of baroque churches of seventeenth-century villas of madonnas who weep from pride and honour the South simmering with tropical heat nocturnal fragrance and jasmine-scented secrets the South of the youthful readings and wanderings of a strait-laced girl from the North.

The relations from Calabria treat her with contempt. She is too sweet too gushing too spinsterish too poverty-stricken for them and every time they see her approaching them with a plate in her hand they edge away sniggering.

Smeralda has come with her brother. She is wearing a loose-fitting skirt and a tight waistcoat embroidered with gold. She moves awkwardly. But she personifies something simple and delicate. I am always astonished by her colouring the red of her hair the milky whiteness of her arms and the violet of her eyes.

Paolo has the look of someone who has already travelled unknown waters half-way towards a future full of promise and surprise. He looks at us as if we were lost to him. Suddenly he finds us small-minded and obsessed with little unimportant things. He regards us as if we have not been chosen by the Lord for a grand or adventurous destiny.

We stamp our feet in the cold. Above our heads facing the Palazzo del Comune with its beautiful flight of steps Marcus Aurelius spurs his bronze horse forward. He is only just out of the hands of the restorers. Two water-gods bent over the fountains – on the far side the Capitolina Museum.

At last Dida arrives in a taxi yellow as the sun wrapped in a cloak of flame-coloured brocade. Her fair hair falling in fluffy curls over her neck and forehead. Her breasts barely covered by a black shawl.

She makes a royal entrance radiating clouds of jasmine-scented perfume an expression of child-like excitement in her blue eyes. She knows – and everyone else knows too – that she is the true bride even if it is Ada who is marrying Nico. She is the focus of attention and desire and she delights in it with the gracious modesty of a real queen.

We stand facing two damask-covered chairs and listen to the mayor delivering his discourse. We sit down. Ada and Nico exchange rings. Nico's mother weeps into a large embroidered handkerchief. Ada's aunt puts an affectionate arm round her shoulders. For her all this weeping merely confirms her rather folksy and novelettish idea of the South: a mother living at home like a lost mole. Gives her heart to her son studying in Rome. Comes now to take part in their final separation. Ill-starred youth chooses to marry a woman reputed to be a lesbian. Rumour has it she's in love with another woman said to be a prostitute. And here the mother is all dressed up in light blue ready to witness this outrage. Mothers do not protest. They accept everything with the humble servitude that is the lot of mothers in the South of Italy.

The ceremony only lasts a short time. The Mayor pale and perspiring from the wedding photographer's lamp goes with Ada and Nico to sign the register. Then he dismisses them and quickly removes the red sash he wears across his chest.

We find ourselves outside in the cold without knowing exactly what to do next. Nico's parents have prepared a meal at the home of one of their relations but they haven't said how many friends are invited and Dida Cesare and Filippo look at each other uncertainly waiting for a sign from Ada. The bride passes holding on to the arm of her father-in-law who looks very still as he escorts her to a classy hired car. She just has time to turn round and beckon us with a gloved hand to follow. Cesare Dida Filippo and I get into one car and Paolo Smeralda Lamberto and Nico into another. We are all sandwiched together in a country procession: the car at the head with two wreaths of white flowers forming a V on the bonnet. The second and third cars each the inevitable dark blue with an artificial rose attached to the radio aerial.

Nico's relations live out at Eur a smart suburb of Rome. The ground floor of their house has large spacious rooms that open on to a well-kept garden crowded with dahlias climbing roses oleanders cedars and fir trees.

We sit on Art Nouveau chairs with our feet resting on soft blue and green Chinese rugs eating *pasta al forno*. The owners of the house work in television. They have lost their Southern accents and they pride themselves on belonging to the select little world of the Italian upper class. Those right-thinking people who are firmly lodged within the navel of Italian history.

Nico is in the middle: country folk from the province of Catanzaro sit stiffly on one side and the smart television set with their Roman sophistication and their loose way of talking on the other. He is closer to the first in the sensitivity of his character in what he loves and what he fears. Closer to the second in his tastes his conversation his dress and his manner. So he is split into two and is bent double as if he were bearing the burden of this painful and exhausting division. With his head he loves these relations with stiff shoes and awkward ways but he hates their moralising their morbid attachment to tradition and their fierce possessive feelings about family unity.

Today he is more hunched-up than usual. His wide-open eyes wander between guests and relations recognising himself in some and hating himself in others. He is waiting for Dida who will appear like a breath of fresh air to liberate him from his nightmares. But she is in the kitchen talking quietly with the youngest of Nico's sisters a little girl of fourteen who is as thin as a post.

Cesare joins Nico. He puts a hand on his shoulder and prods him gaily. Meanwhile the owner of the house in a well-meaning but slightly patronising way has put on a record of tarantella dances from Calabria. But no one seems to respond. He doesn't realise that his conception of popular taste is quite outdated. He identifies the country folk with the culture of their grandparents that has long since become a subject for anthropological study.

One of the younger boys goes over to the record player. He takes off the tarantella and puts on Jimmy Hendrix. Immediately the other young people put down their plates and start to dance with amazing expertise and nonchalance.

Ada too is very ill at ease in her role of bride. She is still holding the bunch of cornflowers not knowing where to put it or what to do with it. She smiles gracefully at Nico's mother and nods in agreement with the portentous platitudes uttered by his father. But her eyes are focused on Dida who passes every so often radiating clouds of jasmine.

Cesare approaches me. I'm trying to cut up a slice of roast beef on a plate balanced on my knee. Some gravy spills on my skirt. 'Wait – I'll help you' he says with an awkward laugh. He doesn't know where to put my glass. In the end he manages to pour water all over my legs. He looks very contrite but already his thoughts are miles away.

'Why didn't she marry me? I just don't understand it' he says looking down at the havoc he has created.

'Because you're in love with her and demand attention and love in return whereas Nico is in love with Dida and doesn't ask for anything.'

96

'But if she has to marry without love she could have just as well married me. I would have cherished her. Just look at Nico how thoughtless he is. Look at him with his eyes glued on Dida. What do you think he'll give her? He'll be a disaster as a husband...'

'But Ada doesn't want a husband.'

'You're all of you so corrupt. Cynical. Rotten. You treat people like goats. What's getting married to do with that?'

'You're so intolerant.'

'And you're all vile. Twisted. Cynical...'

'Does that make you feel better Cesare?'

'Why do people get married at all? Tell me that.'

'You're jealous.'

'All right. I'm jealous. But also disgusted by all this fooling around.'

'Ada loves Dida. Even if she'd married you she'd still have gone on loving her.'

'It would have been a sham – but only half a sham. This is just a joke though. A horrible sick joke. Anyway if she'd married me she would have ended up loving me. I know it.'

'My poor Cesare. If she hasn't loved you up till now what makes you think she would if she married you?'

'Why are you all so fascinated by this girl Dida? She's nothing but a fat interfering cow.'

'You're just being silly Cesare. Come on eat a bit of this delicious tart.'

'Look at the way she dresses. As if she's just going to do some sort of circus act – it's ridiculous.'

'She's very beautiful you know that quite well. Whatever happens Dida is a queen. No one can help loving her.'

'I feel absolutely indifferent to her.'

'If you were you wouldn't be talking like this.'

He explodes into a burst of laughter. He seizes the wine-glass he'd put down on the floor and empties it in one go. He stares at me with eyes as round as if they'd been ringed with a black pencil.

'You don't know Ada. You don't know a thing about her. And Nico knows even less than you do. She's just simply wasted in this

97

fucking marriage. Do you understand that? She's throwing herself away...'

'Marriage won't change her.'

'Yes it will. She'll become infected by Nico's banality...'

I follow his infatuated gaze. Ada is alone. She stands out against the big French window that leads down to the garden. Her shining black hair falling over her forehead her small aquiline nose set sharp against the light. She makes me think of a falcon. Cruel and proud but also very fragile beneath its speckled feathers.

'Do you know how long I've been in love with her?' He gets up and pours himself another glass of wine. He shoves a big slice of tart into his mouth. He comes back and sits down.

'For three years Armida. Three years! Have you ever heard of a man of twenty-five who keeps on loving the same woman without getting any response?'

'But Nico's loved Dida for years without her returning it.'

'Just think how crazy it is. For a year now I haven't made love to anyone. And before that I only went after girls who looked like her. I took them to bed and pretended they were her. I sweated away making love to them in the dark forcing them to keep silent so that they wouldn't break the spell. But in the end I got fed up with it. Now I masturbate. Thinking of her. Waiting for her. If she'd asked me to marry her without ever sleeping with her I'd have accepted. It's her lack of trust that exasperates me. She prefers this cabbage Nico who never even looks at her and doesn't give a shit how much she suffers...'

He pushes another piece of tart into his mouth while tears slide down his cheeks. Drops of passion that edge their way over the threshold of the black pencil lines become elongated and fall gently on to his plate.

98

'COME and fetch your clothes. I've got to shut up the house.'
'I've already taken everything.'
'No. There's still some of your things here.'
'You can throw them away.'
'I want to give you something.'

After supper I go. In a gentle rain that smells of pavements and decaying leaves. I go up the stairs. I ring the door-bell – I returned the key months ago. It seems absurd to be ringing the bell of my own house. I feel as if I am ringing at the door of my past to ask for news of myself. As if I needed to take this heavy weight off my belly.

Paolo is wearing a dressing-gown. His face screwed up with sleep. Testone jumps up and Paolo wraps him in an anxious embrace. They start to dance together in the middle of the room like two bears.

'Were you asleep?'

'Lamberto's not well. I gave him a sedative. Then I took one too because I'm feeling all strung up. And then I fell asleep. Would you like a coffee?'

'No.'

'I did this picture for you.'

He hands me a small rectangle framed in pale wood. I take it over to the light. It's a self-portrait. The chiselled face disfigured by pink and green brush-strokes that are piled up as if to destroy his very self. Angry turbid chunks of colour on a clear translucent canvas. A background of purple that is almost black. Dissolving into this dark background the head as precious as a jewel melting into the shadows. It is certainly the best thing he's ever done.

I kiss him. He clasps his hands round my waist. The pressure of his chest against mine. My cheeks aflame. The familiar heat drowning my belly. In a fever of excitement he lifts me up and carries me towards the bed.

Necklaces stockings sweaters shoes all fly away. I take him with my eyes shut to prevent myself from thinking. From sinking into a past that has the stale old familiar taste – begonias on the palate. We hug each other until it hurts each of us searching in the other for some remote worn-out part of ourselves.

99

Afterwards sitting triumphantly on the bed his eyes rimmed with red Paolo confesses in a tense shrill voice that the telephone call was a trap.

'It worked didn't it?' he asks laughing. 'So now you must admit that I still turn you on.' Another spasmodic laugh. 'To hell with divorce to hell with separation. Now you can come back to me and sling all this rot right out of your head.'

So many little kisses on my feet on my hands on my neck down my back...

'No Paolo it's not on.'

'Why don't you give up all this shitty nonsense? Why are you so pig-headed? Why – when I've shown you how we still attract each other? How well we make love together?'

'No. I don't want to turn back.'

'Then why the fuck did you come here? You knew what I wanted. You knew perfectly well you bitch!'

'I came because you asked me to and because I like seeing you.'

'You're such a bitch. You really drive me mad. You're a cow. I hate you. You've trodden all over my life. You've messed up my plans my dreams you've turned everything upside down by your shitty behaviour. So now you've driven me off to land up in a strange country where I shan't know a soul. All because of your idiotic determination to be independent. Anyway let me tell you this. If you get pregnant by that rotten bastard Miele you'll end up crawling to me for money. Oh yes you will for sure.'

I get off the bed. I get dressed as quickly as I can without a word. I seize my coat and rush out through the door. While I wait for the lift I hear a melancholy drum-beat and Lamberto's desperate weeping.

I don't feel like going back home so I go to see Ada. I'm trembling all over. Testone sniffs my hands anxiously. The cold cuts into my legs – even though we're well into March.

Nico's out. He's gone to have supper with Dida and Cesare. Ada is working at a big table of plain unpolished wood bent over sheets of paper pinned to it with drawing pins. Behind her Don Carlos at full volume on the tape recorder. A glass of wine on a small revolving stool.

'Armida! What's happened?'
'I've been quarrelling with Paolo.'
'Again?'
'He wants me to go back to him.'
'He loves you.'
'He's just stubborn.'
'Ah! The last link in the chain of unhappy love affairs is missing:
Paolo loves you who love Miele who loves...?'
'Well. Who does Miele love?'
'I'm not sure. I think he loves you. But the game requires him to
love someone else. Then the chain would be perfect wouldn't it?'
'Have you got anything hot? I feel frozen.'
'Some mulled wine? With cloves in it?'
'Yes. But let me do it.'
'No. I will. It's good to have a break from working now and again.
My eyes feel as if they were on fire. Did you make love?'
'Yes.'
'That was a mistake.'
'I know.'
'And Miele?'
'He's left for Barcelona.'
'Politics again? That's all he really cares about.'
'Have you any news of Dida?'
'Haven't you heard the latest? She's got a job. As a social worker at
a youth detention centre.'
'She'll have all those delinquent young boys falling in love with
her.'
'Too true. They'll all go crazy about her.'
'Do you still love her very much?'
'You know the best moments are when Nico and I lie in bed naked
smoking cigarettes and talking about her. We talk about her for
hours. Then in the morning when she telephones it seems as if I'd
been holding her in my arms all night.'
'You and Nico live off fantasies. What satisfaction is there in that?'
'Are you saying that satisfaction is essential to love?'
'Well desire is certainly part of being in love.'

101

'When I was in love with Ignazio I used to feel really bad. We were living together and we used to quarrel all day long. When I was loving towards him he was worn out and bored and when it was my turn to feel unresponsive he was seized by storms of jealousy. He tormented me so much that when we left each other I felt as if I were having a re-birth. For months I luxuriated in the pleasure of falling in love with people I'd never seen before of not allowing myself to be bossed around by anyone of eating when I wanted to eat of sleeping when I wanted to sleep of talking to people when and how the spirit moved me. Then Dida appeared and I fell in love with her immediately. But this time I won't make the mistake of trying to possess her. And it doesn't worry me if she's in love with someone else. I love my love from afar without wanting to swallow her up. I wouldn't go back now even if it meant death.'

Cradled by her voice I cleanse myself of the bad feelings that had accumulated in Paolo's place. Testone lies sleeping on the rug his muzzle resting on my feet. From time to time he opens his eyes snorts gently and lays his chin on my shoe with an uneasy sigh.

Ada stops drawing. She gets up. She heats up the mulled wine. I'm full of gratitude towards her for the way she moves so silently and discreetly for the way she talks to me for the way her shining black locks of hair fall down her cheeks while she bends over her drawing.

T<small>HE</small> clock on the bedside table says two. A glimmer of yellowish light comes in through the closed window. It is the murky light from the streetlamps outside. I dreamt that Miele greeted me from on board a boat. I was sitting on a rock and he was a black dot on the horizon. The boat was a walnut shell. I waved to him with a feeling of panic. Where are you going? Puffs of white smoke came from the boat as if shots were being fired from little hidden cannons. Turning round I realised that Miele's greeting was not for me but for someone behind me. . . .

Then I woke up with a start. I get up. I go into the kitchen and fetch a glass of water. I go back to bed. Sleep has vanished. On the bedside table is Miele's last letter. Ten days old.

I open it. I read it again. Loving but evasive. He writes not a thing about himself. He is being swallowed up by the Moovement, as he pronounces it lingering over the first 'o'. I hadn't realised that the name of the hotel – Hotel Assuntion – and its telephone number are written almost invisibly at the bottom of the letter.

I lift the receiver and dial 'International'.

Number engaged.

I go back into the kitchen. I get another glass of water. I re-dial the number. It rings but no answer. My ear fishes for an answer in the shell of the receiver. Finally when I am just about to put the phone down I hear a metallic voice.

'What number do you want?'

'A Barcelona number.'

'What is the number?'

At once I am seized with uncertainty. Supposing I wake him up? Suppose he's only just got to sleep? Maybe he's sharing a room with someone else? My voice won't come out of my throat. The telephone operator is getting impatient and repeats 'What is the number?'

At last I get it out hurriedly all in one breath. I hear a click and then silence. I put down the receiver. I wait. I want to pee. But what if it rings back while I'm in the toilet? I hold myself in. My bladder stings. I bite my lips. The telephone rings impatiently. A woman's voice speaks to me in Spanish. I ask for Miele faltering over his

103

surname.

The room telephone rings faintly. A click.

'*Hola?*' A female voice. So unexpected that I am thrown into a panic.

'I want to speak to Miele.'

'*Quien?*'

'Mi-e-le.'

'*Ah no esta aqui.*'

'Where is he?'

'*No sé . . . no sé . . . Otro numero.*'

'What is the number? Could you give it me please?'

Needless to say I can't find a pen. I sweep the alarm clock and a glass of water on to the floor while I rummage around the bedside table for one.

'Give me the number' I shout hoping I shall be able to remember it by heart. But the voice goes on monotonously repeating '*No sé – No sé.*' and then – click – the phone goes dead.

Do I call back or not? I pick up the pieces of glass and mop up the water with a cloth. I put the alarm clock back in its place after making certain it is still working. I find the pen – it was right under my nose all the time between a little box of sleeping pills and a pile of books.

I re-dial 'International'. Engaged. I go and get a notepad so as to be all ready to write down the number. I keep the pen within reach of my hand. I try 'International' again. Ten . . . twenty times. Meanwhile my need to pee comes back. I'm just about to put down the receiver when a plummy male voice replies. I give him the number of the hotel in Barcelona. He says:

'Put the receiver down and I'll call you back.'

'Will that be soon?'

'I don't know. There are a lot of personal calls booked.'

'So late?'

'Do you imagine we go to sleep here? There are hundreds of people like you who ring up at night instead of dreaming . . .'

I rush into the bathroom. I sit on the lavatory seat. At that very moment the telephone starts to ring. I stop peeing half-way and rush back into the bedroom. As I lift the receiver I slip and end up on the floor with my foot in agony because I've banged it against the corner of the bedside table.

Same number. Same room. And now at last it's Miele who replies.

'Miele!'

'Armida! Hullo... has something happened?'

'No I only wanted to hear your voice. When are you coming back?'

'I don't know. In about ten days. Soon.'

'Were you asleep?'

'No. I've only just got back.'

'You haven't written to me. I was worried about you.'

'Of course I've written to you.'

'Yes. Ten days ago.'

'I've had a terrible lot to do.'

'Will you send me a telegram when you arrive?'

'Yes my love... Why ever aren't you asleep at this time of night? Have you been tearing around?'

'No... I mean yes. I've been to see Ada.'

'I've got a feeling you're being unfaithful to me – is that what's up?'

'I made love with Paolo. But I'm not ringing you because of that.'

'I know you're still in love with him... But – well I'd rather not think about that... it makes me feel bad.'

Click. Cut off. In a hurry to end the conversation. And I told him everything while he never said a word about himself.

I pull the receiver towards me. I dial 'International'. With my other hand I cut the phone off. I lie down. I pick up a book. I read it without understanding it. I try to recall the drowsy voice of that woman. To figure her out. A woman who's not all that young. Around forty perhaps. Even if her voice was hoarse from sleep it's a voice that's completely at ease. Confident. What else? Perhaps a moment of alarm at that nocturnal phone-call but no obvious signs of curiosity as if everything were an accepted fact. She there. I here. A man divided. Right through the middle. Without a qualm.

But that's enough. I must get some sleep. Tomorrow morning at nine o'clock I've an appointment with a young director who wants to put on one of my plays. I turn off the light. I close my eyes. But sleep refuses to come. I forbid myself to fantasise. I count dogs who all look like Testone jumping over a fence. One two three twentyfive eighty two hundred six hundred... But it's no good.

I turn on the light. I take a sleeping-pill and put out the light again. I turn over between the ice-cold sheets. My feet are frozen. If I don't do something immediately they'll drop off like two lumps of ice. I get up to make a hot-water-bottle. I sit perched on a stool waiting patiently for the kettle to whistle.

...No sé... otro numero...

Impossible to understand the mystery of that number which should be different and instead is the same. A ploy of the woman to throw me off track? Are there two communicating rooms? Or does she really believe he is somewhere else?

I get up. I take another sleeping pill. I swallow it. I shut my eyes. I open them again. I look at the alarm clock. Half-past four. Another three hours of sleep. Is it worth it? My stomach is in turmoil. It says no.

I re-dial 'International'. I'm determined to get things a bit clearer. Engaged – luckily. I put the phone down.

I decide to get dressed. Testone looks at me with surprise his whiskers bristling his eyelids heavy with sleep. Are we going for a walk? This early? He gets up grudgingly. He stretches. He elongates his hind-legs with the movement of a dancer. He follows me looking miserable and dejected. I put on wellingtons. I button up my raincoat. We go out. It's still dark outside and the cold air cuts my face. I take deep lungfuls of the reddish mist that rises up from the pavement.

Testone sniffs the air uncertainly. He turns round to look at me as if to say that it isn't daylight yet and we must have made a mistake. But when he sees I am quite firm he goes ahead of me and trots along slowly and calmly. He stops at the first plane tree. He lifts his leg. He waits for me. He frisks around. He stops. He sees a cat roosting on the roof of a car and barks without enthusiasm.

'... Jealousy is a physical activity in the worst possible taste...' Cesare's voice sounds frayed in the freezing air. 'Everyone must be free to sleep with whoever they like whenever they like even if they are in love. For fuck's sake above all when they are in love. Or else love is nothing but possessiveness. Don't you agree?'

Testone places his front paws on my chest. He covers me with earth. I scold him. He goes off mortified with shame. He turns round to look at me with plaintive eyes. I call him back. I make a fuss of him. I throw a stone for him and he rushes to retrieve it.

'The only reason our lot are honest about being unfaithful is because bourgeois people are so dishonest about it.' Cesare licks his lips like a wise old cat. 'But that's a lousy way for us to carry on. It's the height of cheap melodrama.'

Dida is more cautious. She has her doubts. 'Mmm . . . a great show of honesty . . . hasn't it an element of sadistic pleasure in it? Can you deny the cruelty behind some confessions?'

'This is how I see the new morality dear Dida. Freedom conditional on keeping one's word. Trouble is you can't impose fidelity in the same way. As for possession it doesn't exist. When you love another person you love them. That's it. You can't ask more than the other is willing to give. Jealousy's an outdated fossil. Do you understand that? It's a small-minded relic of former times. We must free ourselves from it as soon as possible . . .'

So – faced with this relentless intruder from the past we all do our best to find rational reasons and pretexts to hide from other people – and from ourselves – that we are inhabited by such an ill-bred guest.

So lots of people run away from love just to avoid falling into the clutches of this unwelcome visitor. Some people sneer at her and call her bourgeois, almost as if she'd been born out of the wars and affluence of a prosperous Europe. They say that once she has appeared in a family there's no getting rid of her. So the best thing is to shut every door and leave her chattering outside in the cold.

Having saturated myself in this dubious new morality I can kid myself it's his lack of honesty not his unfaithfulness. If he'd only told me at once . . . But it's too late now. The guest has already slipped in through the door. She's sat down. She's taken off her hat and got herself ready for her first nocturnal feast.

NATURALLY by nine o'clock next morning I'm dead beat. My throat's burning my eyelids are like lead. And I have no desire whatever to meet the talented young producer. But then he conquers me with his Neapolitan charm and we talk together till midday. One martini follows another while Testone snores away underneath the table. He invites me to become the playwright for his company. He's quite shy but he also has a gentle seductive way with him.

'We're going to put on grassroots theatre in a working class district. We shall build a new cultural centre for a new public. We shall overrun the horrendous attitudes of the bourgeois theatre.'

In his enthusiasm he spills half a martini all over me. He orders another. He starts playing with the olives. He makes them jump into his mouth. He laughs. Then he becomes serious.

'We've had enough of the authoritarian hierarchy of popular culture and highbrow culture enough of community centres and conferences and the commercialisation of poetry... We shall start right at the bottom with all humility. We shall spread the word to those who have never had it before. We'll become involved with the rejects of society with immigrants the deprived the poor...'

At half-past twelve we are joined by his girl-friend. A beautiful actress with black hair and coral lips. We eat a pizza together and talk about the theatre.

'Doesn't Ernesto ever make you jealous?' I ask the girl when we are together for a moment washing our hands.

'Yes he does. But I keep it to myself. All hell breaks loose if I talk about it.'

'And him?'

He comes in looking at us with embarrassed curiosity. He washes his hands in the same washbasin as us.

'What were you saying?'

'We were talking about jealousy.'

'Jealousy doesn't exist. It's an invention of the chicken-hearted.'

'We're all of us a bit chicken-hearted at times' she says sourly.

'You're free to do exactly as you please. And so am I. I love my freedom as much as I love yours. I loathe the idea of couples. To own someone else's body fills me with horror.'

'But you don't tell your wife about me' she replies insistently. It is at once obvious from the way she looks at him that she is the victim of his carefree exuberance and daring ideas – more loving than loved.

I get back home staggering on my feet. I am so tired that I can't see straight. I think I see Miele go by. I call him. I run after him. When I catch up with him I discover it is someone else who doesn't look like him at all.

I throw myself down on the bed. But tiredness doesn't bring sleep. I'm obsessed by the temptation to pick up the telephone dial 'International' and ask for the Hotel Assuntion in Barcelona room number 26.

I can see that room immersed in a golden light the slats of the venetian blind half-open two long white curtains swelling out with the breeze a large double bed of light wood with over-size pillows and two naked bodies stretched out and abandoned after making love.

I wake up with my head throbbing. A throb that reverberates in the aching empty sockets of my temples. I look at the clock. It's five in the morning. I poke a foot outside the sheet. I give Testone a shove. He is sleeping all curled up in a ball. I get dressed. We go out. The bars are not open yet. The newsagent is taking in packets of daily newspapers. A fat blonde woman is arranging flowers in metal containers behind a green stall.

I walk quickly along the Tiber trying to get warm. Clouds of vapour emerge from my mouth as I call Testone. If this were a comic strip one of these clouds would have written on it 'Fall in love and you end up in the fucking soup my love.'

I wait with my feet numb in front of a bar till a youth in an Afghan jacket finishes rolling up the slatted blind and opens the steaming windows.

I am alone at the counter. The coffee machine is still cold. I read some of the headlines in the papers while I wait for the boy to take out a cup get some fresh milk and heat it up.

The boiling hot coffee slips gently down my throat. Testone lies stretched out on the floor sleeping with his head transfixed beneath a paw. Someone comes in. A worker from the bus company with a well-

109

groomed moustache. He is served a boiling hot coffee. He asks for news of the Roma Juventus match.

I give Testone a kick. He rouses himself and follows me home with an ill grace. The lift is broken so we go up the seven flights of stairs on foot pulling each other up.

I go into the kitchen. I feel hungry and cook myself a fried egg. But then I can't eat it. The smell disgusts me. I give it to Testone who licks it up happily dipping his muzzle into the white and orange stripes. I sit in front of the small table my hands on the keys of the typewriter. The play is in front of me almost finished. I begin to type. My dry mouth makes me cough. I get up and go to the balcony. The city is beginning to wake up. Men all muffled up emerge from doors along the street and step inside their cars pearly with the damp. The engines fail to start. They keep on trying. They look crossly straight ahead.

Women wrapped up in layers of clothes take their children to school. The buses begin to run more frequently. A cat has climbed on to the bonnet of a car and performs its morning toilet one paw stuck straight up in the air its diligent tongue rasping through its fur.

I shut the window. I am cold. I light the stove. I pick up a book and open it. I sit down in the worn armchair. 'That mental feeling of being in two places at once affected me physically as if the mood of secrecy had penetrated my very soul.' It is the slightly astringent voice of Conrad. I read eagerly. I am calmer. My breathing is almost regular. My double becomes palpable. I also am two separate people simultaneously: the first patient and controlled the second enslaved to the devil.

The telephone rings. My hand leaps out. For a moment my fingers linger in suspense over the receiver. If the fly that's buzzing round lands on the book it will be him. . . .

It is Ada inviting me for supper. I immediately feel better.

Under the ash-yellow gaze of her calm eyes I pull myself together. I return to being recognisably myself.

'The trouble is that if there isn't someone loving me I don't love myself. If I'm not desired I despise myself. If someone isn't looking for me I disappear.'

110

'Couples – what a stupid concept: Adam and Eve Penelope and Ulysses Tristan and Isolde Romeo and Juliet . . . and you still believe in happy mutual love.'

'What can one do to avoid suffering Ada?'

I sit there entreating her advice as if she were a goddess of wisdom. I drink in her words hoping for a miracle cure.

'As I see it love is a work of delicate craftsmanship. It's best executed in solitude. Work for the sake of working. Without any expectation of reward or validation. Useless to fool ourselves about relationships. We are all alone in our walnut shells on a stormy sea. We have to learn to navigate. Navigation even in a walnut shell can be a pretty valuable skill. The sight of another nut-shell with another desperate soul struggling to keep afloat can give you a feeling of warmth and happiness. But nothing else. Don't try to reach for it. Above all don't think of getting on board anyone else's walnut shell. That way you would both drown . . .'

Her scepticism has the sweetness of camomile tea. I take her hand. I squeeze it. Her laughing eyes sparkle with movement.

After days of listlessness I eat with gusto as I listen to her talking about love. Her head enclosed between two black wings has the white transparency of a jellyfish.

'Whether he likes it or not Miele is part of the world that's kept us prisoners Armida. The world of the father. That magnificent fascinating world with which we are all in love.'

'I'm not in love with his world. I'm in love with him.'

'But he is the darling son of that world. The most gifted . . . the most handsome . . . Now the family has fallen apart. The ancestral home has been destroyed all the valuables have been sold. But the tips of his shoes still point heavenwards. And there amidst the imminent danger of collapse sits a gentle old father who protects and adores him. The tip of his nose enshrines the memory of ancient victories just as we hold with the tips of our hair the remains of ancient defeats. And what's this son and heir of the dead patriarch looking for? He's looking for a little girl to mould and look after according to his own fantasies and his own image . . . and you've fallen in love with this diabolical plan. You say you don't exist unless someone loves you.

111

Too true! That's precisely the way you should be according to his patriarchal world: "You shall have no other father but me. You shall have no man but me. You shall have no other love..."'

I listen to her spellbound as if she were the sibyl of Mount Athos with scorching eyes and forked tongue. Her minute body has taken on the gorgeous splendour of a gigantic prehistoric serpent.

At the door of the restaurant she kisses me lightly on the mouth. I seem to draw from her breath the strength to move in a new direction.

THE ten days until Miele's promised return have gone by. Not one letter. Just one telephone call. I decide to ring him up again. I dial 'International'. Immediately I feel better. Free of the silly constrictions that I have been imposing on myself and that have made me ill.

The phone rings. I grab it with both hands.

'Hotel Assuntion in Barcelona on the line.'

'Hullo. Room 26 please.'

'*Un momentito.*'

A faint ringing through the walls. A distant hissing. No reply. Then suddenly:

'*Hola?*'

It sounds like that same voice hoarse with sleep with its intonations of sensuality: '*Hola hola . . .*'

'*Queria hablar con Miele*' I say mixing Italian with the little Spanish I know.

'*Ah Miele . . . un momentito . . .*' A rustling. Bubbles explode on the line. A prolonged buzzing. And then here he is miraculously grasped from beyond the seas.

'Miele is that you?'

'Armida! What's happened?'

'Nothing. You said you'd be back in ten days. I want to know when you're actually coming.'

'Things here are a bit complicated. The comrades have asked me to take part in their public meetings. I've been elected leader of the delegation. And then there's a comrade who's in prison and risks being garrotted and we must think of some way of getting him out. The police here never take their eyes off us. But I must get back soon because I've run out of money.' His voice sounds as if he's said all he has to say. The next thing will be 'Well bye-bye love' and he'll ring off. And I still haven't asked him about the woman who keeps answering the phone. I try to gain time:

'Do you want me to send you money?'

'No love. There's no need. Ines and Migual have helped me a lot. If it hadn't been for them . . . You know that Ines is expecting another baby?'

I was mistaken. It's him who is taking his time. Almost as if there was something more he wanted to tell me. . . .

'I've had some real successes. They were all clapping like mad the other evening when I was speaking . . . I'm definitely learning the art of speaking in public. I used to think I was a disaster as a speaker. And you my little one? If you only knew how much I want to see you!'

'Who was it spoke to me on the phone first Miele?'

I've said it at last. A worm of indiscretion. Cesare would eat me alive . . . With an expression of infinite sadness and horror he would twist his lips in that way he has and he'd say: 'Armida you're so hopeless!'

'Amparo?' I hear from down the phone. 'She's my interpreter. Armida – might you be a little bit jealous? If you only saw her! She's sixty and looks like a sack. I've never got time to look at girls. I'm always working. And when I have got a moment to myself I spend it writing . . . Do you want me my love?' But he doesn't give me time to answer. 'I'll send you a telegram before I leave. So you can come and pick me up. I long to see you. And now sleep well, I love you so much. . . .'

I put down the receiver. I fall asleep quite suddenly. After nights and nights of insomnia. I sink into a dark and welcoming womb that closes protectively around me.

I wake up with the door-bell ringing and ringing. I throw a coat over my night-dress and go to open it. It is Ernesto Caputo the young producer. He stands in the doorway with a carton of olives and a bottle of *grappa*.

'Still asleep at this hour? Do you know what the time is? Two o'clock. May I sit down while you make yourself a coffee? It stinks of dog in here – can I open a window? Well I've read your play. I like the first half but I don't care for the second. Don't get annoyed. I always tell the truth . . .'

'Would you like a coffee as well?'

'You must re-write the second half. Tomorrow there's a meeting of the company. Can you come? Then you can get to know everyone.'

'What don't you like about the second half?'

114

'I don't like the way she becomes the unchallenged protagonist. She doesn't have the qualities for that. It throws everything out of balance. It doesn't work.'

'It doesn't seem like that to me . . .' I say but already I'm thinking that he is right and that it's me who's got it wrong.

He gives a boisterous laugh. He doesn't reply. He's said what he had to say. He takes on a preoccupied look. He gets up. He walks up and down. He looks at me. He looks at my books. He takes one from the bookcase. He opens it. He closes it with a dry thud.

'Well I'm off Armida. Get down to work. Till tomorrow. Goodbye.'

'But – '

'If you want the play put on you must do as I say. You must trust me. I've had more experience than you. In any case everything for the company goes through me so don't go canvassing the others to take your side. I ask you to trust me and to put yourself entirely in my hands. We'll do some good work together. *Ciao* darling.'

I haven't time to say goodbye before he's gone.

A T five o'clock a girl from Ernesto's company comes to pick me up. In a ramshackle Fiat the colour of burnt sand. We drive towards Monte Verde skidding on worn tyres. I look surreptitiously at her profile against the dirty car window. She is fair and her hair is cut very short. A famished look. Age indeterminate – between twenty five and thirty five. She drives absent-mindedly heedless of halt signs and rights of way cutting corners recklessly. She doesn't utter a word during the whole journey.

At Ernesto's the others have already arrived. He introduces me to the company in a decisive voice.

'This is Armida Bianchi the author of the play.' Then he continues addressing me: 'This is Marcella who you know already. She's really good at playing the part of a woman who abandons everything for love. This is Giancarlo who came from the Academy last year. He's a little over-zealous. Once he gets over that he'll be okay. This is Nicola the elder brother of the company. He comes from the Stabile Theatre in Trieste and he's the perfect actor. A shade dull maybe but we think we'll make him a brilliant one. He has too low an opinion of himself and he's a bit earnest – that's what makes him dull. As for Sara the enigmatic Sara who brought you here . . . perhaps she's too intelligent to be an actress and should be a producer. However unfortunately it's me who's the producer here. And then we've got Ilario Sabatine and Giovanni but they're out in the kitchen with my wife Domenica making a delicious *sangria*.'

The house looks out over a small garden enclosed by a high wall of encrusted bricks. Pots with lemon trees and red geraniums add a bit of colour to a small shrivelled lawn.

'My wife looks after the garden. She's an amazing woman Armida I'd like you to meet her now. Come with me.'

He takes my hand and pulls me along a narrow passage and through a sliding door. The kitchen opens out like a small well-kept cupboard. The three actors are sitting on the table while she busies herself in front of a big decanter filled to the brim with red wine.

'Here's Domenica. This is our playwright Armida. I've been married to Domenica for ten years – isn't she beautiful? She's a marvellous woman. I don't deserve her. I'm too mean and selfish and uncaring. But she always forgives me. Without her I wouldn't survive.'

Domenica dries her hands on her apron and comes forward smiling. She has a soft friendly voice. Her chestnut hair falls gently round her pale forehead. Her large mouth has a tragic cast. Her eyes are still and almost expressionless as if a long habit of dissimulation had deadened them.

'And now let's read your play aloud so that if anyone has any comments to make they can speak out. Is that all right?'

It isn't all right for me at all. But I consent. What else can I do? The actors make a circle sitting either on the floor or on chairs or on the window sill. Meanwhile Domenica comes in and out silently carrying glasses mats and plates heaped with small cream cakes.

'But who's going to read it?' I ask in alarm.

'You darling. They don't know it and they'd be too preoccupied with avoiding mistakes in the reading to get the full meaning. Don't worry. We'll listen religiously.'

It seems a really bad idea to me. But there's no choice. I begin reading. My voice is strained. Sweat trickles in long rivulets down my neck on to my chest. I feel everyone's inquisitive gaze fixed on me: sometimes hostile sometimes indifferent. I read badly eating the words in my haste.

I finish as quickly as I can. I lift my head. I have swallowed a rock and now it won't go either up or down. I force myself to smile as if I were quite calm but what emerges is a painful grimace. I wait patiently for them to say something. The silence becomes piercing. Domenica comes timidly to my rescue:

'I think your play is lovely. I really like it.'

'What do you know about it Domenica? You weren't here while she was reading it. Don't take advantage just because I said you're intelligent. Are you trying to make a hit with the author?' What uncalled for aggression! I try to catch Domenica's eyes so as to thank her. But I see them escaping to shelter behind that veil of dissimulation I've already noticed in the kitchen.

'Come on everyone let's have your opinion. Then I'll have my say'

117

urges Ernesto goodnaturedly.

'Well I think it's a load of crap' says Giancarlo taking care to avoid my eyes.

'Why?' asks Ernesto in an amused tone of voice.

'Because it isn't clear what she's trying to say. The political line is a mess. The ideology is flabby. The language is too literary and doesn't fit the characters.'

'And you Nicola? What do you have to say about it?'

'I like it. I can see myself in it. But I don't know if we could do it – with all those characters it would take a lot of money.'

'You Marcella?'

'As far as I'm concerned it's fine. I like the way the two sides of the woman are brought out. I think we should do it.'

'And you Ilario?'

'I think it'll do. But it needs cutting. It's far too long.'

'Anyone else?'

'You're right Ilario. There's a lot of repetition. I'd cut out all that first part which frankly I find pretty boring.' Santino has plucked up courage and looks into my eyes defiantly while he talks.

'No. The first part's all right. It's the second that doesn't work' said Ernesto dryly. For a moment everyone is speechless. Then things start to boil up. A resolve to challenge the authority of the producer. A determination to speak their own minds to be uncompromising to be ostentatiously sincere.

'No no. It's definitely the first part that's wrong. It limps along. It's tedious.'

'You stupid oaf. I'm telling you it's the second part that's up the creek.'

'I think it needs more humour.'

'But you were doing nothing but laugh!'

'It's true I was laughing. But it needs more guts to it.'

'As far as I'm concerned there's too much . . . too much aggression. It gets on my nerves.'

'I feel the action in the second part is much too harsh. It's too. . . . middle class.'

'Are you suggesting the working classes aren't harsh?'

118

'The working classes understand toughness. Consequently they're less intolerant and judgmental. The working classes have stood for justice throughout history.'

'What do you think revolutions are made with then? Kid gloves?'

'As usual you misinterpret me every time I speak. You don't understand...'

'Stop quarrelling' interrupts Ernesto. He has stayed silent to listen to this explosion of different opinions. 'Let's get back to the play.'

'I feel it could be done. Since we haven't anything better let's do it.'

'What about Wedekind?'

'We did one of his plays last year.'

'He's an author who's really got guts. I'd do it again every year. We could do Brecht.'

'No. You know Brecht's rights are blocked.'

'That's true. Then why not a new version of Hamlet? I've got an idea: Do away with all the female parts. Have the Queen as a transvestite and Ophelia as a transexual – '

'And what's going to happen to the women?' Marcella's angry voice is heard as she gives us all a savage look.

Ernesto watches them quarrelling in a fatherly way. Every so often he gives me a wink that pierces right through me like an arrow. As if to sound out how far I can stand this trampling up and down over my naked body.

'Well that's enough everybody. You've all had your say. Thank you. If you'd reflected a little more you wouldn't have found yourselves throwing out judgements you weren't able to justify.'

Everyone listens to him in silence. Some are angry at his authoritarian tone but they are forced to accept it because they have to earn their living. Others are seduced by the tone of his voice – so generous so aggressive so firm.

'The play has its defects – that's not unusual. But my impression is that on the whole you're all happy about staging it. It's clear there'll have to be cuts. But Armida is open to that. She's quite willing to accept any necessary alterations – that's so isn't it Armida?'

I nod in agreement. I am incapable of opening my mouth. The

119

sangria heaves up and down between my throat and my stomach. I don't know whether I want to scream or to bury myself alive or simply to vomit.

In the car Sara speaks to me for the first time. She has a pensive ironical look.

'You're left feeling pretty bad eh?'

'A bit.'

'It's the brutality of working in a group. There's a pretence that it's all very egalitarian but in reality it's merely an excuse for the group to practise a sort of ritual sadism.'

'Why on earth didn't you say that earlier? I would have been really grateful.'

'It's a waste of time. I'm always saying it. They don't listen. They call me the duchess. You can't shift this illusion of theirs that they're on the right side of the barricades. This illusion that what they're engaged in is all very democratic and 'collective'.'

'But did you like my play or didn't you? You've never said a word.'

'Do you realise that yesterday we read a play by some other author and a week ago we read a third one also by a woman?'

'I don't understand.'

'They're plays written to order for the company. The authors are given the impression that they are already employed by us. But the majority of the group found the plays bad and so they were turned down.'

'Were they all along the same lines?'

'Of course. I told you they were commissioned for us. For over two years Ernesto has been obsessed with the theme of the Risorgimento.'

'You mean he's commissioned two plays from two other people at the same time?'

'Three if you include yours. So far each author has been as ignorant of the others as you were. They've both of them had to undergo a public reading. They both came out with broken bones.'

'Like me.'

'But they'll do yours.'

'Why? So many of them found it boring and unplayable.'

'You don't know what they did to the others. But in the end

Ernesto's opinion is the only one that counts. He's the producer and director of the group and he has the say-so. He likes it. He'll do it.'

'But do you think he was being sincere?'

'He's no reason to lie about it. We'll put it on and it'll be a success. You'll see. It has some good things in it...'

Gratitude makes me awkward. I embrace her and kiss her on her cheeks beneath the dark rings under her eyes. She smiles enigmatically. She puts the car into gear and drives off without looking back.

SITTING on a small black plastic seat. Hands on knees. Eyes fixed on the arrivals board which indicates that the flight from Barcelona is due at 12.12. But the green light hasn't come on yet. It has already lighted up for the arrival of the following flight the 12.30 from Abidjan. It's now 12.32. I go to the information desk and ask if the flight from Barcelona has arrived. A man looks up at me absent-mindedly.

'The plane's running late.'

'How late?'

'It will be announced as soon as they know for sure.'

'But at least it's left Barcelona?'

He isn't listening any more. He turns his bored eyes to the next anxious traveller.

I go back to sit in front of the arrivals board. I look round. In front of me is an Arab family. The man in a white barraccan. His curly black beard almost purple his eyes soft and gentle. The woman covered from head to foot in a brown habit the hood slipping round her neck. Her head veiled with a black scarf folded across her forehead. Her shapely hands playing with a rosary made of pale transparent golden beads. A very young baby wrapped in a piece of coloured voile with fringes sucking its fingers peacefully. Every so often the woman bends forward and rummages in a suitcase with big black handles and pulls out a handful of sunflower seeds which she passes to her husband with a deft movement of her wrist.

On the other side two hairy blond youths in shorts and T-shirts with open sandals on their grimy feet. One of them is asleep with his head resting against his rucksack. The other dozes leaning his head sideways on the shoulder of his friend.

Three nuns seated demurely on the edge of a bench reading. Their white coifs rise from under their chins. One of the three is an albino and continually flutters her white eyelids over her pale pink eyes.

'Flight number 227 from Barcelona will arrive about sixty minutes late.' An announcement at last! I look at the clock. It is ten to one. So it should arrive in about twenty minutes. I get up and go to the refreshment bar. I have a glass of iced tea. I go back to my plastic seat

122

but I find it occupied. A dark-haired girl looks at me in triumph.

I remain standing and scrutinise the board. The green indicator has still not lit up but the time announced for the delay has already passed. Four green lights come on at intervals announcing flights from Toronto Sofia Monaco and Hong Kong. I turn towards the amber-coloured picture-window and my eyes feed greedily on the gigantic birds with silver snouts gliding along the runway ready to take off for exotic far-distant lands. I become immersed in a state of stupor and don't notice that someone is touching me on the shoulder. He laughs in my face. It's him! The green light indicating the flight from Barcelona has only just come on.

We hug each other. Impetuously. But something isn't right. The impetus seems to come from an act of will rather than the urge of desire.

I drive in silence with his hand on my knee. The landscape rushes past with giddy speed. It is sucked into the funnel of the road where it is chopped up and pounded to pieces and emerges as a discoloured greyness. The silence becomes unbearable.

As soon as we're in his house with the luggage still piled up in the hall we make love without undressing. In desperate haste. Without pleasure. Without even a word.

I pass my fingers over his eyes to rid them of all the places all the people all the things he has seen which still lie heavily under his eyelids. My breath against his cheek trying to get free of the *For Man* eau-de-Cologne he picked up on the plane. Weary lips lost for words.

I caress him slowly tracing the contours of the muscles in his chest feeling the knots of his taut stomach sliding my thumbs along the veins which stand out beneath his skin.

I put my dry mouth on his shrunken prick. I feel it slide out. It swells up and takes shape. I grip it lightly between my teeth when a fart of rotten air wafts up into my nostrils. I sneeze. He laughs shaking his stomach muscles beneath my cheek. I laugh too. We make love again but this time we are in complete harmony.

When I wake up he has already gone out. It is just nine o'clock. I wash and get dressed. I hear Testone whining in the hall. I go and comfort him. 'Be a good dog while I finish getting dressed then we'll go.' Testone doesn't like sleeping away from home. He hates being shut up in bathrooms or entrance halls as happens when I'm staying at Miele's or my mother's. He objects to being locked up or kept away from the places he's familiar with: where he sleeps and has his meals and where the pleasures and parties and love affairs of those he loves are consummated.

While I am looking for my bag my eyes fall on some photographs taken and developed in Spain. Bright colours twice as strident as natural colour: the blues almost purple greens almost black pinks almost scarlet whites almost yellow. He is smiling in the centre of a group of men. Two young sombre-looking women are sitting on a wall next to the group. On the back of the photographs there are signatures.

As I read them I know exactly what I am going to find. I see it among the other names: Amparo. The woman who was sleeping in his room at the Hotel Assuntion in Barcelona. In no way is she the old bag of sixty that he described but a small slender figure with black hair cut short round eyes and a full sensual mouth.

I sit down with the photograph in my hands. My heart has shrunk to the size of a button. Suddenly everything is clear. The coolness when we first met. The lovemaking so fast and furious in an attempt to overcome the difficulty of adjusting to another body the exhaustion the silence the unfamiliar smells.

And then that puff of foetid air which rose from his anus to my nostrils and made me sneeze. And the way he laughed as if this expulsion of badness had liberated him from the last poisons of an alien love.

I hear the door open. Testone runs to see who it is. He doesn't bark. He wags his tail. It's Miele coming back with hot rolls and a thermos of coffee. He is happy and contented. He pours me out coffee and urges me to eat.

'Are you looking at the photographs? Aren't they good! That's me. And those are the international delegates. They come from all over the world.'

'Wasn't Amparo your interpreter?'

'Amparo?' He gives me a sideways look trying to gain time. 'Where did you see her?'

'It's written on the back.'

'Oh yes the signatures. That's another Amparo. There's thousands of Amparos in Barcelona. You could almost say that one woman in three is called that.'

'Don't you have a photograph of the other Amparo?'

'I don't know. I'll have a look.'

But he can't find one. He looks a bit embarrassed. I don't pursue it. I know how predictable and boring jealousy is.

I return home with Testone trying to recollect all Miele's old theories. 'How I hate subterfuge and deception and lies. You must believe me Armida – jealousy is outdated and even if I recognise its importance in the collective unconscious I'm damned if I'm going to be its slave. Two liberated people like us should be able to love quite freely. They shouldn't need to hide anything from each other...'

As I go into the flat I find a note pushed under the door...'Today there is another meeting. Get cracking! I'll come for you at five. Love Sara.'

I sit down at the table with the script of my play beside me. Rewrite the second act. Take out the trial. Take out the part of the protagonist. Why should I? My fingers refuse to move from my lap. I remain drowsily gazing out of the dirty window at the facades of the distant houses as they slowly change colour.

125

Sara sounds her horn repeatedly from the street. I lean out of the window and call a greeting to her. I go down to the front door. She looks more cheerful than usual. In her hair she is wearing forget-me-nots kept in place by a hair-grip.

'Have you been working?' she asks me immediately.

'No.'

'We can't start to rehearse until you've handed over the finished script.

'What's happened to the other two authors?'

'Dead. Finished. Kaput.'

'I'd like to meet them.'

'I wouldn't advise it. They'll hate you. Indeed they hate you already.'

'It's not me they should hate it's you people. It's you who've brought about this silly situation of rivalry.'

'People always hate the wrong people. It's just the same with love – you always love the wrong person. Don't you agree?'

'Who do you love?'

'Myself. And it's the very worst thing I can do. I'm always disappointed. And then I know myself too well. Nothing ever surprises me. But I can't act differently. I've always been so much on the defensive that now I'm shut up inside a solitary shell with only my feelings for company. And you?'

'Me? I'm in love with...' I stop on the edge of a precipice.

'A man or a woman?'

'A man.'

'The same old story. He makes you suffer and you feel bad and you run after him and so things go from bad to worse. Correct?'

'More or less.'

'If one loves oneself at least one isn't trapped in these inevitable and tedious situations.'

'When do you think they'll put on my play?'

'In November. Didn't Ernesto tell you?'

'No.'

'He's acting mysterious. So that he can possess you better.'

'Possess? In what sense?'

'That's what he wants most of all: to possess people. Then to understand them. If he likes you he'll try to possess you. I don't mean just sexually. I mean total possession that involves the spirit more than anything else. He's a sort of wizard with a lot of intuition for other people's talent. He's got loads of charm. If he likes you and if he likes your play he'll do you a good production. He's quite a magician. He can make lions and panthers appear on the stage and then make them disappear inside a hat. They're all in love with him. Didn't you notice that?'

'All who?'

'The whole company. Especially Domenica who as he says is a saint. But like all saints she knows how to practise the most refined cruelty. Then Marcella who'd die for him. Santino too. And Giancarlo – everyone ready to do any dirty trick to gain entry to his slimy heart.'

'I guess you're a little in love with him yourself?'

'I was mad about him. For two weeks. Then I got bored.'

'Did he want to possess you too?'

'He possessed me completely. But that wasn't enough for him. He wanted my total surrender so that I wouldn't just see him with my eyes but with my belly. With my womb. I simply strengthened the lock on my shell and barricaded myself in. Now I'm not afraid of him any more. I'm better off on my own.'

We arrive. Everybody else is already there. Ernesto asks me if I've re-written the second act. I tell him I haven't. He makes a big scene in front of everyone. Eventually he realises he has gone too far and he throws himself down on the divan next to me seizes my hand and kisses it. He loads me with compliments and begs to be forgiven. And he does it all with a sort of demonic sincerity. By this time I feel I don't want to have anything more to do with them. I say that I'm going. But he takes hold of my arm.

'Where are you going? Nothing's settled. Before letting you get off to work you must sign here.'

'What's that?'

'An application form for membership of the Cooperative. Then

127

you'll be one of us. Aren't you pleased?'

'Yes but...'

'No buts. It's an honour we're doing you. It means that at meetings you'll be able to take part in the election of the director. You'll have a vote like everyone else and you'll have your share of the profits.'

'Don't talk such rubbish Ernesto. Tell her what you really want from her.' Sara has plucked up courage and is looking at us ironically. The bunch of forget-me-nots has slipped down her neck.

'What do I want? Nothing... All I want is for us to do something good together. Isn't that so?' He laughs and gives me a wink.

'The truth Ernesto' Sara insists stamping her foot on the floor.

'You tell her then.'

'The truth Armida is that you will be engaged as part of the Cooperative. You'll have to surrender your · royalties to the Company.'

'But the Company isn't some sort of man-eating tiger' Ernesto comes in impetuously.' The Company is committed to paying you the same as everyone else.'

'A payment you'll never see... It's better you should tell the truth Ernesto. Why confuse people?'

'What do you mean by never? Who says she won't be paid? The Government grant will arrive. Maybe not just yet but it'll come eventually and then it'll be divided equally between all of us.'

'You know perfectly well that when the money does arrive there are all sort of debts to be paid first of all. Then there's the interest owing to the bank. It'll all be whittled away in no time. We haven't been paid for three years have we?'

On the way home Sara tries to reassure me. But she looks as if she's quite enjoying herself too. The bunch of forget-me-nots has returned to its place over her right temple even if the little flowers are looking a bit faded.

'Made a fool of and still smiling.'

'This is a power game Armida. You can't do anything about it.'

'Thanks for having warned me.'

'I'm not really much help I'm afraid. It's not your fault. It's just that if you really want to have your play put on you have to stick by

128

the rules. It's only worth it if you can keep your peace of mind. I spelled it out for you because you knew it already. It seemed ridiculous to fabricate a pack of lies to someone you are going to be working with.'

'Don't keep thanking me. I'm no saint. I'm not out to save anyone. I've got a sense of the absurd that's all. And the entertainment is more subtle when the victims are aware of it themselves. Otherwise it's just a common fraud. Don't you agree?'

THE telephone is ringing insistently. I stretch out my hand but I mistake the distance in the dark. I was dreaming: I found myself in room 26 of the Hotel Assuntion. Only a faint light from the street filtered into the room through the closed shutters.

A woman stood facing the open door of the bathroom. Miele was sitting on the bed. He called her and she was about to turn round. At that moment the telephone rang.

I hold the receiver to my ear. A spluttering. I switch on the light. It's three o'clock.

'Hullo. Who is it?'

'It's me. Paolo.'

'Hullo. Where are you?'

'In New York. I'm ringing to ask you to join me. I'm ready to forgive everything. Let's begin again.'

'Join you? But Paolo – how do you mean begin again?'

'For God's sake Armida why can't you let yourself go sometimes. You're never open you never show any affection. I'm ringing you up from the other side of the world to tell you I love you. And I want you here with me. So will you come?'

'No Paolo I can't.'

'Oh go to hell Armida. You're just a bloody fool... I hate you.'

'You know our marriage has ended. It's all over. It doesn't exist any more.'

'What has marriage got to do with it? I'd never re-marry you even if I were dead. I just wanted you to stay with me for a bit. But hell what's the use? It's no good expecting anything from you. So – goodbye.'

'I'm sorry Paolo.'

'You're not pregnant are you by any chance?'

'No of course not.'

'I warn you. I won't recognise anyone else's child and I won't give you a penny. So it's a waste of time trying.'

'Why do you have to be so offensive?'

'Because I don't want to be castrated by you or anyone else.'

'But who wants to castrate you? Anyway I was going to tell you not to send me any more money. I've found a job.'

'It isn't me who sends you money. It's Elizabetta. So tell her. What sort of job anyway?'

'Working as assistant to an English journalist.' Something of a half truth because I was offered the job a year ago. But I know I can take it up if ever I want to.

'So how about it? Will you come?'

'No.'

'Go to hell then Armida. I hate you.'

A click at the other end of the line. He's put down the receiver. The telephone cables continue to carry the silence across the ocean from one side of the world to the other.

'Paolo!'

But his rejection is absolute. I turn from side to side unable to get back to sleep. I try to recapture the dream where I left it. The half-lit room in the Assuntion Hotel the open bathroom door the back of the naked woman the voice of Miele calling her: Amparo!

Silence. The regular bands of bluish light from the street lamps stretch across the floor. The open door reveals ivory tiled walls. A length of pink-striped curtain flutters in the steam rising from the hot water. Now I can hear quite clearly the splash of water as it cascades into the bath.

She is completely still. One leg slightly bent one foot raised as if it had stopped in the middle of a footstep. Narrow girlish hips long back curved at the waist slightly sloping shoulders.

'Amparo!'

The woman half turns. She is smiling out of the corner of her mouth. I look at her in astonishment my gaze piercing the milky darkness. It is my mother who stands there in front of me. My mother at the age of twenty. Long white legs. Neck like a swan's.

Now she smiles ambiguously. Is she smiling at me or at Miele? The twist of her body has brought her right breast into the light: a large delicate breast. With all my soul I long to drink from it.

I move my head. A dull pain keeps me nailed to the pillow. Now I remember. I knocked a hole in it playing between the tables. The stitches keep pulling on my heavily bandaged forehead. She has

131

bathed the wound with hydrogen peroxide and it is trickling down into my ears. It blossomed into a flower of effervescent bubbles at the tips of her fingers as she cut the fringe of my forehead with a pair of nail scissors. She covered the bleeding wound with a piece of gauze and then she wound a bandage round and round it . . .

Now I am a mummy. I have lain undisturbed for centuries inside a casket. A little beige coat. Patched shoes . . . Now my mother and I are walking down the corridors of the museum. There's not a soul to be seen. We stop in front of a statue.

'This is Sicmeth Goddess of Darkness' she tells me and she holds my hand so tight that it goes numb.

Sicmeth on a pedestal of pink stone. Her feet pressed tightly together her hands on her breasts. A peplos of mottled black and green marble loosely covering her body. A woman in the fullness of youth.

My child's eyes climb up the statue from her feet to her head. I stare in wonder at the face of the goddess: an old she-lion with a watery gaze sad mouth and shaggy moustache. We look at each other for a long time spellbound. Rays of dust-laden sunshine slant through the windows of the museum corridor. I fall eternally in love with this mysterious goddess whom my mother has presented to me on that fateful morning.

But now my mother takes hold of my wrist. She guides me between two aisles of gigantic gods and goddesses who stand there with bored expressions. Then she pushes me firmly but gently towards a badly lit glass case.

Beneath the glass smeared with finger-prints I make out a little painted table right up against the wall. Then I see a miniscule body. Layers of bandages blackened by centuries. Framed by the tarred bandages a small shrunken face dry as a withered pear. A perfectly preserved nose. A mouth with lips drawn over a row of flawless teeth. Eyelids stuck down over the pupils. Eyelashes clotted on to cheeks of papier maché.

This macabre sight takes my breath away and paralyses me with fear. In her calm sensible voice my mother tells me about the Queens of Egypt who took all their possessions with them into their tombs.

And indeed there alongside the child mummy are jewels combs carved out of bone tooled mirrors and large pieces of crumbling blackened bread.

'This child was the daughter of a King. Look how they buried her with all her toys. She should have got married. Instead she died . . .'

I stand there. Eyes glued to the glass. Incapable of moving. Stomach turned to stone. Knowing I am dead for ever and ever. From sidereal distances hearing the music of my mother's voice and smelling her delicate scent of magnolia . . .

A sacrilegious thought obsesses me. A painful thought. Indeed more than painful: terrible. I am tantalised by it: the thought that time has stopped at the same moment for both of us in that empty museum. She and I silent bandaged mummified for an eternity of perfect love.

Amparo has the same she-lion's face as Sicmeth the same fierce sad look the same smell of magnolia that I have always loved.

I wake. I am sitting up in bed with perspiration running down my forehead. A feeling of suffocation. The telephone has been ringing and ringing. I can hear it reverberating in my head still heavy with those bandages. I am still gasping still incapable of finding my voice. I lift the receiver.

'Hullo Armida?'

I manage to force out a yes.

'What's the matter. Are you all right?'

'I've just had a nightmare!'

'Wake up. It's ten o'clock.'

'Yes?'

'Yesterday Dida Ada Cesare and I met up and we decided we'd all go together to Helsinki to celebrate Nico and Ada's wedding. We can join the International Youth Festival there. So we've already registered you as working in the theatre. In return for their hospitality they'll expect you to give a short lecture about the theatre. Is that O.K.?'

'Yes. That's fine. When do you leave?'

'In a week. On the first of August.'

MIELE and I striding confidently towards the station. Suitcase on my head. Flowered skirt flapping round my knees.

'Have you got the hair dryer?'

'No.'

'Scatter-brained as usual. And some books to fill in time?'

'Yes. Lots.'

'I feel quite light-headed.'

'I can't say I do. Not with this suitcase on my head.'

'Give it to me. I'll carry it.'

'No. I'll manage.'

He comes round in front of me and makes me put the suitcase down. He grabs it and gives me a kiss. Grasping a suitcase in each hand he balances himself and runs forward.

The station is crowded. Hundreds of people coming and going. Hippies with their hair tied behind their necks with string. A flock of nuns. Soldiers sweltering in the heat – the atmosphere of an army tent. Trains running late. Platforms changed at the last minute without warning. Young people sitting on the ground smoking and leaning against their rucksacks. Others sleeping with their backs against the walls. Passers-by striding cautiously over their bodies.

'Where are we meeting the others?' asks Miele.

'Platform Five.'

'Are you sure?'

'Absolutely certain .'

'Have you got the tickets?'

'Yes yes.'

'Let me see.'

Miele puts down the suitcase. He takes the tickets and reads pronouncing the words one syllable at a time: 'Tri-este Vi-enna Ki-ev Vil-na Ri-ga Tall-in Hel-sink-i. Have you ever seen such a fucking journey? I bet you've never done a trip like this in all your life. Still we'll make it...'

I put the tickets back in my shoulder-bag alongside my passport my make-up a clean handkerchief and a little roll of dollars. I shield it with my hand. For fear it might escape! The magic bag that now enfolds all those miraculous unknown cities.

Ada and Nico are already on Platform Five with two military green kitbags on their shoulders. A little later Cesare arrives with a pigskin case marked with his initials. Dida is late as usual.

Meanwhile an avalanche of other Festival-goers arrive. A banner high above the platform proclaims: *Youth Festival Train – Welcome.* Boys from the South with peasants' luggage and hair curling on their necks put on a carefree manner but actually look a bit lost. Country girls from near Rome wearing brand new white trousers. A swarm of people all jabbering in different dialects dragging suitcases rucksacks leather satchels bags and parcels.

'Have you got seats you apes?' shouts Cesare from where he's looking after the luggage.

'Nico's gone to do that' says Ada who isn't looking at the train but at the entrance to the platform. She is waiting to see Dida appear. 'It's nearly time to leave. Shall I go and phone her?'

'No use. If she's still at home she's missed the train. She'll be on her way.'

'The train leaves in six minutes.'

'Here she is!'

Dida walks up the platform with a buoyant step even though she has a suitcase in one hand a bag slipping off her shoulders and a bundle of newspapers under her arm. She is wearing one of her full gathered blouses open down the front.

'I've been having heart attacks. Why on earth are you so late?' Ada takes her bag. Dida full of excitement and happiness embraces everyone. We board the train amidst a confusion of arms luggage and bawling voices. On the dot of six the train starts to move. Hundreds of faces lean out of windows to say good-bye to relations or simply as an act of defiance – good riddance to Rome and its heat and its traffic and its summer shambles and its stinks and its political and social chaos.

We have a compartment all to ourselves. Six seats with six couchettes that open out at night to fill the small space in which we shall be living for eight days.

We stow the luggage away. We open the windows. The train

threads its way out of the city and through the wide Roman countryside made more spacious by the lengthening afternoon shadows.

Miele sits opposite me. He looks at me. He is happy. He smiles. In that moment our love is so full it overflows to infinity.

My heart takes up the rhythm of the train. The rhythm of a country dance. A jump and a hop two steps to the right a jump a hop two steps to the left and so on and so on round and round in a circle one step and a curtsey another step and a curtsey hop hop hop. . . .

'SUPPER will be served at eight o'clock in the restaurant car at the rear of the train. Will you please form a queue for meal vouchers. Supper will not be served to anyone without a voucher.'

We are a bit late. The queue already stretches as far as the fifth carriage. We wait more than three quarters of an hour leaning against the lurching sides of the corridor. The wind blows through the window in bitter smoky gusts.

Miele stands next to me shoulder to shoulder. Behind is Dida singing in the middle of a group of fresh enthusiastic faces. Her soft blouse flakes off her. Her hair hangs down her shoulders like a waterfall of golden ringlets. Ada and Nico can't take their eyes off her. Cesare sits by himself playing patience. He lays out the cards on top of a newspaper folded in four which he's spread across his knees.

I peer into the darkness letting myself be sucked into the gusts of air that swirl in and out dishevelling my hair. I am in a state of peaceful euphoria. I could spend the whole night here being monotonously jolted. I imagine the train seen from outside: a chain of lighted squares snaking through the countryside. How often have I craned my neck to watch enviously a lit-up train as it disappears from sight. Now I am inside it. Lazily I follow the rectangles of light as they glide over the trees over the walls over the rails over the fields. This time the train does not melt into the horizon but will be with me night and day hypnotising me with its repetitive rhythm.

After about an hour the queue finally reaches the restaurant car. They have run out of vouchers but they let us in all the same. We are tired and famished. We sit down at a table stained with wine.

'What is there to eat?' Dida signals the dining-car attendant with her bare arm. In fact he is simply an impoverished student earning the trip by working.

Ada cleans the table with a paper napkin. There is a smell of boiled eggs and rotten apples.

'There's nothing left in the kitchen. If you like I can get you boiled eggs and some bread.'

'And to drink?'

'Beer.'

137

Stale bread and eggs as hard as marbles. We eat it all up hungrily and wash it down with two bottles of luke-warm beer.

While we are returning to our seats the train gives a long-drawn-out moan and stops. Barking of orders in an unknown language. Stamping of military boots. A soldier in greenish uniform appears his face framed in the carriage window. He calls out in laboured Italian: '*passaporti prego.*'

Outbursts of swearing at the train's abrupt stop. Tousled heads peering out from the compartments with couchettes. Feet waving in the air. A prolonged whistle. The train gives another jolt. It moves. But it doesn't get far. It halts again with more screeching of brakes. Someone falls. Loud swearing. Laughter.

I hear a nasal voice: 'This is the Yugoslav frontier.' Someone with catarrh hawks and spits into the darkness. Curses in Serbo-Croat. A soldier with a red nose comes to inspect passports.

'No one may leave the train.'

The night around us is no longer soft. It has become thorny and prickly. Orders are rapped out. The train waits to leave. A sound of footsteps. An angry shout.

'What's the delay?'

'Some imbecile has lost his passport.'

'They're interrogating him.'

'Interrogating? Why the fuss if he's only lost it?'

'They're saying he's a spy.'

Murmurings from the shaded light of the carriages. The voice of one of the organisers is heard protesting:

'Excuse me but they are all students. They're young people coming from all over Italy to the Festival. We are not stopping in Yugoslavia. We are going straight to Helsinki where they are waiting for us. I assure you that no one will be leaving the train.'

An irascible voice answers him in Slav something that corresponds to: 'I don't give a damn whether they're students. If he doesn't produce his passport the train doesn't leave.'

The argument goes on for a good half-hour. Meanwhile Dida has started singing again. Some girls from Naples join with her. Half-heartedly at first then louder and louder. A soldier sticks his head inside the carriage and holds up his finger in front of his mouth as a sign to shut up. Dida defiantly continues singing on her own. When she has finished the song she stops and lights a cigarette. She moves from one window to another puffing the smoke out into the darkness.

At length the train takes off. We never know whether the passport turned up or not. Some people are already snoring. Clouds of black smoke swirl in through the window. Miele turns over and over in his berth below mine.

'Can't you sleep?'

'I'm not sleepy.'

'Would you like a cigarette?'

'Yes.'

I hand him the packet. He takes it pressing his fingers for a moment against my palm. I lean out of the sleeping berth. But he has already turned towards the wall. He hasn't even lit the cigarette. I go back to looking at the ceiling eighteen inches above my nose. The inside of a barrel painted white. At each curve of the line small mauve reflections of light flicker up and down.

I have hardly got to sleep when I am woken by a series of sudden rapid jolts.

'What's up?'

'Klagenfurt! Klagenfurt!'

'We're in Austria. Out with your passports and no fooling around unless you want to be skinned alive!'

More stamping heels. Orders in German. But this time the stop is brief. People continue sleeping.

AT six o'clock next morning we are in Vienna. We are woken up by loudspeakers. We dress hurriedly and rush outside. We shall be stopping here for one hour.

'What shall we do?'

'I want to wash.'

'Have you seen the queues in the corridor? Let's go to the toilets in the station.'

'There are queues there as well.'

'Let's go and get something to eat first before yesterday evening gets repeated.'

Dida is already on the platform drinking coffee out of a paper cup. She greets us with a kiss. She has washed and dabbed on scent and brushed her hair. Curls are dancing round her forehead.

We go out of the station. We cross a street full of shops. Cesare goes in front taking big strides from one paving stone to the next. The pavements are already touched by the sun. It's warm even though it's barely half-past-six. The shops are still shut. An old man with a sailor's beret pressed down on his head is selling freshly boiled frankfurters in a little booth by the entrance to the station.

We rush towards him and order twelve sausages with mustard and fried chips. But the potatoes aren't cooked yet. They lie in the boiling oil shrouded by swarms of small crackling bubbles.

'What a fucking breakfast. I'll be down with gastro-enteritis!' grumbles Cesare. He makes to move off but as soon as Dida hands him a hot sausage spread with mustard he seizes it and bites into it with gusto.

A moment later we are joined by other groups who take the booth by assault. The old man who was initially jubilant at the thought of so many customers is antagonised by the uncouth haste of all these over-excited Italians who grab boiling sausages and unsliced bread out of his hands.

We have already learned that if one wants to get anything on this journey one has to be first in the queue. The difficulty is that others know it too. So the days consist of a need to be permanently on the alert followed by a strategically planned rush. Everyone except the

140

first-comers has to put up with left-overs. And the queues start two hours in advance.

As we are about to pay for the sausages we realise we haven't got any Austrian money. The old man watches us in dismay. He gabbles at us angrily. We don't understand. Finally Cesare decides to make use of the little amount of German he knows. He explains that we don't want to go away without paying but we've only got Italian money to pay with. The man gets really angry. But by now the sausages have been eaten so he is forced to accept the liras. Then he hurries to shut the booth before the next wave of hungry students arrives.

The train begins the long day's journey. The first whole day of the trip. People come and go. Get bored. Set up volley-ball matches between carriages with balls made out of crumpled paper. There is a lot of singing. Many have guitars and there is always a circle of onlookers ready to improvise a chorus. Others play cards on any seat that is momentarily vacant. Some have fierce political arguments. I prefer to pass the time reading. I don't feel bored. I sit next to the window with the book on my knees. At times I raise my eyes and let them glide over the ever-changing landscape.

At midday we reach the Czech border. The train stops with a groan. Barbed wire. Rifles on shoulders. Steel helmets. Deserted platforms.

A soft female voice repeats continually 'Znojmo Znojmo' sensuously dragging out the 'Z'. I imagine a woman with a sylph-like body consumed with passion. A moment later I catch sight of her. Legs wide apart the megaphone held up to her mouth a gigantic woman with large lopsided features wearing a straight grey skirt and on her head a grey cap with gold braid. 'Znojmo Znojmo' she repeats into the megaphone sounding as if she were on the point of fainting.

'Don't we go through Prague?'

'No love nowhere near Prague.'

'But it says Prague in the timetable.'

'No not Prague. We cut straight up towards Leningrad. We don't even see Moscow.'

'Not Moscow!'

141

'No my love not even Moscow.'

Snatches of conversation that reach me while I read. I turn the page. I turn back. I start again at the beginning.

'Have you seen Federico making a pass at that fat girl?' The malicious voice of an excitable boy filters through the small curtain that divides the compartments from the corridor. I prick up my ears.

'Which fat girl? There are so many' replies a rather insipid woman's voice.

'The beautiful one with fair hair and a sexy look.'

'How anyone could find her beautiful I don't know. She looks to me like a great porpoise.'

'She's really beautiful. She's got the loveliest face I've ever seen. It's a pity she's quite so plump.'

'She's O.K. as she is' interrupts a hoarse drawling voice. 'I'd make her any time!'

'What taste for Christ's sake!' Laughter which merges into the rumbling of the train. A whistle. The train slows down. Through the window come gusts of heavy viscid air – we are going through an industrial zone. Desolate factory chimneys break the whiteness of the midday sky. Long grey buildings with windowless walls. Barbed wire. Rows of dirty mud-stained lorries.

'Brno Prostejon Ostrava. What fucking names! How the fuck are you expected to pronounce them?'

'They know how to.'

'Thanks.'

'Stupid clot.'

'So are you a clot.'

'I'd shove your face in but I can't be bothered.'

'Try it then.'

The two go on quarrelling all day without ever shifting from their seats or moving their legs bent up under their chins.

'Have you noticed the difference now we're out of Austria?'

'No I can't say I've noticed anything.'

'What a wanker! You're not even aware that we've passed from a capitalist country to a socialist one?'

The two voices get sharper. I look up from my book. I glance absent-mindedly at the landscape bristling with tall chimneys.

'No. I didn't notice a thing.'

'Weren't you aware of a sort of ostentatiousness in Austria? Can't you feel that here it's different? Nobler. More austere. How people are concerned with mankind's destiny? Whereas there they think only about what they can sell!'

'And you spotted all this from the train while it was moving?'

'You've got eyes too you arsehole. Use them.'

'Arsehole yourself!'

'Have you yet seen anything gratuitous superfluous or vulgar since we've been in Czechoslovakia?'

'I don't know what you mean by vulgar.'

'I mean all the consumerism.'

'No I haven't. I haven't seen a thing.'

'Because you don't want to see.'

'And you see what isn't there. I don't know which is worse.'

'You're accusing me of being an idealist?'

'I hate fanatics of any kind.'

'Haven't you noticed the factories? The queues of workers waiting to go inside? How disciplined and serious they look?'

'Yes so serious they've become as grey as the grey cement!'

'It's the grey of revolution comrade. The grey of justice. The grey of happiness. You're dazzled by the glittering colours of capitalism that bewitch man before subjugating him. You're a cretin. Brainless. You consist of nothing but a mouth at one end and a prick at the other. All you want is to eat and to fuck.'

'You don't eat and fuck I suppose?'

'I eat and fuck but I don't make them my only reason for existence. I want to change the world and if anyone isn't with me so much the worse for them. To the wall!'

'*Extremism: the growing pains of communism.*'

'Don't say such fucking stupid things!'

'Actually it was Lenin who said it.'

'When did he say it and where?'

'It's the title of a book.'

Silence. An irascible cough. Then footsteps down the corridor. The

143

two have shut up at last. I turn to the window and look out. To the right is a lake radiating a phosphorescent glow. A long boat with black sails glides over the placid water. I hear the calm voice of my mother reciting:

> My ship goes by black sails unfurled
> Black sails unfurled across the storm-tossed sea.
> My heart lies pierced
> Pierced as you laugh to make it bleed.

When the boat comes nearer I can see a woman sitting in the prow. She turns round and gazes with astonishment at this train full to bursting with young heads and arms stretching out of the window to embrace the world in a wild fantasy of omnipotence.

I T is half-past five in the morning. I slip out of the sleeping berth and jump bare-footed on to the floor so as not to wake Miele. I put on a Japanese dressing-gown with big green dahlias and walk towards the toilet. There is always somebody who has woken up first. But the queue is still short: only two or three people. They all have towels hanging over their arms and a toothbrush and a piece of soap in their hands. We barely greet each other. Drowsiness slows down our movements. No one feels like talking. Everyone else is asleep. Many are still snoring. Someone is preparing to grab a place in the restaurant car where coffee finishes after the first four sittings.

I open the door. I find Dida inside.

'Armida come in too.'

'No. There isn't room for both of us.'

'I've almost finished. Just a minute' she says passing a brush through her fair curls.

'You look lovely Dida. How do you manage it always looking so fresh and scented? When I wake up I feel like a used rag with rings under my eyes a pain in my back and my mouth like a birdcage.'

She smiles as she fixes a coil of hair on her neck with four hairpins.

'Are you happy?' she whispers in my ear.

'Yes. Very.'

'Me too. I believe Cesare is coming round to me. He actually listens to me when I talk – he never used to do that. Do you think he might end up loving me?'

'Ada's the one who loves you. And Nico as well.'

'Ada . . . I really like her a lot. But I couldn't ever love her.'

'Why not?'

'She loves me too much. If I returned her love I believe I'd disappear.'

'So you too are pining for a solitary love that never gets returned?'

'No. I really want Cesare to love me. And he will. One day he will.'

'But meanwhile he doesn't.'

'He will love me. He will.'

'And with him you aren't afraid of disappearing?'

'No because he'll never love me in the way that Ada does. He's

145

incapable of that.' A sad laugh. Two dimples in her cheeks.

'Dida if I didn't love Miele I'd love you. You're the most fascinating woman I know.

She kisses me lightly on the tip of my nose. She laughs happily. Her fair hair falls in ringlets down her cheeks. At that moment Miele comes in. He has heard our voices. He looks at us suspiciously. He grabs my waist. He searches for my tongue with his. With unusual fervour. Stirred up by jealousy and his will to possess me totally. Dida goes out silently closing the door behind her. He pushes me against the wall but the truth is it's too cramped to make love in there and outside people are knocking on the door so we go back to our seats holding each other's hands.

We have changed trains. This one goes more slowly and reverberates with a different rhythm. The carriages are larger and wider. The sleeping berths are solider and are upholstered in wool and leather. When they are closed up a snow-white hand-embroidered antimacassar hangs at the level of our heads. The restaurant car is more spacious with red leather seats. Each table has a lamp with a parchment shade. The food has changed too. In the morning they give us bread and butter and tea without milk. At lunch vegetable broth with meat balls and green vegetables cooked with garlic. In the evening bean soup bread fresh cheese and beer.

We have all lost weight from having to skip meals when we arrive too late to get our vouchers. In spite of rushing all the time this happens very often.

The landscape has changed again. Expanses of watery green stretch to the horizon. We pass through woods of birch trees with milky white trunks. We are in the middle of Poland heading towards the Soviet Union. The train stops at every station and every time there is a resounding welcome. Hundreds of banners. Posters with *Youth of the World – Welcome to Socialist Poland.* We leap off the train *en masse* and rush to grab maize fritters and honey which are held out for us by the peasants. We drink acid fizzy cider brought to us in mess-tins. Everywhere kisses and hugs. Political songs. Out come the cameras. Everyone poses to be photographed alongside the station signboards.

146

In the larger stopping-places like Krakov and Lodz we are taken to rooms where we are given light refreshments. Hundreds of shining glasses filled with water or cider. Hundreds of portions of home-made custard tart. Festoons of coloured paper. We all fling ourselves forward like locusts and devour the lot within a few minutes under the indulgent eye of the organisers. They are very fair with red necks ill-cut hair and gentle curious eyes that fix us with avid stares – we the travellers from Europe from the exotic land of Italy which they've only heard of from schoolbooks.

'Italy . . . Italy . . . Venice?'

'Rome.'

'Ah Rome . . .' and they almost fall backwards. The city of Nero and Virgil. The city where the Pope raises slender arms in white to bless pilgrims from all over the world. 'Ah Rome!' They sigh not knowing how to express their admiration. They are friendly awkward idealistic ingenuous enthusiastic curious. They want to poke their noses into our handbags and suitcases so that they can hold up in front of the astonished eyes of their friends blue American jeans blue and white nylon underwear transparent as dragonflies' wings white canvas shoes with sea blue edges. Everything of ours fascinates and enthrals them.

Some astute person has set up a barter business based on smiles and gestures. One pair of trousers for a balalaika. Four pairs of lace-trimmed pants for a record. A flesh-pink petticoat of artificial silk for three packets of cigarettes. A box of chocolates for two pocket-knives. A leather bag for a magnifying glass. And so on.

The train departs with heads leaning out of windows arms stretched up in a salute and fists clenched. Banners flapping barely filling out in the breeze of a damp sultry August day. Standing erect in a line along the platform all the people who welcomed us with so much enthusiasm turn their faces after us with genuine sadness. They continue to wave even when the train is no longer in sight.

In some places there is not even a station. We stop in the middle of a sun-drenched countryside. The students jump down precipitately in a desperate hurry to see what there is to barter. Now they have only rubbish to pay with – mother-of-pearl buttons biros necklaces of

Murano glass beads gold belts and handkerchiefs imprinted with a picture of the Colisseum.In exchange we are provided with fritters hot bread plum liqueur fresh tomatoes very small pears with a sharp taste bunches of daisies and big cotton headscarves with colours that are already fading.

'Aren't you ashamed selling such rubbish?'

'All the worse for them if they get cheated' cynically replies a lad from Rome with a dome-shaped belly. He has been the organiser of the sales centre and acts as go-between for peasants and travellers.

'How about letting me have some of your books?' he asks in a conciliatory self-satisfied tone.

'No.'

He makes an obscene gesture which means 'Fuck off then'. The Polish student who is waiting for the books from me and for a pair of canvas shoes that belong to Cesare smiles disconsolately revealing two gold eye-teeth.

Amongst the 'new youth of Europe' the five days of travelling has seen the formation of alliances hierarchies friendships and associations that divide the train into the privileged and the under-privileged. First of all there are the 'mafiosi' who can be found right throughout the train. They know everybody they know where to lay their hands on anything. They do business with anyone blackmailing seducing threatening in order to maintain control over the train. They are the ones who are certain to have a seat in the dining-car. They are the bosses. Then there are their vassals and clients who don't have the unscrupulousness or the cheek of the bosses but who are happy to cash in by acting as intermediaries in selling a pair of old tennis shoes for three hundred times their value or a French phrase-book or an old pair of knickers in exchange for food or local handicrafts. They are the ones who buy black market meal vouchers for the dining-car and sell them at a profit. They spend all day in their compartments eating drinking playing cards and intriguing to capture the best-looking girls on the train about whom they know every detail.

Then there are the hard-liners like the Stalinist who sleeps in the compartment on my right. He doesn't acknowledge the existence of the business rackets or the mafia but goes on blithely pouring out a

148

soliloquy on the 'great destiny of socialism'.

There are also the dim-wits who live from day to day who let themselves be robbed with a smile and who embrace the welcoming hosts at the stations as if they were brothers. Each time the train leaves they explode in noisy farewells. They spend hours and hours at the window watching the landscape go by and waving their hands as they greet every shepherd every stone-cutter every rice-picker they catch sight of in the distance. As if they are desperate to find some rationale for this amazing journey which has wrenched them away from their families their ill-smelling kitchens their village streets where everyone gets together on a Sunday in the village square to play football or to go to mass.

Finally there are the aristocrats. Too anarchical and too snobbish to get involved in trading they tend to keep themselves to themselves in a closed circle talking their own language made up of bookish quotations keeping themselves above the common herd maybe even giving up a meal so as not to lower themselves in the mad scrimmage for a seat in the dining-car.

Our group is part of them. We spend the day reading books on history or sociology in a way that has something self-consciously serious and heavy about it which gets on the nerves of the others. We don't shout we don't rush off from the train quarrelling we don't grab food at the welcome parties we don't shout to each other from one carriage to the next we don't play cards we don't sing folk songs together we don't fill up our suitcases with postcards handkerchiefs balalaikas and wooden dolls. We take care of our own things and we wouldn't dream of bartering a pair of second-hand trousers for a childishly painted icon.

Only Dida escapes from any stereotype. She makes friends with everybody. She refuses to get involved in buying and selling but one day we find her bartering a small tortoise-shell-coloured plastic comb for a basket of apples.

'Even you Dida' says Nico softly in a disappointed voice. Dida lifts the rush basket. She shows us the top layer of perfect apples and underneath a mass of rotten ones. We burst out laughing.

'You see: we aren't the only ones who are crafty.'

'If they'd palmed it off on that boy from Rome with the big gut he'd have stopped the train to throw it at their heads.'

We share the few good apples. We throw the others out of the window. Dida peels an apple for Ada. Nico watches her jealously. Cesare buries himself in a big book of poetry. Miele is writing something in an exercise book with a marbled cover. Cesare looks around him.

'What a cosy family scene' he says bitingly. 'So who's father and who's mother?' We exchange glances. Dida is suddenly enthusiastic about the new game. Nico bites his nails. Ada scrutinises her travelling companions with half-closed eyes. Miele lifts his head from the exercise book with an amused expression.

'Dida's mother' I say.

'No. You're the mother Armida' says Nico categorically. And everyone else agrees with him. Only Miele stays silent.

'Why me? I'm the youngest of the lot of you.'

'Because you're the most motherly. Age doesn't come into it.'

I look down at my hands not knowing whether to be offended or to glory in this. 'Do you find me maternal too?' I ask Miele who is ruminating to himself. He twists his mouth and speaks between his teeth as if every word cost him an effort.

'Yes you're someone who needs the needs of others . . . in that way you are maternal.'

I've been hit in the midriff. By words that have come as a complete shock. 'A need for the needs of others'? Where has he got this insight from? Something I'm not even aware of myself.

'And who's the father?'

'Nico's the father' says Dida smiling at Nico affectionately as if to reassure him that she's not trying to upset him.

'It's true. Nico's the most fatherly of us all. He's got fatherhood in his blood.'

'That's not true at all' protests Nico. 'I've never wanted a son and I don't think I ever shall.'

'That's not the point. It isn't necessarily the person who's actually a father or who wants to be one who is really fatherly.'

'Who is then?'

'A father's someone who's forbearing towards other people and who loves without expecting to be loved in return.'

'If that's so there aren't many fathers on this train' I say. 'But I do know some people who love without asking for love in return. Ada for example. Or Cesare. And Dida too.'

'But they love like children. With the total egotism of childhood' says Miele with ponderous sarcasm. 'Because they know that in any case everyone is in debt to them.'

'Not Ada. Ada is a perfect father' I say avoiding the weight of his ironic amber eyes upon me.

Ada raises her head. Her look cuts the air like a flash of lightning from between her thick dark eyelashes.

'And how do you love you self-satisfied bastard?' She bursts out turning towards Miele who up to now has been in command.

'I love like any man does. With all the contradictions and ups and downs that everyone experiences. I'm not a purist like you. For me absence doesn't make the heart grow fonder. I love in the here and now. And I want my love to be returned.'

'Thank you very much. Considering you're the one who's always absent. So fuck off and good riddance.'

'Where shall I go to then?'

'Go where no-one can reach you in your bright ordered world of lies and deceit.'

'And who's the grandfather among us?' I interrupt to calm the mounting tension. Miele and Ada glare at each other angrily.

'There! Look who's mother now. Armida the archetypal mother. Concerned above all with peace in the family – we've caught you in the act!' Everybody laughs. I blush. I can hear my mother's voice saying 'The more you grow up the older I become. For God's sake shut up Armida. You sound so sensible you're my mother.'

Suddenly the train stops with such a jolt that Dida bangs her head against the window.

151

As we enter the Soviet Union the stops become longer and our reception more official. Every station is decorated with flags and there is always a delegation to greet us with speeches and clapping. The loudspeaker announces the programme of the day in several languages. The times for the train's departure are written in large Russian lettering on a blackboard. We are served more complicated meals with salted cucumber salami sausage fried chicken blackcurrant jam and vodka diluted with water.

Sometimes there is a forgotten portrait of Stalin in the depths of a dark station.

'You see' says our friend of the next carriage. 'The people don't forget their beloved father.'

The hardliners complain because they aren't able to talk politics with their Russian comrades. As soon as you open your mouth the Russians reply with a smile and a barely perceptible nod. To avoid any danger of subversive conversation. To avert indiscreet questions. Even those who can speak Italian smile and shake their heads as if to say 'I don't understand'.

They are friendly but inhibited and impenetrable. They respond to the enthusiasm of their Italian guests with calm deferential gestures. They will pin a badge with Lenin's face on someone's lapel and then edge mysteriously away.

A girl dressed in dark clothes with a big blonde pigtail reaching right down her back talks to us about Kruschev with a look of exaltation. Immediately a small crowd collects round her. She is showered with questions. Everyone wants to photograph her either because she is a real 'Russian beauty' and therefore almost a manifesto in herself or because she seems to be willing to communicate with us beyond the official level of reticence.

But later in the evening we learn she is no longer among the interpreters. They have sent her home. The cynics take advantage of this to make stupid sneers at the expense of the hardliners. Others feel remorseful: what will they do to her because of us? Still others ask themselves whether this is a 'revolutionary' way of behaving.

'But hasn't there been de-Stalinisation?'

'Yes but they still use spies.'

152

'What's the need for spies amongst us?'
'To keep control.'
'Of whom?'
'The people.'
'And who controls the controllers?'
'The Party.'
'But the Party isn't the Police. After all, there's free speech now isn't there?'
'Not with us apparently.'
'Why not?'
'We're the others. The outside world. Capitalists. The Bourgeoisie.'
'I thought we were the renewed hope of socialist youth!'
'We're the shit that's what we are. Even if they have lots of their own shit to shovel different kinds of shit don't mix.'

The further we go the more isolated we are. It is forbidden to talk to railway workers or to the peasants or to the students. Only the interpreters are allowed to speak with us and then always in front of witnesses. Imprisoned in the Youth Festival train we pass through a countryside yellow with ripe grain. We carry with us our two diseases: our inquisitiveness and our hard bargaining. Anyone approaching us is kept under observation. Any words spoken are registered in the disciplined memory of some observer. Only the bartering of the traders is permitted and even then unofficially. The authorities avert their gaze from smallscale trafficking. Indeed it is often the police who start it by offering liqueurs and Russian dolls in exchange for knick-knacks from Italy.

One morning we are all bundled helter-skelter out of the train. We have reached Kiev the capital city of the Ukraine where we shall be staying for two days.

'It's just like Naples' cries Dida forging ahead with great strides.

'Why Naples? This place has got wide streets and new fascist-style buildings. What is there like Naples about that?'

'It's got something Neapolitan. I think it's the smell: fry-ups feet mass poverty cheap ice-cream pigs smoked fish illness gossip...'

'Don't talk such crap. Don't you know this is the mother of Russian cities? One of the most important stopping places on the *"Amber Route"'* intervenes Cesare showing off his knowledge and full of self-importance. 'When Liszt came here to give a concert in 1847 he said that its three hundred and sixty golden domes made it a "city of light". Then in 1941 the Germans came. After two years of occupation they left nothing but ruins and ashes. And two hundred thousand dead. Do you understand that? Two hundred thousand corpses! If you look you can still see them walking through the Khrechtchalik with faces flushed from their long sleep.'

'How dreary you're being! Let's go and have an ice-cream in these gardens.'

'These aren't 'gardens'. It's the Park of Culture and Rest.'

'What a bore you are Cesare! You're just like some text-book or other.'

'I am a text-book. I've read it all in the guide. Sometimes I get a kick out of showing off!'

Dida smiles indulgently. But Cesare is busy scrutinising Ada's face. All his talk is aimed at attracting her attention. But she is oblivious of him and has eyes for no one but Dida.

We go up a steep flight of steps that brings us on to a flowered terrace. All around us are tall modern buildings. We sit down on wicker seats dark with age. We buy jumbo-size raspberry ice-creams.

'Aren't we going to see Santa Sophia? The others are waiting for us there.'

'Yes we'll go now ... But let me have one more ice first.'

Dida is greedy for ice-cream. After a raspberry one she orders chocolate and then another of strawberry and vanilla. Several ice-creams later we reach Santa Sophia to find that the others have already gone.

'It's better this way' says Nico. 'Now we can enjoy it on our own in peace.'

But no one wants to move. We flop down on a low brick wall and stay there relaxing and admiring the thirteen shining domes that breast-feed the sky like the breasts of thirteen giantesses.

In the evening we go for a walk and come to a restaurant. The tables have table-cloths with red checks. We make signs to ask whether we can have some meat. They don't appear to understand. Miele seizes a pen and a small piece of paper and draws a chicken pecking the ground. The head waitress shakes her head. Miele draws an ox with twisted horns like ones we have seen from the train. Laughter from the regular customers. Someone starts mooing. The waitress shakes her head. By this time a small crowd has gathered round our table. Miele draws a fish with conspicuous scales an open mouth and a comical expression of fear. More laughter. Someone mimics the action of swimming. Once more the woman says no.

'What is there for Heaven's sake?' we ask in desperation. The woman says something incomprehensible. One of the customers takes the pen out of Miele's hand and draws an egg – a little too round but unmistakable. Miele opens the egg and makes the head of a baby chicken poke out of it. The laughter becomes louder and more uproarious. Someone starts clapping. A large fat youth offers us a drink. We are giving a performance!

At that moment a neatly shaven man enters cocooned in a dark suit. He carries a large shoulder bag. His long pointed collar of dazzling whiteness is open at the neck.

The regular customers change their attitude without even appearing to see him. They hasten to sit down in their places. The waitress also hurriedly puts on a distant expression. Everyone stops laughing.

Miele draws two eggs in a dish and makes a sign for them to bring us one dish each. She nods 'yes' and disappears. The man with the pointed collar passes by our table and looks over Miele's shoulder at the drawings. He sits down quite close to us and takes a notebook out of his bag.

A little later four fried eggs arrive on two small dishes. We share them between us. A minute later another four arrive. Then another four – another four – another four. In the end they occupy the whole of our quite large table. We make signs to the woman to stop. But she pretends not to understand. She goes on bringing dish after dish. Slices of raw onion wink on top of eggs that are less and less cooked.

Finally there arrives an enormous bill. Our protests are useless. She takes refuge in not understanding our language. In the end we pay up giving her all the money we have just changed this morning.

I WAKE up with a sensation of angst. I look at the time. Three o'clock. I hear a noise in the bottom berth. I lean over to see if Miele is sleeping. But the bed is empty. I look up. I see the door being closed from the outside. I'm just in time to see Miele's bare feet behind the half-closed door.

I wait for him to come back from the toilet. But after half an hour he still hasn't returned. By now I am wide awake. I get up. I grope my way down. I put on my sandals. I set off down the corridor. I pass two boys smoking in the dark. There is no one in the toilet. For once it is dark and empty. I take advantage of the fact to have a pee. I go forward falling against the sides of the carriages thrown about by the jolting of the train which seems to be racing along at a hectic pace. I walk holding on to the edges of the windows. Every so often I'm assailed by a gust of warm air. The floor has never seemed so unsteady and slippery. Every time I pass from one wagon to the next I seem to be thrown headlong into the void. The walls of waxed canvas bellow in and out like a harmonium revealing ancient cracks and black abysses. The two iron plates beneath my feet converge and separate sliding back and forth on each other with a rotating movement which throws me off balance. Advancing each foot cautiously I edge forward. Imprisoned between the two heavy doors I am seized with panic. Then with all the strength I can muster I push open the carriage door in front of me and pass forward into the deserted corridor.

After having gone through a dozen carriages I find myself facing a door. I push down the handle to open it but it does not budge. I push my forehead against the glass. I see the rails gleaming in the moonlight as they race away from me. I have reached the end of the train. Miele is not here.

To undertake the return journey seems beyond me. How can I pass back through those dark corridors that seem to swallow you up and throw you headlong into the night? I take in a mouthful of air at the window. My eyes fall on a square of light that runs skimming along with the train. Inside the square two shadows are clearly silhouetted. Two heads kissing.

It is Miele. I recognise him from the shape of his head with its chestnut tuft of hair and from his nose as it encounters the smaller nose of a woman. I rush towards the first compartment and open the door. I find myself in a closet full of dirty sheets and metal buckets. The light doesn't work.

I go back to the window. I lean out. The square of light has vanished. As if it had never been.

I lean back against the shaking walls. I let myself be jolted by the violent rhythm of the moving train. I don't know how long I'm there. It seems as if I can do nothing except stay there glued to those walls for ever. Only when dawn comes do I summon the strength to find my way back.

In the carriage the first thing I see is Miele sleeping with his arms round the pillow. He doesn't wake up when I put my feet on the edge of his berth to climb up to the one above.

In the morning I wake up to find his face an inch from mine. He smiles at me. I open my eyes wide. I must have a silly expression because he bursts out laughing.

'What is it?' I ask anxiously.

'Nothing. I was watching you sleeping. Mayn't I?'

'Why were you looking at me?'

'Because I love you.'

'Shhh. They'll hear you.'

'Who cares? I want everyone to hear. I love you Armida! How's that? I'll always love you.'

'Always? Isn't that going a bit far? It's enough that you love me now.'

Shyly I put my hand out to touch his face. His skin is soft and scented. I put my open palm round his cheeks. I pull him towards me. I kiss him. He bites my lips gently. We are interrupted by a shrill voice shouting: 'Helsinki! Helsinki!'

157

THE train has stopped alongside some wooden sheds and hoardings outside the station. I join with the others walking along the platform with our suitcases on our heads clambering over sleeping bags and bundles of waste paper. Our group all walk together. Dida fresh and full of energy. Ada in a black mood her eyes deeply sunken. Cesare's sardonic voice criticising the city he hasn't even seen yet. Nico's tender eyes fastened on Dida. Miele walking cheerfully just ahead of us.

We queue for the customs. The organisers wearing red bands on their arms shout and direct the crowd first to the right and then to the left. Hundreds of young people dressed in the most outlandish garb leap from one platform to another trying to understand where they are meant to go.

In the square outside the station huge coaches gleaming with silver and chrome stand waiting for us. But the doors are locked. We settle in the shade of one of these giants and wait. Dida sings softly drawing on the pavement with her foot. Ada leans back against a colossal wheel the colour of wet coal. Cesare's eyes follow a little group of girls distributing rosettes.

'Have you ever seen such girls?' he mutters shaking his head. No one takes any notice of him. Nico has curled up on the ground his head hunched between his shoulders his eyes shut.

'I say have you seen those lovely cunts?'

'What on earth's the matter with you? You're behaving like a small-town yobbo. We come all the way to Scandinavia and the first thing you do is to get all worked up about every girl you see.' Miele speaks with his mouth full of mints which he found in the bottom of his pocket and which from force of habit he chases tirelessly between his teeth.

'I've never seen so many blondes all at the same time.'

'You're talking like a slob of the fifties.'

'Where are we now then? In the eighties perhaps?'

'It's the late sixties Cesare. And in a little while it'll be the seventies. And there's no Stalin with his moustachios in the air and there's no Churchill and no De Gasperi. Everything keeps changing. Only you stay the same.'

Cesare spits on the ground and laughs sarcastically. He spits again. He can't tear his eyes away from the girls in shorts and their bare legs. 'Fifties sixties who gives a damn! My prick is ageless. When it sees so much lovely flesh it hoists the flag and then – goodnight it's bedtime!'

'It's all so obvious. You're behaving like an Italian clown!'

'Clown yourself! You're like a hairdresser. Always so polished so chiselled. Yes you're a real hairdresser Miele.'

'Are you in love with Ada or aren't you?'

'Everybody knows that. She doesn't care a damn about me – they know that too.'

'And how do you think she likes the way you're carrying on?'

'I don't imagine she does like it. If she wants me she'll take me as I am or not at all. Anyway she won't have me because she's a fucking lesbian bitch.'

Nico jumps and rushes at him. He hurls him to the ground with a violent tackle. Cesare kicks back. Nico throws himself on top of him and starts beating him up. A sudden silent hand to hand fight which leaves everyone stunned.

'Chuck it you cretins chuck it in.'

Dida watches them apprehensively but doesn't lift a finger to separate them. I try to stop Nico who's got his hands round Cesare's neck. But all I get is a kick on the shoulder. Miele comes to my help and manages to pull Cesare away from under Nico's legs.

Ada stays motionless. She watches in silence sitting propped up against the wheel of the bus her sphinx-like amber eyes devoid of expression.

'It's exhaustion' says Miele. 'We're all knackered after eight days in that damned train without being able to have a bath and not getting enough food and what we did get was horrible and all that shambles and confusion.'

I put my arms round Nico and use a clean handkerchief to dab a wound by his ear. He thanks me tearfully. Cesare has moved away behind Dida. She swears never to speak to him again.

At long last the doors of the coaches are opened. But we are suddenly separated: men on one side women on the other. I try to get

159

a seat near Dida and Ada but Ada has disappeared. I see Miele moving off among the other men and vanishing behind the line of metal giants. I've no idea where he will be staying. I wait for him to turn round so that I can give him a last wave but he doesn't. The whiteness of his crumpled trousers imprints itself on my retina. I shut my eyes and lean my head against the headrest. As the coach leaves I retrace his image as if I were watching a slow-motion film. The curve of his legs the breeze flapping his trousers against his ankles his chest thrust forward as if to overcome the force of the wind the collar of his shirt dancing round his thin neck his dark bronzed head that from a distance expresses something frail and lost mixed with a childish and incorrigible obstinacy.

Kaivokatu Annankatu Lapinlandenkatu... the coach heads rapidly down wide white streets bordered by trees. In the next seat Dida turns her head right round fascinated by the novelty. They put us down at the entrance to a state school. A big building on two floors with large windows which reach right up to the ceiling and doors which open on to an uncultivated garden. More delays seated on the ground in front of the doors of the school. We are waiting for the other coaches with their coachloads of women. After a few minutes six coaches arrive. They throw their doors open to let out an avalanche of girls from 15 to 25. One coach for the French one for the Spaniards another for the Germans and so on.

Eventually around ten o'clock the organisers arrive and give us each a piece of paper with a number written on it. The big doors of the school are opened. We can enter. Everyone stampedes up the wide stone stairs in a great rush without a clue where they are going. As we chase around pushing and panting someone shouts 'You've got your numbers so what's all the hurry? There's a bed for everyone so there's no need to rush.'

I look at the number I have in my hand. 415C. In each room there are thirty tiered beds – each bed with three bunks just like the train. I notice some arrows: the Lower Ground Floor ends at number 380. For the 400s one has to go upstairs.

'What number have you got?' I ask Dida.

'320. And you?'

'I've got 415. We're on different floors. I've got to go up and you've got to go down. I'll see you later.'

I watch her as she disappears frowning down the corridor with its pale yellow tiles. Her lilac skirt flaps heavily round her ankles. I go upstairs. The passage echoes. Voices fly up to the ceiling. Multiplied a hundred times they rebound uncannily amplified as if above the crowd of women scattering and scrambling up the stairs there was another crowd upside down high above us. I go to the end of the passage and into the front room. The large classroom has been transformed into a dormitory and resembles a barracks. There must be about 40 beds each with three bunks.

402 403 404 . . . the beds come to an end at the far wall. I go out and walk further. The walls are lined with tiles the high ceiling is bordered with mouldings of pine wood. The long windows remind me of a gymnasium. The light floods in a little shrouded even though it is only eleven o'clock in the morning. Eventually I find my bed. It is the topmost of the bunks on bed 415. First is bunk A then bunk B and at the top is bunk C. That is mine. Two girls each unrolling a rucksack. They greet me with a smile.

'Italian?'

'Yes. You too?'

'I'm from Genoa. And you?'

'Rome.'

We shake hands. I look at the other girl who seems not to understand. I think that maybe she is foreign. But it turns out she is from Udine.

'I reckon everyone in this room is Italian' I say.

'It's like a concentration camp. There aren't even any bathrooms.'

'How do you know?'

'I've looked. Would you believe it there are only five lavatories for each floor. That'll never be enough. It'll be nothing but queues just like on the train.'

'A girl from Naples told me there are showers but they're in the basement.'

'What about sheets?'

'Sheets! This isn't exactly the Grand Hotel! There's one army

161

blanket each and a cotton towel and a little bit of cloth to lay on top of the pillow and that's it.'

'Would you like a liquorice?'

The girl in bunk A is looking hard at me. At the same time she's taking out of her case two rolled up shirts a pair of blue bedroom slippers and a short flowered dress.

'Aren't you a friend of that plump blonde girl from Rome?'

'Dida. Yes.'

'She's nice. She's got a lovely voice. There was someone in my compartment who was mad about her.'

'Everyone is mad about Dida.'

She gives me an earnest look. Then she returns to her suitcase. I also pull out the few clean things I have left: a white shirt a pale blue skirt a pair of socks. I leave everything else in the case. There are no wardrobes and no clothes hangers.

'Attention everyone! Meal tickets will be distributed by the entrance at twelve o'clock sharp. Everyone must bring the piece of paper with their bed number on it. The distribution will go on till half past twelve so we advise you to be punctual.' The voice on the loudspeaker has a strong Venetian accent. The announcement is repeated in Spanish French and English.

'If you don't hurry to get your tickets you don't eat till tomorrow. What sons of bitches!' grumbles the girl from Genoa as she does her best to stuff her things back into her suitcase.

162

'WHERE do we wash?'

'Over there. At the end of the corridor next to the stairs.'

I go over and find myself in a wide lobby. Opening out of it are five spring doors without locks or keys and only a single lightbulb. The light rains a cloud of dust from above. Opposite is a row of white porcelain washbasins attached to the wall. No mirrors. No shelves. I take my place in the queue for the lavatory behind a dozen other girls who are looking completely lost. Many have never had or even imagined a similar experience. It reminds me of my boarding school. There too were queues for the bath queues for chapel queues in the dining room. It isn't a new experience for me.

'Is it true there are showers somewhere?'

'Apparently there are some but no one's seen them yet.'

'I've been dreaming of having a shower for ten days.'

'There are saunas in the town.'

'I know. But you have to pay for them.'

'How much is a marco worth?'

'It's markka with two ks stupid.'

'I've only got liras.'

'You can always give your cunt!'

Subdued laughter. The girl with the liras stands with her legs wide apart outside the queue face to face with the one who spoke last. 'Which would you rather – I slapped your face or spat in it?'

'I'd prefer a kiss. I don't like fighting.'

'Then take back what you've just said.'

'I take it back I take it back. I always offer my own cunt even if I don't get much for it. I really didn't mean to offend you.'

No one knows whether she's joking or being serious. The other girls look at her shocked and fascinated. She's a small fair muscular girl with the blackest of eyes a fine imperious nose a bright mischievous smile and a face that is a perfect aristocratic oval.

'What's your name?'

'Me? Selvaggia – the Wild One. And you?'

'No that can't be real.'

'You've got to recognise I always speak the truth even when I'm telling lies. I swear that whatever I say I'm always sincere. On the other hand the truth as you can see is hellishly boring. It's the monopoly of priests and revolutionaries.'

Her provocative energy stupefies the others who look at her open-mouthed without knowing what to say.

'She's a nutcase' I hear someone whispering behind me.

'She's no nutcase. She's a snake in the grass' says someone else.

'I like her.'

'Shhh. Keep quiet or she'll clock you one!'

It seems as if everything has returned to normal. But then out she comes from the queue once more to show the small audience of women a key she's carrying on a string round her neck.

'Is that the key of your safe?'

'No it's the key to my room.'

'You've got a room!' Suddenly the faces become attentive. Someone immediately starts shouting about favouritism.

'I told you. I can lay my hands on anything I want with what I've got here.' She places a small slender hand on her crutch and gives a coarse laugh. The women don't know how to react. A few laugh. Others look indignant. 'Have you seen your precious companions sitting on the lavatory? Look at their feet. You can see them beneath the door all lined up two by two. You're all behaving like slaves! Now I'll show you how to piss with style and originality!'

She jumps up on the window sill above our heads. She pulls up her skirt and holds on to the framework of the window. Laughing defiantly she slips down her pants and pees out into space.

'She's really crazy' the first voice repeats.

'Make her get down from there. She could fall' shouts another.

'You deal with it. I'm shit scared of her. She's quite capable of laying you out flat. What a lunatic!'

Meanwhile Selvaggia has climbed down. She puts her hands under the open tap and splashes water between her legs. Then she smells her fingers and makes a cheerful grimace.

'Smells good! Stale sex! I bet none of you lot had it off in the train. I did. Every night. And then I washed in the guard's cabin. What are you all looking at me like that for? I suppose you think I'm daft? My

164

cunt is the real rebel. It's an anarchist. Take a look at it.' Saying this she sticks her fingers under the nose of another girl who leaps backwards. She gives a boastful laugh.

'Smell it? Didn't you like it? It's the smell of freedom. Does it offend you? Make you shrink back? You're a pretty feeble little yellow-belly with silly round eyes aren't you? Do you know what this place reminds me of? Prison. But there at least all the cunts had balls. Strong women possessed by the devil. Here it's like being surrounded by cooked pears. Boring boring boring. I'll tell you something just between us. I'm not called Selvaggia but Beelzebub. Do you like that name? No? All right then I'll confess I'm really called Anastasia – Asia for short. And with that I'll say goodbye. I'm going back to my room. I'm under the stairs on the left. Knock and the door shall be opened. I never deny anyone a shot of vodka even if it's three in the morning. Goodbye sheep! Go on as you're going . . . and you'll end up with your throats cut. Goodbye!'

She's gone like a flash of lightning. We see her in the distance sliding down the banisters. We look at each other in amazement. One girls points a finger at her forehead as if to say the woman needs her brains looking at. Others treat it all as a joke. Still others reflect on the weirdness of her behaviour and ask themselves whether it was all just a big act. But after she has gone there's a drop in the temperature. Boredom returns. We start to yawn. Slowly and steadily the queue grows shorter. A diffuse grey light comes in through the window.

Some of the women have stripped to the waist and are bending over the washbasins splashing water and washing themselves. Others stand dazed watching.

The row of feet are still sticking out from under the lavatory doors. It's true that the whole scene has something grotesque about it. It was Asia who managed to convey that in her short performance. I make up my mind I shall call her Asia. I feel the name fits her like a glove though I don't know whether it's her real name or not.

A quarter to twelve and I am downstairs. The entrance hall is crowded with women shoving and scuffling round the organiser's table. Two women with agitated expressions on their faces try to maintain a minimum of order for the distribution of tickets. They are

165

not accustomed to Italian pandemonium to girls stretching out their hands without waiting their turn to women who laugh and push and trip people up and who plonk their bottoms on the organiser's table or who bend double over her chair and pull her by the hair.

I go in search of Dida. However bed 320 isn't in the basement as I thought. I go back to the ground floor. But her bed is empty. I pass by the lavatories. There's still a queue. The washbasins are already filthy and the floor is awash. I go back to the entrance and catch sight of her in the distance among a group of French girls who are arguing by the main door.

'Dida!'

'Have you got your meal ticket?'

'No. Where's Ada?'

'I don't know. Let's queue and look for her afterwards.'

Eventually I reach the table. Someone pushes a cardboard voucher into my hand. I hardly have time to grasp it before being pushed roughly from behind. I leave the throng clasping the ticket: a small card folded in two and roughly stapled with numbered slips of paper one for each meal.

I sit down on the outside steps to wait for Dida. Large semi-circular steps of white granite mottled with green.

'Hullo.'

'Ah so here you are. Where have they put you?'

It is Ada. Standing at the bottom of the steps. Fagged out. Cigarette drooping from her mouth. Looking despondently down at her naked feet in sandals.

'In the garage outside. Do you want to come and see?'

'Dida said to wait for her here.'

'I know where she is. She won't be here for another twenty minutes. Dida's hopeless at queuing. She lets everyone get in front of her. So let's go.'

I follow her along a path of round stones set into the soft sandy earth. We cross a courtyard with a fountain in the shape of a shell.

'Look at it. It's like a house of ghosts. Take care!'

At the end of the path can be seen a long low building covered by climbing plants with small violet flowers. From a distance they look black. The windows are buried beneath thick dense foliage. We go in through a big sliding door. Four rows of pine beds are lined up along the floor. Two bunks each – one upper one lower.

'You're lucky. Where we are it's three bunks to a bed.'

'It's damp.'

I look up to the rectangular windows which reach right to the ceiling. Down the panes of glass small green serpents grip the smooth surface with minute gelatinous suckers.

'It's sinister.'

'But at least it's quiet.'

'My hunch is that someone will be murdered here during the night.'

She looks at me smiling mysteriously. Quite still with the wing of black hair falling down the side of her pale forehead. She herself has something spooky about her.

'And as I don't want to be among the victims I've decided to join the assassins.'

She takes me by the arm and leads me towards her bed underneath a window which sheds a violet light striped with green. 'I've decided to kill that stupid dark depressed woman who answers to the name of Ada.' Her voice has something so determined about it that I feel quite scared. But I hear her laughing silently.

'Why is it Ada that you carry your ghosts with you wherever you go?'

'But if I killed myself for love would you find that less threatening?'

'You must find a lover who returns your love. Then you wouldn't want to kill yourself.'

'That's not so easy. Mutual love's easy enough. But it's invariably followed by possessiveness – which may gratify me but also disgusts me. Genuine love means this: to want the greatest good for the other person. And do you know what the greatest good is? Freedom! And one can't want freedom for someone and at the same time want to imprison them with your love. Love which is possessive is like murder and I don't want to kill anyone – only myself.'

'Oh Ada you're so beautiful! Come on let's go. I'm desperate to get

167

out of this place. It's like being in an aquarium.'

We go back to the courtyard. Dida is sitting on the steps waiting for us surrounded by a group of admirers who are listening while she talks.

'She's already found her fans' says Ada smiling. 'Let's stop a minute and watch her while she's still unaware of us. Have you ever seen a more perfect beauty?'

I stop. My eyes on Dida's junoesque body. But then she lifts her head and gets up smoothing her skirt with her hand. She comes towards us smiling confidently.

'The city belongs to us' she says putting her arms round our waists.

WE walk along the esplanade breathing in the light raw air. The sky is quite different from our skies: high high up bleached of colour distant yet at the same time looming strangely above our heads. The atmosphere has a rarefied and brilliant consistency each particle of light reflecting its neighbour creating a sensation that we are inside a luminous explosion – almost an atmospheric cataclysm.

The fountain of all this light remains invisible: the sun is hidden behind transparent veils drowned in a dense heat haze. We glide through the light as if moving awkwardly through water.

We reach the Merikata and make for the sea. The street is broad and spacious brushed by the wind. A double row of poplars rustles gently with the noise of smooth silk. The shops present a sober façade of double windows and double doors behind which they look distant and closed. A few have hoisted a sun-blind coloured rust or bottle green. On the pavement in front of them plants are bent by the wind.

A large bridge with granite parapets spans a channel through which a river rushes seaward forming a lake and a harbour. There is a strong smell of rotten fish cut grass engine oil and fresh paint.

'Look there's an Italian ship!' Dida points in the direction of the harbour. In amongst the largest ships with their exotic names there is a prow painted blue with the ship's name written in black capitals 'Carmelina'. On the mast a red green and white flag.

'It makes me feel all sentimental' says Dida leaning on the parapet of the bridge. 'It reminds me of sitting on my doorstep in the sun talking about the price of beans.'

A sailor with a pear-shaped head walks along the bridge carrying a pale blue bucket. He leans over the railings and empties the dirty water into the sea. He looks round for a moment sniffing the air. Then he disappears.

Every so often Ada takes out of her pocket the meal voucher on which is written the address of a restaurant and shows it to a passer-by who smiles and gabbles a hurried reply and then goes off wishing us several good-byes. But we don't understand a word and we do not like to badger them.

It is almost two o'clock by the time we arrive tired and hungry at the Vasa restaurant. We check the address: yes, it is the right one. We push through a big wooden door that opens on to an inner door made of glass.

Inside it is like a madhouse – worse than at the school. Students are eating at the tables sitting two to every seat knee to knee. Others are standing and chattering while they wait their turn. Some lean against the walls looking ravenous while they watch the lucky ones who have got a seat. And others are perched on high stools at the bar drinking beer while they wait for a place to become empty.

Walls of wood. Ceilings also of wood. A sort of spacious Alpine chalet with a worn floor full of cracks and holes. A row of red paper lampshades suspended from a length of cable strung along the ceiling. A smell of beer and frying fat.

'Dida!' a male voice rises from the back. It is Nico waving. We make our way through the throng of bodies and reach a table next to the kitchen. Cesare and Miele are there as well.

'Where have they put you to sleep?'

'In a school.'

'Same with us.'

'Where?'

'Not far from where you are.'

Miele makes a place for me. Nico squeezes up against Cesare so that Dida can sit down. Ada squats on Cesare's knees.

'You have to go to the cash desk with your voucher.'

'That's impossible. You'd have to fly over everyone's head to get there.'

'I'll go.'

Miele takes our vouchers and disappears among the crowd. In a little while we see him popping up with a tray. On it are three glasses of beer slices of bread and butter and smoked herring.

'Is that all?'

'The goulash is finished. We should have got here earlier.'

'Who'll swap an ice-cream for a slice of bread?' A pale spotty youth appears from between everyone's knees to make this offer.

'I don't fancy an ice-cream. But I'll give you some bread in exchange for an apple.'

170

'O.K. I'll get you an apple pronto. Do you want a yellow one or a red one? Keep the bread till I come.'

'Are we back to bartering all over again?' grumbles Cesare irritably. 'We're not still in the train are we?'

The pale-faced youth reappears with a little white plate on which jolts a diminutive red apple. Dida gives him a slice of bread. He thanks her and goes off. I've already eaten my slice of bread and smoked herring but I'm still hungry.

'Surely one can have more if one pays?'

'Not here. Only in town. Tomorrow we'll go to a proper restaurant and eat till we burst.'

Miele grasps my hand under the table. He squeezes it. He puts his mouth close to my ear.

'I can see there's no chance of making love here. Is there a hole we could creep into where you are?'

'No. I'm in a room with thirty or forty beds.'

'It's even worse where I am. What are we to do?'

I don't know what to answer. I feel his fingers interlaced with mine. And the tender excited look on his face.

I EMERGE from the lavatory to collide with Asia who is rushing by
impetuously bare to the waist with her key dangling from a string
round her neck.

'Oh it's you Armida. I hear you write for the theatre. What's that
like?'

'Who told you?'

'I always know everything. Do you need any meal vouchers?'

'No.'

'Come to me if you need to change money on the black market. I'm
in room number 16 underneath the stairs. Bye.' She goes to the
lavatory singing at the top of her voice. Shortly afterwards I see a roll
of lavatory paper whizzing out from under her door. It stops right at
my feet.

'I scored a bull's-eye didn't I?' she laughs.

'You know everything?' I ask nervously scared of her tempestuous
manner. 'Can you tell me how to get to the men's school?'

'Ah! So you're in love too are you? What a balls-up! All these
women losing their heads over some hairy prick. One plays around
with men one doesn't fall in love with them. Love is just crazy. It leads
straight to marriage and that's like being tortured over a slow fire. Oh
don't look at me like that. I'm not a witch. Have you noticed that low
yellow house at the bottom of the street? When you get to it turn right
and then take the second on the left. One day you'll say "You were
right, Asia. Love is shit and I spit on it!"' She spits on the floor. Then
she realises that it's landed right on my shoe. She bends down quickly
and cleans it off with the hem of her skirt. She gets up and goes off
without saying goodbye. A girl who has been watching the scene
shakes her head in commiseration.

'I shouldn't get mixed up with her. She's a nut-case' she says. But I
like Asia and I am curious about her.

I go back to my bunk. It is still quite early. Everyone is asleep. And
if I go down I shan't even find anything hot to drink. I climb up on to
the top bunk and lie down on my back and look up at the ceiling. It is
the absence of darkness that makes sleep impossible. A strange
impression of being suspended in a luminous void padded with cotton

wool. And then it's never quiet in this large room. Many people smoke till late in the night. Some eat surreptitiously using their blanket as a shield. Others play cards or lie on their beds gossiping in twos and threes.

Looking round I can see bodies curled up under blankets arms clasping pillows. Backs naked. Heads buried beneath sleeping-bags. In my imagination a nun's discreet footsteps ... her breath on my hair. She hands me a tin mug with a scalding liquid in it. 'Drink it up Armida it'll do you good ... If you go on lying there awake how will you get up in the morning?' My lips touch the metal and I swallow the concoction bad-temperedly. It smells acrid and bitter. It is very sticky. An infusion of lime flowers boiled up with essence of poppy and rosewater. I saw her preparing it in the kitchen. It emits a mildly sickening smell. But the sister has blind faith in its miraculous powers. Fragile and inexorable Sister of the Bleeding Heart stands over me until I have swallowed up every drop and scalded my tongue in the process.

'It's good isn't it?' she says with a pat on my cheek.

'No sister. It smells of shit.'

A sharp slap greets this remark.

'Don't you dare to use that word Armida.'

'What am I to say then?'

'You should say excrement.'

'Well then: the lime-flowered tea smells of excrement.'

'Don't try to be funny. Go to sleep.' She strokes my hair hastily and goes off with her rosary jingling on her hips.

There was no need for me to go on looking for Miele. He came to me bringing me a packet of aniseed-flavoured biscuits and some apple-juice 'in case you still feel hungry.' Outside Cesare and Nico are waiting for us. Soon Dida arrives followed by Ada. Together we make for the centre of town.

'Shall we go along the esplanade?'

'No let's go by the harbour.' We end up having an argument in front of a restaurant on two floors with big gilded windows looking out onto the street.

'Well – shall we go in or shan't we?'

'We'll have to pay through the nose.'

'It doesn't look all that expensive.'

'Let's try it then.'

'It's time we had a decent meal.'

'O.K. Let's go in.'

We enter intimidated but self-confident. We take our seats noisily and the head waiter gives us dirty looks from afar. A ravishing waitress with hair the colour of milk comes up to us with a notebook. What will we have? We look at each other in perplexity. The menu is in Finnish. The woman talks to us in broken English. We don't understand a word. We point to a sumptuous-looking dish on a neighbouring table.

In a short time there arrive six oval plates heaped with all kinds of fish dressed in an exquisite pink sauce. We ask for bread and then later for more bread. We eat as if we were starving. We hunt for every little scrap on our plates greedily. We wash it down with dry German wine.

The bill arrives. We look at each other in consternation. The total is enormous. When we've paid up we're left broke. We go out feeling resentful and angry.

'No more restaurants friends. We're bankrupt.'

'What shall we eat then?'

'We've got the vouchers.'

'That means queuing for hours for a plate of boiled potatoes or burnt goulash. No thanks.'

'We can have fish and chips. Have you seen how they sell it on the street?'

'I've had some of their fried fish. It gave me the shits.'

'The big shitter!' Dida's rippling laughter infects us all. The seagulls fly low screaming. It seems as if they are calling to us. We walk slowly in the direction of the harbour.

When I get back to the school I find a note pinned to the black notice-board by the main door: 'Armida Bianchi. Report to the head office at 3 o'clock.'

I run to fetch a jumper because outside the weather has turned cold. It is drizzling. I find my bunk turned upside-down. The biscuits and the apple juice have vanished. I look inside my suitcase. The gold bracelet I wear occasionally on my wrist has disappeared too.

I rush out and go to see the organisers. There is only one who speaks Italian. I tell her about the theft. She shrugs her shoulders.

'You Italians are all thieves' she says. 'Settle it among yourselves. We can't do anything.'

I go out and make my way towards the festival office. First I am directed to one room then to another. Finally I discover the person who sent me the note.

'Are you Armida Bianchi?'

'Yes.'

'You write for the theatre?'

'Yes.'

'Your talk is scheduled for this evening at seven o'clock at the Palladium. There will be simultaneous translations. Can you let us have the text of your lecture.'

'I don't have a text. I'd rather not give a talk.'

'I'm sorry but it's scheduled in the programme. If you don't give it you'll forego reimbursement for your ticket and accommodation.'

'Can I improvise?'

'The regulations don't authorise it but if you can't do anything else . . .'

I've never in my life given a public lecture. I'd completely forgotten about it but I don't tell them that for fear of seeming stupid or rude. I ask where I can lay my hands on a typewriter. They show me a small room and I get going. The tables with typewriters are all occupied. I stand and wait holding a blank sheet of paper in my hand. In front of me with her back towards me sits a small child her nimble fingers assiduously striking the keys. Her nails are painted red. Her fair hair comes halfway down her back. Suddenly she turns round and I can't avoid a start of amazement. She is not a child at all but an old woman. A wrinkled monkey with a child-like grace. I look at her curiously. She smiles at me. I smile back at her. She tells me that she won't be a moment and shows me her last sheet of paper. She smiles again. She turns round and quickly resumes typing.

As soon as she has finished she gets up. She gives me a little bow and

175

points to the chair. She only comes up to my chest. She has very small feet thrust inside a pair of high-heeled shiny pink shoes. She goes away walking stiffly her curtain of fair hair bouncing up and down her back.

I sit myself down. I put the sheet of paper in the typewriter. I try the typewriter out. I say to myself: 'That's fine now I can begin.' But nothing comes. I hold my head in my hands. I swallow. I glance at the bent heads all around me. I can hear the noise of a waterfall. I put my fingers in my ears. I tell myself that it is the noise that stops me concentrating. It's not true though. My head is empty. Completely empty.

After half an hour I'm still there. Feeling so weary weary. Without having written a thing. Two people are waiting and giving me nasty looks. I must absolutely write something or leave. I begin reluctantly. It reminds me of doing essays at school.

While I am getting more and more entangled in incoherent sentences I feel my eyes being drawn to the window. I look up. I see Miele laughing. With him a girl who looks like a plainer version of Ada. Her head leans languidly on his shoulder. He is kissing her forehead.

I rip the sheet of paper out of the typewriter and rush outside. But Miele has already gone. So has the raven-haired girl. Three streets lead out from where I am standing. I go down one. Nothing. I turn back. I go down another. Not a sign. It's no longer any use trying. I walk back quickly towards the school.

176

T HE first person I meet is Asia. Bare legs. Sweater coming down below her hips. A pair of red and white gymshoes on her feet.

'Where are you off to, Armida? You look like a corpse. How about a shot of vodka?'

I don't feel like talking. I make for the stairs but she puts out an arm to stop me. 'Don't go upstairs. They're cleaning up there.'

I struggle free and throw myself up the first few steps. Then I get stuck. My legs refuse to obey me any more. I sit down on the staircase. I can't get my breath. I want to be sick. Asia looks up at me ironically. She clambers up the stairs. She puts a cool hand on my forehead. She helps me downstairs and takes me to her room. She opens the door with the key that hangs round her neck. She pushes me into a small wicker chair.

'Which would you rather have? Vodka or tea with rum in it?'

I shake my head. I don't want anything. I only want to be sick. She looks at me intently for a long time.

'I know those symptoms: it's jealousy. You've just seen your boy-friend with someone else. I told you – love is shit. You can't put your life into the hands of a guy just because he's tall and handsome and good in bed.'

She puts a drink in my hand. She forces me to drink it. The taste of alcohol makes my tongue tingle – then my chest is shaken by retching. She presses her glass filled with ice-cold drink against my forehead.

'Once I was ill just like you; that was out of jealousy too. I was desperately in love with my uncle. But all he wanted was to look at my naked body from behind. He used to gaze at my arse for hours on end. I'd weep from pain and jealousy. I'd have given him my life – anything but my arse. But he said I wasn't androgynous enough for him: my breasts made him feel sick. Then one day I tried to slash him with a razor-blade. My mother ran at me screaming and managed to stop me. They put me in a strait-jacket the bastards. They gave me electric-shock treatment and I turned into a sort of vegetable. I ended up saying 'yes' to everything. So they declared me cured and threw me out. No way was I going back to my mother so I decided to travel.

I went off without telling a soul. That's when I got the nickname 'Selvaggia' – the wild one.'

'I was phased out – really depressed. I was crazy. I got a job as a porter. Then I became a chauffeur. Then a road-sweeper. But it never worked out. In the end the only thing people wanted was my cunt. So I said "O.K. if that's what they want they can have it – at a price". And in no time at all I'd made myself a sackful of money.'

She laughs as she gulps down the drink. She pours another vodka into my glass. She loosens the collar of my blouse which she thinks is constricting my throat. 'Drink up Armida. It'll do you a power of good.'

So I drink. The heat burns my throat and then floods softly and sensuously into my body.

'But I got bored with being a prostitute. I rang up my mother. She'd assumed I was dead. I made a date to meet her in a bar. Guess what she did the bitch. After having first kissed me and hugged me and wept all over me she sent for them to come and put me back in a strait-jacket. That didn't last long – next day I escaped. For a time I sold little bead necklaces. I made good money too. But there was a snag – my boss was always pestering me for a fuck. Day and night. In the back of the car in dark porches in a cupboard full of junk beneath the stall under the big umbrella flat on the ground in the toilet. Then a friend of his turned up who'd decided to go to India. "I'll come with you" I say. So we set off together. But halfway there he gets viral hepatitis and we end up in hospital in Aleppo.

'I gave up and came back to Italy. I was completely broke. I hadn't got a thing. I survived by raiding dustbins for food. Then one day I was hitching on the motorway and not a single car would stop. I thought I'd die of hunger and boredom when a big dark girl pulled up. She was called Amparo – '

I raise my head when I hear that name. Asia breaks off and pours herself another vodka. Then she lies down on the bed and kicks her shoes in the air.

'Are you feeling better?'

'Yes.'

'I've been going on about myself to distract you. And you actually

178

have been distracted. It's done the trick.'

'I think it has.'

'Drink up and have some more.'

'Go on with your life story.'

'Where was I? Oh yes – Amparo.'

'Where was she from?'

'From Barcelona. I had a terrible crush on her. I was infatuated. I'd have eaten her alive. But she wasn't so faithful as I was. After we'd been together for a month she went off with an Argentinian volley-ball player. Come on drink. Let's see that colour coming back into your cheeks. Would you like me to go to your boyfriend and do the dirty on him so that he'll never dare look at anyone else but you?'

'You sound like the Mafia!'

'Perhaps I am a bit of a witch. . . . I know how to mix up a drink that makes men impotent. Would you like to have some?'

I watch her with her sleek hair twined like serpents round her expressive face. Asia has a hundred different faces: each one more difficult to decipher than the last.

'Drink up Armida you'll see how much better it makes you feel. Go on drink.'

So once more I drink. She fills my glass. I swallow it down in one gulp. The vodka loosens the knots in my guts. I raise my eyes. Everything is misty and clouded. I shall never be able to get up out of this chair. Asia has bound me to it with her serpents.

Something catches my gaze. I turn round and focus my pupils slowly. For the first time I see that the room is an alcove under the stairs. The ceiling comes straight down and divides the already cramped space into two halves. There are no windows. Only a ventilation shaft. An electric light bulb in the shape of a glass flame rests on a chair and illuminates a small hospital bed.

She watches as I focus my eyes. She smiles sardonically. She swallows half a glass of vodka.

'Well, what do you think of it?'

'It's a bit of a dungeon!'

'Better than being squashed together like sardines in some huge room with thirty other people. Here I'm my own boss and that's what

179

I want.'

Nails on the wall... Various garments hanging from the nails... On a smaller nail a little dog collar of red leather... Next to it something that gleams. I feel I am on fire slowly smouldering away. My cheeks burning. My eyelids weighing a ton. Suddenly I realise what it is hanging on the wall: my gold bracelet.

'I nicked that from the floor above. I don't know what I'll do with it. I may even chuck it away. I'm keeping it for the bad times. When there's no more booze and I've got fuck all to do.'

'It's mine' I say in a weak voice.

'Yours? Then you're an absolute idiot. Leaving a gold bracelet in an open suitcase in full daylight in a room with eighty people in it. Haven't you got any brains at all? You're lucky it was me who took it. Anyone could have nicked it. Whereas now you've got it safe... When I do sell it I'll give you half what I get for it. Is that O.K.? Anyway let's drink to its recovery.'

She pours me out more vodka. My hand shakes as I raise the glass up to the neck of the bottle. She laughs – but her hand isn't too steady either. She doesn't notice when the glass is full and the liquid overflowing. She goes on pouring and it runs down over my shoes on to the floor. We are both laughing as she tilts the bottle over my raised glass.

'Look what you've made me do! You aren't concentrating. Drink up before it all runs away. I'm going to drink straight from the bottle. Shit! There isn't any left.'

'You've tipped it all over the floor, that's why!'

'I what? On the floor? You must be joking! It's you who upset it. Why didn't you warn me to stop when the glass started to overflow?'

'My feet are swimming in vodka.'

'Let's see.'

She grabs one of my feet. She smells it. She takes off the shoe. She tips it up on to her tongue. A few drops trickle into her mouth. She coughs in a fit of laughter and I laugh with her. I rest my feet on the slippery wet floor. Suddenly I remember that at seven o'clock I have to give my talk at the Palladium. I tell her and she claps her hands gaily.

180

'I'll come with you. Don't panic. There's nothing like being pissed
if you've got to give a talk. You'll be brilliant.'

I reach up to take my bracelet from the nail. She stops my hand.

'Let's keep it for a rainy day. I swear that I won't cheat you.'

I draw my hand away. To hell with the bracelet! I'm croaking with
thirst. There's no way I'll go and give that talk. But she pushes me
through the door. She takes me by the arm. She drags me towards the
entrance. We leave the school staggering together.

I AM sitting in a small velvet armchair. At the Palladium. I try to figure out how the hell I got there. My thoughts are all mixed up with memories of Asia. I look for her next to me. She has disappeared.

Miele arrives with a small cup of coffee. With gentle yet compelling gestures he forces me to swallow it. I look up at him at his eyes a streak of the gentlest black sepia at his nostrils infinitely dilating.

'You're drunk Armida. You're completely pissed. At any moment it'll be your call. What the hell are you going to say to them?'

'I love you Miele.'

'Go and see the organisers. Tell them you're ill. You can't show yourself in this state.'

But I don't hear him. All I want is for him to kiss me. Now. At once. I tell him so. With a gesture of long-suffering patience he bends over me like a mother.

At that moment I hear my name called through the loudspeakers:

'Armida Bianchi please come up to the platform. The Italian playwright Armida Bianchi will tell us about the problems of social class in the world of the theatre.'

Miele gives me a sideways look. He doesn't offer me a hand as with enormous effort I pull myself upright. I set off holding myself rigid so as not to stumble. Hundreds of eyes are turning towards me. The effort to walk straight is so great that I don't give a thought to my terror of the microphone or the fact that my head is totally empty of ideas.

I reach the platform. I lean on the lectern with both hands. Somehow I manage to prop myself up. I can breathe. Someone shoots a spotlight into my face. I can no longer see anything or anyone only this metallic object immediately in front of me: the malevolent head of a snake. I must show it that I'm not afraid of it otherwise it will put out its forked tongue and kill me. I must put it under a spell with my voice. I must mesmerise it with words.

I begin to talk at random without thinking. Then my tongue takes over on its own. I don't really know what I am saying. From time to time I realise that I am talking about the journey and about everything that happened during the ten days of travelling through

Europe.

The silence becomes palpable. Tense. I can't see a thing. But I sense they are listening. I don't know whether they are exhilarated or aggravated or scandalised or amused. I am keeping my eye on the snake's head which every so often rears up menacingly and then becomes calm and drowsy and shuts it silver eyes with their enormous chequered pupils.

I hear occasional outbursts of laughter. I don't know whether they're laughing at me or at what I am saying. I continue undaunted. I concentrate my attention exclusively on the snake.

In my mind I am really talking to Filippo and I am telling him about our disastrous journey and the bartering and the queues and it all seems quite hilarious but I am deadly serious because of the snake. I hear Filippo splitting his sides and around him lots of other people bent double with laughter at what I am saying.

Then suddenly I am aware of the snake beginning to get restless. It opens a minute cleft in that coral mouth of shining scales and out shoots the sharp gleaming tip of its tongue.

I draw back. I am struck dumb. I fall silent. I am met by a thunderous roar of applause. I hardly have time to turn away before the reptile shoots out his whole tongue of prodigious length. I jump down the four steps from the platform in one bound. I land on all fours. I hear more laughter. I get up with dignity. I dust my sleeves. Stiff as a ramrod I make for the exit.

Miele catches up with me. He pushes me against the wall and shakes me by the shoulders.

'You're absolutely mad!'

'Why? What's the matter?'

'You've behaved in the worst possible taste. A really vulgar display of histrionics. You've talked about things you should never have mentioned... the dirty deals... the bartering... you're mad!'

'But why shouldn't I?'

'You're a guest here. Just imagine what all the right-wing journalists will make of it! You've fucked up the whole festival. You've given it a kick right up the arse. You've exposed it to ridicule. The least they'll do is to boot you out.'

183

'I only told the truth.'

'They'll send you straight back to Italy with an expulsion order like they do prostitutes!'

'Will you come with me?'

'You stupid fool. You drunken half-wit! What on earth entered your head to go and get pissed like that?'

I nearly tell him: 'You did. You – by making me feel so bad.' But I bite my tongue and say: 'I don't know why I got drunk. I don't know.' We go out together. I hang on his arm . . . his smell in my nostrils . . . I forget the snake . . . the threat of expulsion . . . I surrender myself to being dragged along on his seductive arm.

The alcohol has made me feel randy to a degree that is quite unusual for me. Seeing a half-open door I suddenly push Miele through it. He is taken by surprise but he doesn't resist. He stands there immersed in black thoughts. I kiss him in the cool darkness of the entrance hall. I smell his cheeks. I squeeze his waist. I clasp his head in my hands and kiss him. He lets me. I do not know if he wants me or not. It doesn't matter to me at that moment. My pride is buried deep down drowned in vodka. I clutch him in a frantic grasp.

We are prized apart by a small boy running precipitately up the stairs dragging a dog on a lead. The dog barks loudly at us. The little boy looks round with amazement. Then he calls out at the top of his voice: 'Mam! Mam!'

We hurry out holding each other by the hand. We set out in silence towards the school. I walk over bits of board and rubbish and I keep stumbling. But nothing matters. I cling to Miele's hand and push ahead blind and happy.

'You've ruined everything for yourself . . . You're a bloody fool.'

'But everyone was clapping.'

'Of course they were. You know what a kick people get when some half-baked cretin spouts out things that no one else dares talk about.'

'Then I did the right thing.'

'Did you hell do the right thing! You did the very worst thing possible. Politics doesn't function in that sort of stupid off-hand way. It requires intelligence – a sense of strategy. You acted from irrational impulse. You thought with your arse.'

184

'You mean heart.'

'I mean arse. Instead of a heart all you've got is an arse. Here it is.'

I laugh at this grotesque image. Then a few inches away I see his face swollen with anger his eyes shooting out flames like some prehistoric dragon.

'I'm not here to fool around, Armida. Through this holiday we've become part of a vast political movement whose aim is to spread socialism amongst young people everywhere. All the socialist countries have contributed towards this fantastic festival... including these angelic Finns who aren't part of the socialist block at all. But they understand what it's all about and have really fallen over backwards to help us. Well then. In this programme of intellectual solidarity and reconciliation your drunked tirade tastes like boiled cabbage for breakfast or rather like poison in the soup. You'll pay for it. That's inevitable. You'd better prepare yourself for something pretty ferocious. And don't expect me to take your part either. You're in the wrong, Armida, you're rotten, wrong and rotten...'

'Will I be tortured?'

'Are you trying to be funny? Though actually that's just what you deserve.'

'I'm not a political animal Miele. I just told them what had happened, that's all.'

'No Armida, you engaged in politics without thinking about it without giving it a thought and that's the most *abominable* thing to do. You gave yourself away as a real reactionary...'

'I described things as they were... nothing else... and they were amused... that's the truth of it.'

'Truth is dangerous when it isn't properly directed. The truth you described could be turned against us.'

'You're talking like Comrade Stalin with his great macho moustaches – who is now dead and buried and being eaten by worms.'

'In politics truth doesn't exist, Armida. What exists is strategy, long-term planning, common interests, discipline, tactics...'

'Our forbear Machiavelli thought like that. But he didn't have big moustaches and he didn't set out to change the world.'

185

'There's no point in trying to be facetious. You make me weep.'

'Why are we arguing like this, Miele? I don't want to quarrel with you. All I want is to make love with you.'

'I don't like drunks. When you're sober again come and find me. Good-bye.'

'Where are you going?'

He doesn't answer. He turns his back on me and walks off. White against white. In the nothingness of the damp misty evening . . .

I sit down on the ground with my head in my hands. I fall asleep. I dream there is a puddle of muddy water immediately in front of me and I am sinking sinking into it. I am a worm and I enjoy plunging into the darkness of this muddy water but I am also conscious of my abysmal weakness and fragility.

I meet some obstacle and it seems insurmountable. I raise my eyes. It is the pointed toecap of a shoe that is threatening me. I look at my soft and elusive body with the most intense pleasure and fear. I want to remain immersed in that soft mud with its exquisite aromas. But the shoe is there to squash me. I cower in the slimy depths. I feign death as I wait for the final blow . . .

'Armida! Wake up wake up! What on earth are you doing lying there on the ground? You'll catch your death of cold. Get up! Get up! Let's go what's the matter with you?'

My eyes open but I can't see. Something blue is shimmering in front of my wide-open eyes. With great effort I manage to distinguish pale blue shadows which slowly take shape and form.

'Ada!'

'It's long past supper-time. Have you eaten?'

I shake my head. I am dazzled by her blue dress which seems to be made of dancing pieces of mirror.

'I've heard you were great at the Palladium. People were enthusiastic. They say you gave an uproarious account of our journey and that everyone was in hysterics.'

'Miele says they'll expel me.'

'What a pity I wasn't there. I'd no idea you were giving a talk. Why didn't you tell me?'

'I didn't even know either. Do you think they will expel me?'

'If they do I'll come with you.'

I summon up the energy to heave myself to my feet. I give Ada a smacking kiss on her cheek. She squeezes my arm. She propels me towards the school. I accompany her making a huge effort not to fall asleep against her.

'ARMIDA Bianchi to come to the Festival Office! Armida Bianchi to come to the Festival Office!' The voice on the loudspeakers reaches me in the lavatory. I've only just sat down after queuing for half an hour. My anus closes up tight on me. There's no way I can force anything out. I clean myself with a piece of cotton wool. Here bidets and bath tubs don't exist.

I go out feeling embarrassed. I know everyone is looking at me. I start going upstairs. Half way up I see Asia coming towards me her hair done up in lots of little plaits tied with red elastic. She is wearing a boiler suit ten times to big for her.

'You look green.... You're scared eh?'

'I guess they'll throw me out.'

'Well as soon as you go in just pull up your skirt and fart in their faces. That'll shake 'em.'

'It's all your fault, Asia. You got me sozzled and I came out with a load of shit up there in the Palladium.'

'You were extraordinary. Just imagine how boring you'd have been without the vodka. Instead you really made the sparks fly.'

'Did you hear it then?'

'Of course. As you were sitting down I shot off to go and get a sandwich. When I came back you were up on the stage as solemn as a pumpkin spouting away and making everyone piss themselves with laughter.'

'But what did I say?'

'A little exhibition of comic theatre. A farce. You were fantastic you had everyone in hysterics. I mean it – really. Everybody wanted to know about you. They were asking "Who's that big cunt stinking of vodka a mile off?" and I was biting my tongue off so's not to give the game away that it was me who got you pissed – how you and I had got blind drunk right in their faces.'

'I must run if I'm not to be late.'

'Let them wait. Make yourself a bit important. You're always so fucking submissive. Act humble and you end up wiping their arses. We need to be queens not slaves. Queens and gangsters. Otherwise we finish up squashed like flies.'

'Would Armida Bianchi please come to the Festival Office' repeats the voice of the loudspeaker insistently. I am about to rush upstairs when Asia grasps my arm and holds me back.

'Listen. I did the cards for you: King of Diamonds. This man will bring you suffering. Three of spades: Disaster! Better you leave him at once. There are complications with health too. Seven of clubs: a brush with death. Maybe you'll be lucky and escape but if you want my advice leave him at once.'

'Thanks. I'll think about it.'

'No you won't think about it at all. You're a stupid moron. You're as obstinate as a mule. So good-bye and don't say I didn't warn you.'

I dash upstairs and immediately forget her dark prophecies. I arrive at the Office panting and out of breath. I knock. A voice shouts something in a language I don't understand. I assume it means I am to go in. I turn the door handle softly. I go through into an empty room lit by neon lighting with two tables placed alongside each other. At each of the tables sits a man. I am unsure which to approach. I stop in the centre of the room and wait.

'Please sit down' the one on the right tells me. He indicates a seat placed exactly in the middle between the two tables.

I sit down. Each time one of them speaks to me I have to turn my head in his direction. It is as if I were watching a game of tennis. 'You gave a very entertaining talk on the journey which brought the Italian delegates to the Festival.'

'Thanks!'

'However what we asked for was something quite different.'

'I'm sorry.'

'Moreover we got the impression that you were under the influence of alcohol.'

'Well.... yes.'

'You admit it?'

'Oh yes. I admit it.'

'You know it's forbidden in the regulations.'

'Yes. I know.'

'Nevertheless you did it?'

'Well... Yes. I'm sorry.'

'You admit you'd been drinking?'
'I said so.'
'Where did you get hold of the alcohol?'
'A friend gave it me.'
'Who?'
'I don't remember now. Someone sold it me for a few liras and I haven't seen her since.'
'Was it Asia Angeli by any chance?'
'No. I'm sure it wasn't her.'
'You were scheduled to talk about the theatre.'
'I know.'
'You should have been talking about the class struggle in relation to the world of the theatre.'
'I know that. But I'm not a drama critic. I write plays.'
'Why didn't you present a written text like all the other lecturers?'
'I didn't have time.'

My head is switching rapidly from side to side. The game of tennis is becoming nasty.

'We must now ask you to resign from the final plenary discussion for which you'd been nominated.'
'What discussion?'
'On world peace. Signorina Bianchi you are very forgetful.'
'That's all right. I'll resign.'
'You resign spontaneously?'
'Yes... since you've asked me to... Yes I will.'
'You realise that you will forfeit any claim to reimbursement for the journey? You'll have to pay the full return fare.'
'Oh dear!'
'You seem to live right up in the clouds.'
'Have you been drinking again?' the other man chips in.
'No. I don't drink.'
'Don't be facetious.'
'I'm sorry.'
'So you freely resign from having any connection with the international panel convened to discuss international peace and you agree to pay the full return fare?'
'How much will that be?'

'I'll work it out and let you know.'

'The fact is I've no money with me.'

'That doesn't matter. You can pay when you get back to Rome.'

'That's all right then. Can I go now?'

'One moment Signorina Armida. First you have to sign your name here.'

'Yes.'

'And here.'

'What is this then?'

'It's a declaration in which you guarantee not to drink any more alcohol while you are at this Festival.'

I sign. My hand damp with sweat. The pen slides out of my fingers.

'Drunk again eh?' The man sniggers contemptuously. 'It's you Italians who have created the most problems at this Festival. You are all rowdy undisciplined greedy dishonest quarrelsome...'

'Thieves and prostitutes as well I suppose?'

'I didn't say that.'

'Is the sermon over? Can I go now?'

'Not yet. Before you go I want to know where you got that alcohol.'

'I've told you. I don't know.'

'You're sure of that?'

'Absolutely.'

'You can go then. And try not to get into trouble again.'

I rush through the door in a flash. I rush up the stairs four at a time. I rush into the dormitory. I rush straight to my bed. For a moment I don't recognise it because someone else has climbed into it. I imagine I must have gone to the wrong room by mistake. I am on the point of going away.

'Hey Armida! Where are you going?'

It is Asia wearing a silver mini-dress. She sits up on the bed, munching biscuits.

'How did it go?'

'They were determined to find out where I got the drink from.'

'Did you tell them?'

'No.'

'You didn't betray me?'

'No.'

191

'Then you're a real friend. Shit – let's go and drink a toast together. Come on!' She pulls me towards the staircase. But I resist.

'Half a sec. People are keeping their eye on me. They'll know immediately it was you if they see us together.'

'So much the better. If they throw me out we can quit this dump and go and have some fun.'

'No. Chuck it. Anyway I'm off booze. My guts ached all last night.'

'I've got something a bit milder we could drink instead.'

'I've got something a bit milder we could drink instead.'

'No no. Besides I must go to the toilet and at this time there's usually the hell of a queue.'

'I'll come with you.'

I set off for the toilets followed by Asia who munches biscuits and hops along barefooted. Unexpectedly there is almost no queue. I go inside and sit down. But everything's blocked. My bowels just won't move at all.

'I can see your feet. They look so ridiculous. What's your bloke called?'

'Miele.'

'What a shit of a name. Is he handsome?'

'Yes.'

'You love him a lot?'

'Yes.'

'You really are simple-minded.'

I get up. I pull the flush. I give up for today. I go and wash my hands under the tap. Asia circles round me like a buzzing blue-bottle.

'According to the cards it'll end badly. This love of yours wasn't born under a good star.'

'Asia. Stop being such a bird of ill omen!'

'How would you like me to seduce him and lure him away from you?'

'For God's sake! I'd hate you for evermore.'

'All right then. Let him gobble you up. So much the worse for you!'

She goes off in a huff without saying good-bye her little pig-tails dancing up and down on her thin shoulders.

MIELE spends all his time in the Palladium. If I want to see him I have to go there. Ada and Dida have made friends with a group from Holland and they are always out in the town. Sometimes they join us at mealtimes sometimes they don't.

I come across Nico sitting all hunched up in one of the red velvet armchairs in the Palladium. He is rubbing his eyes. His glasses are balanced on the back of the chair in front of him. Cesare is leaning against the wall waiting his turn to give a talk on the problem of young people in agriculture.

'How are you?'

'Bad bad.'

'What's the matter?'

'Dida – I hardly see her at all.'

'And your wife?'

'She's disappeared too.'

We are interrupted by a round of applause. Now it's Cesare's turn. Nico puts on his glasses and focuses his gaze towards the rostrum.

The harsh stubborn voice issues from the microphone and spreads itself in aggressive waves throughout the hall. People listen for a while and then the usual whispering begins. Many get up and go out to the coffee bar. They come back. They sit down. They take notes. They chatter in low voices. They put on the headphones for simultaneous translation. Cesare talks precisely quoting a mass of statistics. He is very outspoken. His cutting voice is not afraid of unpopularity. His vision is a catastrophic one. But he does not try to play on people's feelings or to be sensational. He limits himself to cataloguing the failures of a country which has followed the myth of large-scale technology and industry regardless of its effect on crops, trees and the countryside.

At the end there is lively applause and he returns to his seat well satisfied with himself wiping saliva from the corners of his mouth. His eyes shift continually towards the heavy leather-edged curtain which swells and rustles every time someone passes through it and falls back on itself with a soft swishing sound. He is waiting for Ada. Just as Nico waits for Dida.

193

Now a Frenchman with protruding teeth is at the rostrum talking about the relationship between young people and the peasants in Normandy. He reads from small sheets of paper which he holds in shaking hands.

Then it is the turn of a German with a flabby body and a shrill voice. He is dressed in a blue suit with waistcoat and tie. He hurls himself at the audience full of pomposity and clichés. Few people stay to listen to him.

Nico makes a sign to me and gets up. I follow him and we go to the bar. We order coffee. A little later Cesare joins us. He gets himself a huge ice topped with fresh cream. I can hear a woman's voice in the lecture hall. I push the heavy curtain aside and peep through. I see a child with long fair hair that falls down on to the microphone. Where have I seen her before? Of course – the woman at the typewriter.

She is Greek. I can't understand what she is saying. Her voice is intense reflective thoughtful. A strong rich voice totally incongruous coming from that little body of an ageing child.

I see a lot of people are putting on their headphones. I take one that's been left on the arm of a chair and put it on. I am bowled over listening to her. She is talking about Sappho and how political her poetry was. In the hall there is silence. Some are asking themselves who on earth this little Greek monkey is spouting about some woman who died more than two thousand years ago and was also a great socialist.

When she finishes the applause is timid and half-hearted. Someone whistles. But others go on clapping enthusiastically.

I wait for her in the corridor and stop her. I say 'Bravo!' She smiles. She shakes her head. I make a gesture with my hands of clapping silently. She blushes. Then she goes off looking very small as she totters on her high heels.

More hearty applause. I look up. It is Miele's turn. He goes up to the rostrum with an assured step as fair and handsome as an Apollo. I can't distinguish his words but I know that he is talking about the great problems of world peace. It is obvious that he is an accomplished speaker. He is completely relaxed. He doesn't read from notes. He doesn't dry up. The words flow smoothly and

194

convincingly.

I listen to his voice. It ripples like imperceptible waves on the sea shimmering with many coloured facets blue changing to green changing to violet breaking into coils and fringes splintering into a thousand glittering light-waves. I surrender myself to those waves which transport and enchant me. Now his arguments have taken on the rhythm of a calm laborious march. He never misses a step. He never stumbles. He never slows down. Then all at once he seems to be caught in a gully full of rocks. But he leaps over the boulders and sends them tumbling down without losing his balance and continues his non-stop climb towards the peak which he reaches breathing hard but still unruffled. Once there he bows confidently ready to take the prize for champion climber. The finale of his oration rises to a grand crescendo and is greeted with prolonged applause.

The spotlight follows him down the rostrum steps and along the passage like an opera star caressed by the loving gaze of the public. He pauses by me without seeing me. I don't dare to stop him. A crowd of girls flock round him. He looks pleased and thanks them without arrogance but with a childlike mixture of candour and vanity.

I join him in the coffee bar while he drinks a glass of milk encircled by doting women.

'You were very good' I tell him. He stares at me uncertainly for a moment. I feel it is as if we were meeting over some vast distance.

'Did you like it?'

'You were great. You had them spellbound.' He is happy. He squeezes my arm. He kisses me on the mouth. In front of all the girls. And I'm grateful to him for that. To what do I owe all this generosity?

'Shall we go and eat?'

'Yes. We'll wait for Cesare and Nico and then we'll go.'

'No I meant you and I on our own' he says kissing me on the ear. But we have to give up the idea because just at that moment Cesare and Nico come up and congratulate Miele on his talk. We go off together in the direction of a restaurant.

During the meal Miele holds my hand under the table. I gulp down a fish soup full of bones and I eat rye bread and butter without tasting a thing. Cesare orders potato salad. 'That'll be extra' says the

195

waitress in a firm voice.

'Yes yes we'll pay extra.'

'Do you have the money?'

'We've certainly got a ravenous hunger' says Miele getting out a fistful of markka and displaying them in his open palm. 'Is that all right?' he asks. The waitress nods and goes away with our orders. I look for Dida and Ada at the other tables but I can't see them. Nico is looking for them too. He takes off his glasses that weigh heavily on his nose. He breathes on them and wipes them with the clean tablecloth. Then he replaces them so as to keep watch on the entrance. Eventually he takes them off to eat and then has to put them back on again every time he hears the door squeak.

They offer me a beer. But I refuse. The very smell of beer nauseates me.

'Would you like some apple tart?'

'No.'

Miele is eating greedily and drinking a lot of beer. He stuffs himself with slices of bread and salt butter and smoked herring. Then all of a sudden he looks up at the clock.

'It's almost two. I've got a date with some people from Iran about an international meeting in Teheran.... Needless to say it's forbidden by the Shah but they still want it to happen. Pay my share of the bill. Here's the money. I must go. We'll see each other later at the Palladium. Goodbye my love goodbye...'

He gets up. He gives me a kiss on the mouth and goes off. Nico watches him go out with a melancholy expression on his face. Cesare picks his teeth. He is swearing under his breath. He is jealous of Miele knowing so many people and always being at the centre of everything that's going on.

CESARE Nico and I are kicking the ground up by the Students Union looking for our two vanished friends.

'Suppose we went to the sauna.'

'We've only just had a meal.'

'What does that matter. It's not as if it were a cold bath.'

'You two go. I don't like the idea.' Cesare sets off on his own in a really bad mood. Nico calls him back.

'You've had a sauna before you idiot? Surely?'

'No.'

'Listen. You go into this room . . . it's lined with wood . . . the scent of birchwood . . . and then the steam . . . you sweat and sweat and out come all the toxins in the sweat!'

'That's just words.'

'It's true I assure you' Nico insists.

'Well, goodbye' Cesare goes off picking his teeth. Nico and I remain arm in arm in the sunshine in the middle of the street.

'Shall we go for a walk in the park? I've a vague idea Dida might be there.'

'Let's go then.'

We walk slowly towards the Kaivopuisto. We pass by the Tahititorni Gardens. Every now and then Nico catches sight of a white skirt fluttering round a plump body and stops dead in his tracks.

'Where the hell can she be?'

'Maybe she's somewhere looking for you' I say to console him.

'And I haven't even got Ada to talk to.' We stop in front of a shop window displaying various sexual objects. Colossal penises of red rubber. Vibrators. Dummy vaginas. Plastic breasts. Whole detachable pelvises in artificial skin.

'All these things remind me that I haven't made love for months' says Nico scratching his head. 'Sometimes I think of Dida as if she were an artificial body – imitation flesh towards which I am drawn irresistibly. I've a compulsive urge to take a rubber penis and penetrate her with it.'

'Do you and Ada never make love together?'

'No. She doesn't want it. Come to that, nor do I. It's so good lying naked beside each other and talking about Dida...'

Meanwhile we have reached the Kaivopuisto. We sit down on a bench beneath a gigantic fir-tree with blue pine-needles.

'Pornography is a kind of huge theatre.... Only one has to be very subtle to create good theatre... most of the time it becomes just ham acting... the crudest sort of fantasy....'

'But what is fantasy?' I provoke him stretching out my legs on a lawn of clover. I shut my eyes with a feeling of peace...

'Fantasy hovers between life and death... in a dangerous emptiness... mysterious... artificial. It needs only the smallest push to plunge it into the depths of corruption and it needs a similar push to raise it to the heights of sublime beauty.'

'Nico I really like the way your imagination walks so lightly lightly on its nailed boots.'

'Look over there' says Nico putting on his glasses. 'Isn't that Miele?' I open my eyes in time to see a white car driving along the road beyond the edge of the gardens. Two heads inside. A woman at the wheel. Fair with a beret slanting over her forehead. The other certainly could be Miele. I get up. I'm about to call to him. But Nico pulls my sleeve.

'Let him be. You'll spare him having to tell a pack of lies.'

'That makes a lot of sense.' Already the car has slid downhill with its mysterious car-load. 'Perhaps it wasn't him.'

'I think it was. But no matter. Unless you really want to suffer.'

'Why do you want to suffer Nico?'

'I don't but when it happens to me I try to confront it.'

'So do I. But Miele doesn't give me the chance.'

'Perhaps he only wants to provoke you.'

'Perhaps.'

We exchange moody looks. Without the protection of his glasses Nico's eyes look fragile and unhealthy. For a long time I stare at him fascinated. He returns my look with listless despair.

'Let's go and have this sauna Armida. It'll do us good.'

We start walking towards the town centre. He says he remembers a sign for a sauna in a street near the Palladium. Soon we come to it. A white sign-board hanging from a blue metal post. We enter. A woman with a white cap on her head greets us with cheery brusqueness. She takes our money. She throws two clean towels over our arms and opens the door to the small room lit by neon lighting. With her big muscular arms she pushes me behind one curtain and Nico behind another. She gesticulates to us to undress.

I emerge naked covering myself with a small towel. I see Nico in front of me naked and without his glasses. He looks embarrassingly white and I burst out laughing. The woman laughs too. Then she pushes us both roughly inside a small room with wooden steps made out of planks. In one corner a cast iron stove is spewing out boiling steam.

The heat burns our nostrils. I can't keep on my feet. I sit on the highest step and watch Nico timidly groping his way to a place lower down. Then he turns his head blindly towards me.

'How much of me can you see?' I ask him.

'A white thing with two legs.'

'I can see you quite clearly. You've got a beautiful body Nico even if it's so white that it hurts.'

He laughs in embarrassment. He lays his small towel on the step and lies down on it. But suddenly he sits up with his arms round his knees.

'Has she locked us in here do you think?' The alarm in his voice is muffled in the aromatic steam.

'Maybe she has?'

'Suppose we die of suffocation?'

'Of course we shan't. I was joking. She hasn't locked us in she's just put the door to.'

'I feel as if I'm going to faint Armida.'

'Shall I open the door?'

'No no. I'll do it. I can't get my breath . . . but I feel better now.'

'Lie down Nico.'

'I'm scared.'

'What of?'

'Of dying.'

I climb down the stairs that separate us. I put my hand over his heart. His heartbeats are slow but firm.

'You're not going to die. It's the heat. Do you want some cold water?'

He shakes his head. He holds my hand to his chest. I feel his sweat running down my fingers. I see him swelling between his legs. I lie down gently on top of him mingling my sweat with his. I don't think of anything while I press him to me. My throat is parched my lungs on fire.

'The ultimate make-believe...' he says bitterly.

We clasp each other in a long agonised embrace.

IT is Saturday morning. I wake up with a tickling sensation on the sole of my foot. I take off the head band I wear against the light. I see Ada standing on the metal steps that lean against the side of the bed. She is touching my foot.

'Armida! Wake up! We're going to Savonlinna.'

'What's that?'

'A place on Lake Saimaa.'

'I don't think I'll come.'

'Get up! It's a beautiful day.'

'I don't want to go. I'm tired. I couldn't sleep last night.'

'We're all going. Cesare Nico Dida Miele and me. Come on!'

'Miele too? Are you sure?'

'Certain. We're meeting at seven thirty at the School entrance.'

'What's this place called?'

'What does it matter? It's a lake with lots of islands. And we'll all be there. Isn't that enough?'

All at once I am overtaken with enormous curiosity to see this unknown lake. The light that streams in through the window seems less hostile and threatening. It suddenly fills me with the impetus to get up.

'I knew you'd change your mind.' Ada gives me an amused look. Balancing on the step below she passes me my clothes.

'Ada I must tell you something. Yesterday I made love with Nico. Has he told you?'

'No.'

'Do you mind?'

'Of course not. You know it's Dida I love. Nico and I don't make love at all.'

'I know that. But after all you are still his wife.'

'I haven't got any sense of ownership.'

Someone protests against our subdued voices with a shhh! It is still early even though the room is filled with light. I get down from my bed without making a noise and go to the toilets. For once they are completely deserted. I bend down over the wash-basin to wash. I dry myself. I comb my hair. I breathe in great lungfuls of fresh morning

201

air. I put on the only clean blouse I have left.

Miele is the first to arrive. I see him from a distance with his usual white trousers his chestnut hair falling over his eyes and his swaying buoyant walk. He smiles at me. He gives me a hug. He smells faintly of lavender. He sits next to me and leans his head on my shoulder.

'Do you love me Armida?'

'And you?'

At that moment the others arrive. Cesare looking quite a fright in a pair of outsize red trousers. Nico ill-shaven his ears full of soap. He kisses me in an embarrassed way looking in the other direction.

Ada is happy. Darker and more petite than ever. Dida comes behind her wrapped in a filmy white and lilac dress that makes me think of a big tropical butterfly. Her breasts peep out from beneath lacy folds. A red shawl is thrown over her shoulders.

'Here we are all together once more!' Cesare says jumping around in his new tennis shoes. He is obviously happy. He doesn't take his eyes off Ada. 'It's a hell of a time since we've all seen each other' he goes on. 'Dida and Ada lost in wonderful feminist friendships. Nico and Armida lost in the erotic steam of the sauna. Miele lost in his ambitious political machinations...'

Miele looks at him with annoyance. But then he laughs and puts a hand on his shoulder.

'And where were you lost Cesare?'

'Me? In lust...'

'Lust for that French girl with the big snub nose?'

'Everyone knows it's Ada I'm in love with. And I'm faithful. With a faithfulness that's all the more heroic because it's unasked for. As for those trifles my prick gets up to they've got nothing to do with me.

'Anyhow they are insignificant... merely delicious little inanities.' While he speaks he thrusts out his stomach and points disconsolantly to his unruly alter ego. As if it were a degenerate son whose goings on he prefers to ignore.

'I can't be responsible for all his lecheries. What he does is his own affair. All I can do is to keep my distance: I ignore him. He follows every wind that blows. I stay put.'

'Actually you're completely split' says Ada. 'A perfect division

202

right down the middle like a rotten water-melon.' She looks at him sarcastically blowing cigarette smoke in his face.

'Do you want me to castrate myself? Do you want me to cut my balls off to prove that I'm yours – yours till you're sick to death of me. If you'd let me make love with you do you think he'd still go looking for other skirts to sniff? He's less patient than I am that's all. He's satisfied with surrogates. I'm not . . . It's you I love Ada and you only. In my heart of hearts I'm faithful as a saint. I've told you – I'm not in control of my prick but whatever it does it'll never own me – never!'

The red and blue bus arrives and stops right in front of us. Almost at once another twenty people join the queue. The bus doors open with a hiss like a submerged whale. We board it. We take seats at the back. The windows are hermetically sealed and the tinted glass makes it possible to see without being seen. The driver gives out the tickets. He makes the student guide sit beside him and puts a microphone in his hands. We set off. The guide tells us the history of the country – the Ugro-Fin tribe which probably came from the Urals . . .

Someone passes round a thermos of hot chocolate. Someone else starts to sing. Many fall asleep. Or smoke. But the smoke is quickly sucked out by the air-conditioning.

'I made love with Nico.'

For a moment Miele looks at me angrily.

'When?'

'Yesterday in the sauna.'

'So now you feel pleased with yourself?'

'Yes and no. It was you I really wanted.'

His face clears. I see him smile. He takes my hand and crushes it between his legs.

'Do you still want me?'

'Very much.'

'I really think we'll be able to make love this evening.' He buries his nose in my neck. He covers me with small wet kisses. I shut my eyes longing for time to stop like this for ever.

We arrive in Savonlinna towards the end of the morning. Then we walk through thick dark woods between hundreds of pools and lakes some quite small some very large. We catapult ourselves across dangerous bridges suspended in mid-air. Since time did not stop I take note of little signs . . . tracks so that I can rediscover that walk in my memory: here a narrow path in the sand into which my shoes sink with a gentle creaking . . . over there bell-shaped flowers hanging from a strange mauve plant . . . an artificial pool . . . ducks with green and gold plumage . . . a bar with seats made of wicker-work.

We sit down and have tea. After a long wait it arrives black as coffee and flavoured with cinnamon accompanied by cakes that are as hard as stones.

Later we are taken to a youth hostel with a low red roof. A building of pinewood with large rooms cluttered with beds. The smell of pine is mingled with the sweetish smell of pork fat. In front the ground is sandy and dotted with juniper bushes. At the back is a wood of dwarf pines wafting a good smell of resin and toadstools.

There are some large rooms of thirty beds with stable doors and windows without shutters. There are also games rooms with tables in them and lavatories.

'Quite impossible to make love here.'

'We'll manage. Even if we have to disappear into the forest.' Miele whispers into my ear.

W<small>E</small> saunter through the streets. We sit in the bar. We visit the mediaeval fortress. The underground dungeons. The local history museum. We smoke. We sing. We argue. We drink. Always together. Nico possessed by a feverish euphoria. Hand in hand with his wife on one side and the woman he loves on the other. Cesare always grumpy but obviously excited as he tries to capture the eyes of his Ada. Miele and I inseparable.

I wait anxiously for the night. What if we don't manage to be on our own? The woods don't look very welcoming. The ground is damp and muddy and bristling with prickles. Supper lasts for hours. I can't eat a thing. I watch Miele who is calmly putting back a large plate of barley soup. Cesare is battling with some fish from the lakes which is cramfull of bones. Ada watches Dida with fascination as she dips her spoon into a mountain of creamy chocolate mousse. Nico is watching Ada. He follows the direction of her eyes and her gaze falls on Dida's plump hands.

Afterwards we go through the gardens by the harbour walking on a layer of gravel that sparkles in the light of the arctic night. The smell of rotten fish mingles with the smell of juniper trees and of the pine-trees that begin to breathe in the night air.

We meet a group of Finns who are dancing round an improvised fire. We too start dancing and stamping our feet on the gravel. Every so often a hand reaches out for a bottle and someone takes it up to their mouth before passing it to their neighbour.

I dance with Nico and with Ada while two Finnish boys bared to the waist leap up and down next to us. The others sit round in a circle clapping their hands.

'It's the night of August Bank Holiday Armida!'

I drink and pass on the bottle. On my tongue a strong taste of plums. Someone has lighted a joint. The scent of hashish rises up into our nostrils. Nico's eyes search for Dida and light on her in the centre of another circle dancing on her own. Her feet bare. Her breasts uncovered. Everyone's eyes fixed on her.

I circle round in search of Miele. I can't see him. I stop all of a sudden stupefied. Someone knocks my arm insistently with the bottle. I can't manage to lift my hand to take hold of it. Immobilised by painful forebodings. At that moment I see him emerging from behind a bush with a girl with long bare legs. They pause in front of the fire. They say good-bye. Then he comes over to me and pulls me by the waist.

'Armida! Don't make such a face.'

'Can't you ever stay with me for five minutes? Without running after someone else. If you fancy that girl why don't you go with her?'

'What girl Armida? I went behind the bush to have a pee. I don't even know who the girl was. Anyway she's gone off now . . .'

A moment of uncertainty – trying to take stock of my frenzy from outside. Is it possible to deny the evidence? I look at him in a daze and at the same time am already preparing to blind myself in an effort to believe him.

'Let's go Armida . . . I want you . . . Let's go.'

But there aren't any single rooms in the hostel. The big dormitory is full of people already asleep. Discouraged I sit down on a bed. But Miele doesn't lose heart.

'Wait for me here. I'll go and prospect.'

He comes back in a little while beaming. 'I've found it' he says. He grabs Dida's sleeping bag and goes towards the stairs with me following. We creep down the steps in the dark and find ourselves in a cellar. We grope our way through it and come out suddenly in a courtyard. On the far side is a door.

'Don't make a noise and be careful of the apples! Go on.' I open the door and am met by a powerful and pungent smell of fermenting apples. On one side are barrels of cider. On the other boxes of smoked fish.

Miele lays the sleeping bag between two barrels with the end against a box of smoked fish. The floor is made of wood full of worm-holes and tarred with pitch. The sleeping bag has the sweet smell of Dida's jasmine.

We clasp each other's bodies. With our clothes on. Impetuously. Then we separate again and look at each other from a boundless distance. Then we come together as if someone were pushing us from behind. We join belly to belly chest to chest mouth to mouth. Again

206

we distance ourselves and look at each other. Time and again we embrace obsessively.

I place my hand on his sweating chest. His heart is beating rapidly. I take his nipple between my lips. I can feel him smiling in the dark. The smell of apples grows more obtrusive.

We are one single body with two heads and four arms and four legs. We roll over on the floor regardless of the cold and the various obstacles we encounter. Sinking into a void we plunge down a thousand feet overcome by the delicious terror of our fall but without the shock of ever crashing on the bottom. We plunge and plunge for minutes on end in a cloud of dust and apples and smoked trout and milk and pitch.

We separate for the last time. We remain apart. The smell settles down and loses that smarting spiciness that was intoxicating us. We are no longer suspended in the void in a mysterious space between heaven and earth between bursting apples and flying fish but shut into a cramped cellar without enough room to move without air or light or breath our bones bruised and tender semen sticky on our naked stomachs.

In the dark all I can see is the red tip of Miele's cigarette.

'I saw you yesterday in a car with a girl.'

'Where?'

'By the park.'

'Are you sure?'

His voice becomes uncertain. The little red point trembles round and round. Something bitter catches in his throat. He takes his time.

'I also saw you kissing somebody in the train.'

'When?'

'I could understand it if you told me that to love me you had to fancy other women. But do please come clean. It's your refusal to be honest about it that upsets me. You deny all the evidence.'

Silence. His arm pressed against my belly trembles slightly. I realise he's finding this all very painful.

'I haven't anyone apart from you Armida. I'm not interested in anyone else.' He says it with absolute calm. The assertive tone of his voice is just like that of someone used to improvising in front of large

207

hostile audiences. I have a sudden lightning flash of certainty: these denials are necessary to him. He needs them more than I do. They constitute his personality – his secret – the secret of Miele.

In forcing the truth out of him I could ruin everything. That is an absolute certainty. I must leave him as he is shut away in his own mystery that is like a second skin. He is invulnerable because he is a complete loner because he lives in a shell because he will never reveal himself absolutely.

I must not touch his Achilles heel. If I worm out of him the secret that makes him invulnerable I will reduce him to the level of ordinary men inextricably split between truth and lies. Whereas he exists between certainties and uncertainties between spells and dreams between sudden appearances and sudden disappearances. In a tantalising rhythm of unpredictability and doubt.

I don't say any more. I bend down to kiss his navel. Relic of an old wound all that is left of a fateful and far-distant bond. Between those tiny petals of flesh I come upon a hint of faint familiar smells something sweet and hidden almost like the slightly cloying and secret sex of certain flowers.

OUR last day in Helsinki. Coming back from the long queue for the lavatories I find an envelope on my bed – 'Armida Bianchi'. I open it. 'Signora Bianchi is invited to attend the farewell party of the Youth Festival which will take place at 7.30 p.m. in the garden of the Villa Hummeri. The bus will leave the school at 7 o'clock.'

I look round the other beds. A white envelope is conspicuous on every bed. We are all invited. There will be a multitude of people But what can I wear? All my clothes are dirty. I decide to go and buy myself a clean blouse. Maybe I can find a second-hand one.

On my way downstairs I pass Asia's door. I decide to go in and say 'hi'. I knock. There is no reply. I am just on the point of going away when I see her face appear through a dark gap in the woodwork. Her hair sticking to her forehead the imprint of a fold in the sheet cutting her cheek in half and dark rings under her swollen eyes.

'I'll leave you to sleep. I only wanted to say "hullo".'

'No come in.' She pulls me inside and shuts the door behind her. The atmosphere is suffocating. A potent smell of soap vodka and indigestion.

'Are you ill?'

'I'm never ill. I can die but I can't be ill. I die and then I come back to life like some weeds . . . Are my breasts all right? I felt them hurting yesterday evening. I had it off with someone who kept biting me as if they were made of marzipan.'

She throws open her pyjama jacket and reveals two full breasts hanging down with their pink tips turned impudently upwards. Two bruises encircle her nipples like collars.

'They're beautiful. But you're crazy to let someone treat you like that. Look at those bruises!'

'He was so happy though. Like a puppy sucking milk. The trouble was he had sharp teeth' she says laughing. She makes a grimace of pain. She buttons up her pyjama jacket over her breasts.

'You know we're leaving tomorrow. The Festival's over.'

'Yes I know.'

'What about you?'

'I'm staying. I've got friends here. They'll put me up.'

209

'What will they want in exchange though?'

'Nothing.'

'Are you coming to the party at the Villa Hummeri this evening?'

'I haven't got an invitation.'

'I'll give you mine.'

'I don't need invitations come to that. I'll put a little feather over my cunt and I'll go. I'd like to see anyone chase me away!'

'You always want to shock. You scare me sometimes.'

'They're all so boring boring.'

'Have you had much to drink?'

'As much as I need. By now I know the exact dose. I like to feel the death agony in my mouth rising up from my throat. I like the way it presses down on my gums. I could prolong it for ever... Then I take Charon's boat down the river and I know nothing more about myself until tomorrow...'

'To put it in a nutshell you're a zombie!'

'No. Zombies are dead. I pass from one state to another. More like a vampire. It takes a lot of effort but I like ringing the changes. How are you getting on with your handsome revolutionary what's-his-name?'

'All right.'

'Have you managed to find somewhere to have a fuck?'

'Yes.'

'Was it good?'

'Yes.'

'Here's a mystery that I'd like to clear up. When I'm dead I make love very well. I'm a really sensitive liberated corpse. When I'm alive I make it just as well but I'm completely detached – a spectator. I like to watch myself while I make love to see how brilliant I am. It makes my flesh creep – but the trouble is I'm not there.'

'So what's the mystery?'

'The mystery of pleasure.'

'If you're watching yourself from a distance you can't be experiencing much pleasure.'

'The truth is that pleasure isn't confined just to life or death but to something in between. Ecstasy is a tedious state within reach of every

210

little boy with a hard on. It doesn't interest me.'

'It's pride that fucks you up Asia. Horrible fucking pride!'

'Oh shit on it Armida. Why don't we have a lakka together? Do you know what it is? It's a liqueur made from raspberries. Yesterday evening I met a really nice guy. He was around fifty with three children and married to an amazing woman who was only a few feet away kissing someone else... a champion drinker quite capable of downing a whole bottle of lakka without batting an eyelid. We had a really nice time... would you like me to introduce you to him? He's not handsome like Miele but... listen – why don't the two of us make a pact: I'll teach you to drink and you teach me how to enjoy sex...'

'A fine exchange!'

'I'll teach you to get outside yourself and then come back. What do you think of that? It's the secret of so many ancient religions. To go down quietly slipping gently into the valley of self-oblivion and then to come back slowly like a rocking of the boat into your own bed while life smashes you in the face: the smells the tastes the people running the people singing the good familiar smell of a wet dog...'

'I'd die straight away. I haven't got your strength.'

'You could write marvellous things about your journey to the world of the dead when you came back and returned to your senses.'

'Anyway alcohol makes me sick.'

'Sickness is just the right companion for the journey.'

'Why don't you come to Rome with us?'

'Rome's fine for the dead. It's a city of ghosts. But I'm alive and I don't like it. It smells too much of elderberries.'

'Do you like elderberry wine?'

'When I'm broke. But it's too sweet it gives me indigestion and then that transparent taste of aniseed that floods right through my veins... It reminds me of abandoned football fields drains people in the streets bald heads nasal voices...'

'Have you got enough money to stay? Do you want a loan?'

'There's only one thing I want from you Armida; your cunt.'

'Don't talk like some gormless youth.'

'I talk as I please. I want you to teach me to make love with joy...'

'Wife for duty boys for pleasure melons for delight... It's an old

211

Arab saying.'

'I'd like to torture you Armida. I want to bite your clitoris till it bleeds. I want to fuck you. Christ I want to fuck you till you're dead.'

'I like love to be gentle.'

'You're a sentimental little shit. Go away. I'm fed up with you.'

I get up and go to the door. Her aggressive voice reaches me on the doorstep.

'I sold your bracelet but I'm going to keep all the money. Is that clear? Now go to hell.'

I go out and shut the door behind me. I can still hear her swearing in the dark. Out in the passage the fresh air makes me giddy. I lean for a moment against the wall beads of sweat on my forehead.

Ada comes smiling to meet me. A new pair of trousers a lovely pink shirt. The shining black wing on her forehead.

'Ada you're always there to save me.'

'What's happened?'

'I've just had a nightmare.'

'Let's go. You're really pale. Would you like a brandy?'

'No. God forbid.'

I lean on her arm. We walk slowly towards the entrance. We sit down on the curved steps. The morning light consumes me drowns me.

'And Dida?'

'She's ironing her best embroidered blouse. Are you coming to the party this evening?'

'Do you think Miele will show up?'

'I expect so. Miele likes parties.'

'And Nico?'

'He's asleep. We were awake all night talking about Dida.'

'Did you make love?'

'No.'

'You're crazy.'

'You too Armida – soon. Very soon. I see you walking with great strides along the road of solitary love. You'll find out how much yearning and happiness can come from one-sided love...'

'Helena loves Demetrio who loves Hermione who loves Lysander who loves Helena...'

'Nico loves Dida who loves Cesare who loves Ada who loves Dida...'

'And Titania?'

'She loves an ass's head.'

Vɪʟʟᴀ Hummeri. Half past seven. The garden of the round stones. Light enveloping the garden like water made of minute shining particles scattered over the grass.

The organisers receive us courteously at the entrance to the Villa smiling at everybody. The two men who interrogated me now shake my hand politely and affably. They ask me if I have had a good stay in Helsinki – but they don't wait for a reply. They turn to the next arrival with an identical formal welcome.

I go in search of Miele. But I can't find him anywhere. I meet Cesare. He is in a very bad mood. He is eating toasted peanuts. He gathers handfuls from plates dotted around the tables and stuffs them angrily into his mouth. Nico follows behind him looking depressed his glasses sliding down his nose. He is wearing a smart clean shirt and his usual outsize trousers of blue worsted.

'Have you seen Ada?'

'No.'

'Has Madam Julie put in an appearance yet?' Cesare interrupts in a harsh voice.

'Julie who?' asks Nico distractedly.

'And now John the servant arrives with the master's boots which he has to polish . . . how very clever fascinating brutal and servile!'

'Who on earth are you talking about? Now it's me who's curious.'

'Your true love.'

'Why is he a servant?'

'In this enchanted nordic garden . . . one day in the middle of summer . . . while Madam Julie makes marmalade . . . He's just an animal but obviously a glamorous servant with the heart of a billy-goat . . .'

'Stuff it Cesare. You're just being bitchy.'

'Servant or not he knows how to get the best out of it. It's us from the miserable lower middle-classes who are out on a limb. Ten days in Helsinki and we haven't managed to strike up one friendship with a Finn let alone have a fuck. We always stick with each other always together preoccupied with our own navels. At any rate he's been a politico a sociologist an agitator. On every issue that matters he's

214

been hobnobbing with the intellectuals the politicians the capitalists the beautiful women. You could say he's taken possession of this city just like Strindberg's servant possesses Madam Julie's heart. While we trail around the streets thinking about nothing but our stupid provincial love-affairs . . .'

'So now you've fallen for Miele too?'

'I don't love him. I admire him which is quite different.'

'I admire him too.'

'With your crotch.'

'What a shit you are Cesare' Nico snatches off his spectacles angrily. I think he's going to hit him again but he confines himself to glaring at him indignantly.

'By the way where is Miele? Has anyone seen him?'

'I think he's chatting up the wife of some minister or other.'

'How do you know?'

'That's my guess. If she's not the wife of a minister she looks like it. You should see the strings of pearls!'

I walk away. I have no wish to listen to Cesare's malevolent voice running down everyone and everything. I go down to the end of the lawn to view the villa from a distance. I reach a wood of birch trees. A subtle bitter-sweet scent of cedar-wood guides me along tangled paths. I seat myself on a stone covered with moss and look back at the Villa: with all its windows uncurtained and blazing with light it seems to be suspended in the air like a transparent mirage. The music pours out through the open door flooding the park. The people seem hardly moving as they come and go in a silent swarm.

I don't know how long I stay there held by this vision. Eventually my legs begin to feel stiff and I get up. I am making for the path back to the villa when I hear a lapping noise that draws me towards the bottom of the wood.

I walk fearlessly through the wood my feet sinking into the soft damp grass. I come to higher ground. I look round. In the eternally suspended light of the summer night I make out a winding rushing stream that threads its way between clefts and ravines half hidden by the wood as it reappears with the rumbling of a waterfall. I approach clearing a path through the brambles. I hear the spray falling against

215

the stones gurgling and swirling round inside the hollows of the rocks. Suddenly I see something moving in front of me. I look intently and my eyes fall on two white bodies which take shape in the darkness.

I think of retreating but something about the way they move stops me. They are two naked women sitting beside each other kissing heedless of the whole world. One plump and smooth with luminous flesh. The other small and skinny with a dark head and a raven's wing slipping down over her forehead...

They kiss for a long time almost completely still and silent. Then holding each other by the hands they slip into the water and take turns to splash each other. The warm air encircles them inside a thick dense glass.

I want to call out to them and to jump into the water and bathe with them. But something holds me back. The consciousness of being nothing but an eye watching with the painful impotence of the spectator condemned to remain outside while they act in the glare of the footlights expressing something of which I can only be a witness. I stay silent and resign myself to my role of spectator. And like all spectators guilty of abandoning myself to a seductive emotional passivity.

I COME to with a glass in my hand. Surrounded by a crowd of young people in summery clothes. Ravishing music in my ears.

Miele clinks his glass against mine.

'What are you dreaming about?'

'I dreamt I was searching for you.'

'Don't search for me too hard... You might discover there isn't anyone there.'

'Armida is given to fantasising like everyone with little imagination.' I hear Cesare's caustic voice behind my back.

'I love what I love. Is that anything to laugh at Cesare?'

'At bottom you've got the heart of a shopgirl who believes in dreams and redemption. You reduce the world to a mountain of molasses. Are you happy Miele to be seduced by the heart of a shop assistant?'

Miele smiles and shrugs his shoulders. He kisses me on the corner of my mouth. He pours a small whisky into my glass and makes a sign for me to drink it.

'Now the eternal Madam Julie arrives with her aristocratic sensibility. She will cut off the head of the poor chaffinch with one well-aimed blow. The violence of woman against man will be enacted once more with the perfect innocence of an infant mind.

'Who are you talking about Cesare?' Miele looks at him a little startled. Nico takes his glasses off and nervously puts them back on. He peers into the darkness waiting for the arrival of Dida.

'You know perfectly well who I'm talking about: that little priestess of the cult of Demeter: Ada.'

'And the little chaffinch?' asks Miele amused.

'The little chaffinch is a prisoner in the fragile hands of an aristocrat. It's here!'

With a sudden gesture Cesare lets his glass fall on to the floor. With two feverish fingers he zips open his trousers and pulls out from the trap of his pants his shrivelled penis and displays it to Miele.

'Don't you recognise Madam Julie's little bird? The lower class one whose head is cut off out of spite?'

Miele laughs and looks round embarrassed. Nico puts on his glasses

217

for the umpteenth time. He focuses his short-sighted gaze on the flaccid penis lying recumbent in the open palm of his friend.

'But I'm not going to die friends. I assure you with all my heart. I'll let myself be castrated – sh! with such delicacy. That's my style even if it isn't quite genuine. I like to think that only you Miele are capable of being gentle and fierce at the same time with the unforced naturalness of a God. I am a bird of paradise. My wings are clipped but I won't have my revenge. I won't be angry with my assassin. Oh no. I'll wait for the critical moment to pull out her heart. To peck at it till the blood runs but without ill-feeling only with a rose-scented tenderness.'

'Now put that miserable little prick back in its place Cesare. Everybody's watching.'

But he doesn't do as he's asked. He throws his head backwards with a gloomy laugh. Then he turns his back on us and snickering bitterly to himself pisses on the lawn.

'Would you like to dance Armida?' Nico takes me by the hand and leads me towards the smooth clearing among the round stones where intertwined couples are revolving in circles. He clasps me desperately round the waist and buries his mouth in my hair. He is trembling.

'What's the matter Nico? Are you crying?'

He blows his nose. He does not answer. He seizes my waist once more.

'What's going to happen if the chain breaks?'

'What chain Nico?'

'The chain of love . . . if Dida and Ada fall for each other as it seems might be happening. What are we to do?'

'That's why there's such a feeling of doom in the air tonight.'

'We're living on a knife-edge Armida. If the chain breaks we'll all be fucked up. I know I shan't be strong enough.'

'What makes you think it will break?'

'I haven't told you that we kissed each other that night when I saw her home.'

'Who – Ada?'

'No – Dida.'

'Did she say she loved you?'

218

'On the contrary she told me she still loves Cesare and that when she kissed me she was thinking of him. "I won't take her from you" she said. "Cesare's the only one I love."'

'Then where do you get the idea she's now fallen for Ada?'

'I don't know. I'm scared.'

I think I catch sight of Asia in the distance. I leave Nico and go towards her but it isn't her after all. I go back to Nico and find him quarrelling with Cesare. His glasses dangle from their case out of his shirt pocket and swing dangerously.

I look round for Miele but he has vanished. I go and get myself a fruitjuice. A French boy with long black hair hands me a glass full to the brim. He smiles. He says something to me that I can't understand. He pulls me towards a sofa. We've hardly sat down when he flings himself against me whispering passionately in my ear. I push him away and get up. I go into a corridor with a very high ceiling. I open a door from which light is filtering. I find myself in a library with walls lined with shelves. Books right up to the ceiling. Books bound in red Moroccan leather with blue and silver backs. Ancient hand-painted parchments. In the centre of the room a small table inset with mother-of-pearl. I take down a book and open it. It is in Finnish. I go out. I walk to the end of the corridor and find myself in front of a curved staircase. I go up it and come to another corridor lined with plush. I tread on two or three layers of thick carpets with a geometrical design. On the walls large portraits with a dark background. Lords and ladies with clothes of brocade big rings on their fingers and pearl necklaces reaching to their knees.

I open a door at random. It is a bedroom in Empire style with a Venetian chandelier hanging from the ceiling. A woman asleep in a high four-poster bed with her dress pulled up to her hips. Her empty hand hangs down from her shoulder. On one foot a shoe. The other bare. Skirt rolled up her legs. As if she had been interrupted suddenly in the midst of an amorous struggle. Now she sleeps exhausted. And the other?

A lightning glance towards a pair of trousers hanging on the back of a chair takes my breath away. Crumpled white linen trousers. On the floor some coins that have rolled out of his pockets. I bang the door shut as if my eyes had been cauterised by a scorching vision. I rush down the stairs. I sit on the bottom step to think. I'd like to go back and confront the woman. To ask her about Miele – but what sense is there in forcing Miele's secret? Why pester him? I am tortured by doubt. Supposing it wasn't him at all. How can I know for certain?

I hear footsteps and draw back. I recognise Miele by the stealthy way he walks bending his knees. Yes – it is him! I lift my eyes and look at him unable to utter a word.

'Goodness Armida what are you doing here?' He puts his arms round me and crushes my lips to his. 'I was on the terrace with Vera. She belongs to the communist youth group from Prague. Do you know her?'

His voice so calm so tranquil. Innocent. I look at him dumbly. Waiting for some catastrophe. But nothing happens. He caresses me affectionately.

'Don't you believe me Armida? Please tell me you believe me... You are the only one I love... the only one... say you believe me.'

'Yes I believe you' I say with an effort that leaves me exhausted and empty.

And he is happy. He takes my face between his hands and gives me a kiss full of infinite sweetness and yearning. To seal his most perfect incredible lie.

Here I am once again with my suitcase on my head. Canvas shoes on my feet. Shirt washed but not ironed. Slipping out of my skirt which is now so big that it falls down to my hips. I don't know how much weight I've lost.

Miele walks silently beside me. His face shut off his thoughts far away. Cesare stays by Ada's heels carrying her bags as well as his own. Nico and Dida share the weight of an outsize suitcase each pulling it by one handle. We reach the station and meet up with all the other Italians. Everyone is thinner more exhausted more ragged more subdued quieter. Like us they are lugging suitcases looking dazed and gloomy.

The holiday is over. There is a feeling of emptiness. Of things falling apart. Everyone returning home to some dreary suburban flat balconies festooned with drying nappies pots of basil on the windowsill to mothers eternally cooking and fathers going out every evening to play cards in the local bar to friends for ever full of plans and unattainable dreams. To girl friends who dress up in the latest fashion and are *au fait* with all the American movies and will end up getting married in Church and having four kids and looking full of bitterness muttering to themselves and whose fingers smell eternally of garlic and bleach so that one feels sick just to look at them and to hell with it all....

This time the train seems to go hurtling along towards too many familiar trivialities of daily life and all the belongings and junk that once cost a fortune or that has been bartered or exchanged or bought in sales or stolen. The dirty clothes rolled up in bags the down-at-heels shoes the guts-ache the spotty face the hair that's beyond brushing or combing...

Within a few hours the hierarchy is re-created. The system of bartering starts up again and so do the abuses and bullying of the outward journey but now with even more offhandedness and cynicism. No one argues about politics any more. Most of the time they sing endless songs in Neapolitan or Venetian dialect. They pass round photographs of groups: fair girls in shorts arm in arm with fat young men with moustaches. People sitting in a circle under a

221

makeshift roof in a field or standing in front of the microphone in the Palladium.

Nico has a photo of the Villa Hummeri just as I saw it from the meadow suspended and scintillating like a summer mirage. There are snapshots of cars of garden cemeteries of saunas of streets swept by the wind of shops of the big open tent of colourful crowd of girls putting out their tongues or making V-signs. The journey has faded into the past frozen in these squares of shiny paper that are totally devoid of interest.

Ada appears to have fallen into a timeless sleep. She sleeps on and on leaning her head on Nico's sharp bony shoulder. Cesare watches her with tenderness and longing.

Miele is absent-minded. At times distant and moody. I do not question him. I confine myself to gazing at him. I am learning that 'passion is solitary and feeds itself from its own interior rhythms' as Ada says in her hoarse voice. Nico agrees and adds 'We imagine we can divide those rhythms and merge them into a unique movement but it's only a game of mirrors that can never be resolved.' By this time they talk on an equal footing after all those nights spent confabulating about Dida. 'Mutual love is just a coincidence. In reality all of us live out our emotions in isolation. We're consumed by them without having a clue how much the other shares them. All we can do is to hope that this miraculous coincidence lasts for ever. But naturally it doesn't. One passion burns out first and the other is broken and tottering in the void gripped in the pincers of a bottomless despair.

'Does this apply to me too Nico?' I ask.

'Yes. You as well. Paolo loved you but you stopped loving him to run after Miele. One always chases after a part of oneself that escapes running like a hare.'

But I'm not listening to him any more. He bores me with his theories on solitary love. They don't fit in with my ideas and never will. I return to my book. I am aware that Miele has disappeared. But I don't follow him. I wait for him calmly my eyes drifting into the boundless silvery green countryside.

Miele returns. He sits down. He lights a cigarette. He skims

222

through a book. He falls asleep. He wakes with a start. He goes out again. He returns late. I hardly follow his movements. I respect his mystery. Every day he seems to become more closed and impenetrable. At night I hardly sleep. I wake with every creak and jolt of the train and then I can't get back to sleep again. My throat is sore and my stomach is continually churning with nausea.

Arriving at stations and leaving them again has become a pre-ordained ritual. Everybody leaps down from the carriage. We all meet in the station buffet. The delegate on duty gives a short speech which is greeted with cheers and toasts. Someone grabs a bottle of vodka and re-sells it later that night with furtive whisperings. Sometimes the train stops for half a day. We are taken to see the People's Centre. They sit us down under huge portraits of Lenin and Marx. They fill us with tea and cakes. Then there is a sermon! Then they take us back to the station and give us each a souvenir badge for our buttonholes.

In Budapest we stop for a whole day. There the sun is scorching. We are taken on an expedition to Janos Hegy the highest hill in Buda. A funicular railway. Concentric terraces with gigantic nineteenth century statues which bear a striking resemblance to those in the Tennis Club Bar in Rome where Miele offered me a Daiquiri for the first time. The city looks as if it were drawn in black against an almost white sky. The Danube scintillates as it glides like a serpent to divide the city into two.

Later we drink sparkling ice-cold wine in a boat anchored to the bank of the river. Surrounded by a crowd of shabbily-dressed people with alive inquisitive faces and shy friendly smiles.

A sauna before going back into the train. Solariums filled with boiling steam swimming baths lined with green tiles jets of icy water a gaggle of fat naked women who are dumbfounded by the sudden appearance of a group of chattering Italian girls.

Apart from this I remember nothing of the long journey home. Only a sensation of pain hanging over me and a deep and desperate boredom.

At Rome station we all have a coffee together for the last time. Our faces dark and drowsy. Nico automatically polishing his spectacles and swallowing his saliva overcome with emotion. Cesare stamping his feet nervously. Miele breathing in his native air with an ineffable smile. Dida looking fresh and happy with one of her usual blouses half open over her breasts. Ada still absorbed by disturbing day dreams her head framed by the two black wings.

I reach home. I insert the key into the keyhole. I open the door. I go in. I throw open the windows. The atmosphere is stale. There is a sticky heat. I am assaulted by Testone's fleas which after a month's fast are on the lookout for someone to devour. I search around for some insecticide.

When I see the dog's-bed I feel anxious. I lift the telephone my bag still in my hand. I dial my mother's number.

'How's Testone?'

'He's here asleep. You ask about him first. You don't ask about me. How was the journey?'

'I'll come over and get him.'

'Did you hear he got lost?'

'How do you mean lost?'

'I don't know. He kept looking for you. He wasn't eating. Then I discovered he was going over to your place to wait for you. The porter told me. For days and days he wouldn't let anyone get near him. Finally the porter telephoned and I went to fetch him. Another time he escaped and crept underneath Paolo's house. The porter recognised him there too but he didn't manage to catch hold of him. He's a block-head your Testone.'

I take a small majolica teapot I bought for her in Helsinki and go over to get my dog.

I HAVE begun to work on my play. Sara has phoned me several times to tell me that Ernesto is waiting for it to be re-written. Rehearsals are due to begin in a few days.

I sit in front of the open window. It is still very hot. When I look up I see the top of the plane tree with its fretted leaves swaying in the wind. I see the big houses in front of me changing colour according to the direction of the light.

Testone is curled up beneath the table with his muzzle resting on my feet. He is sleeping heavily. Every now and again he dreams he's chasing a cat or maybe another dog. He utters a muffled bark with his mouth closed scrabbling his paws as if he were running.

The telephone rings. I lift the receiver. I recognise the voice at once. The dark clear tones the cadences.

'Are you working?'

'Yes.'

'I love you Armida. I was thinking this morning in the bath that you're the woman I've loved most in my life.'

But there is a reticence in his voice. Something unsaid that he wants to come out with.

'Have you something to tell me?'

'How do you know?'

'I can feel it.'

'You'd better go and see a doctor my love.'

'Why?'

'You might have a dose of the clap.'

'Me? What do you mean?'

'I've caught it and so you've probably got it too. That's all.'

'Ah . . .' I take my time. A feeling of weariness turns my legs to jelly.

'Are you upset?' The voce at the other end of the line sounds gentle affectionate concerned.

'How did you catch it Miele?'

'I don't know.'

'Don't you catch it from making love?'

'Not always . . . you can catch it from a dirty towel or a dirty lavatory seat . . .'

225

'You don't have to lie Miele.'

'Armida whether you believe me or not I swear I've never made love with anyone except you.'

The painful sensation of a mystery that's self-negating. The mystery of a pointless lie. The madness of someone being pig-headed beyond all reason. To avoid exposing himself. So completely pointless. I realise how futile it is to insist.

'What should I do?'

'Go and see the doctor. Do you have a gynaecologist?'

'Yes. A woman.'

'Go and see her and she'll examine you. It could be that you haven't got it. It isn't absolutely certain that you'd catch it as well.'

'What are the symptoms?'

'A thick white discharge. Burning pains. You'd know if you had it.'

'I haven't got anything at the moment.'

'So much the better. Maybe you haven't caught it. On the other hand it could be you're incubating the infection. So it's better to go and see someone. Anyway I'm treating myself. It isn't serious. You'll be on the mend in no time my love. Don't worry . . . the only snag is that we can't make love for at least a month.'

'All right I'll go and see the gynaecologist.'

'Will you believe me if I say I love you?'

'If you say so. I don't see why you should say one thing and mean another. No – there's no earthly reason why you should say one thing and mean another.'

'No – there isn't any reason. Armida I love you so much. Tell me you love me too.'

'You know it.'

'That's good. Then I'll be getting back to work. We'll see each other this evening. *Ciao.*'

I go and see the gynaecologist. It turns out that I too have the beginnings of an infection and I need to have treatment. I buy a syringe and give myself an injection on my own.

In the evening I go to supper with Dida Ada Cesare Nico and Miele. He is happy. He squeezes my hand underneath the table. He chain smokes. He eats a lot. He drinks one glass of wine after another.

Dida is wearing one of her usual blouses. Made out of nothing. Slipping down over her shoulders like a froth of milk. During a moment of silence she raises her glass and announces:

'I have something important to tell you.' There is an immediate silence. Nico takes off his glasses and rubs his eyes. Ada watches her with laughing eyes. Miele gives me a wink.

'Cesare and I are going to get married.'

There is a clamour of voices. Outbursts of joy. Congratulations. Only Ada is struck dumb. She sits rigid with her knife and fork clenched tightly between her fingers in a painful spasm.

'What's this obsession with getting married?' shouts Miele raising his glass and swallowing a piece of chicken.

'After that I am going to make an announcement' Cesare interjects seriously. 'My love for Ada hasn't changed. Dida knows that if I marry her it's only so that I can have sex regularly. Everyone knows that I'm quite capable of separating sex from emotion. So I shall be fucking my lawful wife and loving Ada who'll have nothing to do with me and is steadily killing me.'

'That's just a load of bollocks. Typical of you Cesare' shouts Miele.

'Listen to who's preaching! Miele you've nothing to teach anyone. You're simply a randy old womaniser. You're completely irresponsible and one day like Don Juan the devil will come and take you by the hand and carry you off to hell.'

'This business of getting married is simply ridiculous. Nico loves Dida and marries Ada. You love Ada and you marry Dida who loves you who loves Ada who loves Dida etcetera etcetera etcetera. What's it all in aid of? How many intertwined adulteries are you all going to end up with?'

'Adultery doesn't interest me Miele. There's nothing secret between us and adultery without secrets isn't adultery at all. Anyway marriages without love are the only ones that work.'

'You're all half-witted. You're mental.'

'Why don't you marry Armida?'

'I love her. So according to your code of morality I mustn't marry her since that would be a marriage of love! But anyway I'm against marriage whatever kind it is. Cesare haven't you always said that it's

227

a bourgeois institution?'

'If it's taken in earnest with all its rules and regulations – yes. But our way of interpreting marriage is at least original...'

'Original perhaps. But why this sudden urge to get married to become subservient to the law and the social contract?'

'You're such a bore Miele... Instead of acting the moralist why don't you join our chain of unrequited love? Armida loves you... you love yourself...'

We drink a toast. Dida gets up and kisses each of us on the mouth. Wafting a heavy nostalgic scent of jasmine. Miele continues pressing my hand underneath the table as if to tell me that we are not like the others. We are better.

At midnight he takes me home. He stops to kiss me in the entrance.

'Is there something you still have to say to me Miele?'

'Yes... I can't hide anything from you.'

'What is it?'

'I've got to go to Paris for a week. I leave tomorrow. I'll ring you from there. Will you wait for me?'

'Why shouldn't I wait for you?'

'Sometimes I'm so afraid of losing you. I lie awake at night worrying about it. I'm afraid you'll get sick of me. You'd be right too... I'm so uncaring. I'm here so little. But whether you believe it or not I know I'll always love you.'

We kiss each other. His lips slipping away into his unfathomable smile so relaxed so wistful.

I AM woken up by Testone's wet nose pressing against my arm. As soon as I open my eyes he starts wagging his tail. He snorts and squirms in paroxysms of joy. I get up. I wash. I get dressed. I take him out. But I don't go too far for fear that Miele might telephone while I'm out. Testone is fully aware of this. He runs on ahead from one plane-tree to the next and waits for me to catch up with him. I call him. I glance at my watch. He turns round. He looks at me with pleading eyes all ready to spring forward. But I restrain him. I scold him. I call him to heel. Against his will he turns to follow me stopping at every tree to sniff where he has urinated all the time hoping that I will change my mind.

I buy the papers. From the delicatessen I buy bread a few slices of ham and some mozzarella cheese. Then I return home. I sit in front of my typewriter and fill one sheet of paper after another. By two o'clock my back is aching. I leave the table and make myself a solitary meal. As I eat I watch Testone who does little turns to amuse me. One of his favourite performances is to be a pointer and hunt flies. He points a fly with his three paws well planted on the floor the fourth bent up in the air his nose suspended absolutely still and alert pointing towards the wall where a little black dot with wings is visible. As soon as the fly moves Testone springs forward with a quick jump opens his mouth and snaps it shut with a click that jars his teeth like the clank of a metal gin-trap a noise that always surprises him far more than it does the fly.

The insect almost always flies calmly away. And Testone turns his head slyly towards me with his ears folded back his black lips stretched into a kind of comical forced grin. He comes over and lays his muzzle on my knees. He looks up at me raising only his eyeballs with an effect that is both playful and pathetic.

I stroke his head and call him 'Good Dog' 'Big Boy' 'Old Chap' and 'Little Fellow'. He wags his tail happily and leans his head on my knees. Meanwhile out of the corner of his eye he observes that the fly has alighted on the edge of the table quite near us and he takes up his stance as a pointer once more.

After having eaten and given Testone a big feed I lie on the bed

229

reading. The telephone within reach of my hand. I'm getting on with reading Jane Austen. I follow the logical geometries of her ironical imagination. Quite the opposite of the fevered Brontë sisters with their tangled way of seeing the world whom I used to love so much when I was a child. Now I am travelling through an ordered landscape composed of small everyday events: short conversations about what muslin is in fashion about carriages about an invitation to take waters at Bath about meeting a gentleman with penetrating eyes about gossip between bridesmaids about marriage to a good-hearted man who is both well-to-do and aristocratic. In the end it is the person with courage honesty and a good dose of bourgeois irony who wins out. The losers are the foolish the fatuous the cunning the vain the dishonest the cowardly.

I can almost see Jane Austen dressed neatly in a straw hat with a silk ribbon never at a loss for an answer her eyes tender and malicious her lips pursed ironically and eighteenth century England spread out beneath her penetrating gaze a landscape that is both peaceful and cruel both obvious and disquieting.

At five o'clock I get back to my typewriter. Always with an ear on the phone. Testone lies under the table feeling sorry for himself. Every so often he jumps up turns a rapid somersault throws himself on to his back with all four paws in the air and his tongue hanging out. He looks at me as if to say 'Aren't we going out?' At seven I take him out. The moment I go into the bathroom to comb my hair he's aware of my intentions. He seizes his lead and brings it me wagging his tail. 'Testone wait!' I say. 'Hang on just a minute.' But his impatience has reached its limit. He can't wait a moment longer. He plonks himself down with his nose in the air where I can't fail to see him. He utters a little growl in the back of his throat always keeping the lead tight between his teeth.

When we reach the front entrance I let him go free. Otherwise he'd drag me off my feet. Sliding his nails on the marble floor he can pull with the strength of an ox.

As soon as we reach the pavement he flings himself backwards and forwards in a frenzied race round the first big plane tree as if he were about to throw himself at it. But at the last moment he brakes and swirls round with his bottom arched up in the air. Shaking his head with pure happiness he rushes back towards me. As soon as he comes up to me he sets off again in the same reckless gyrations.

I follow him enjoying his antics. When he goes too far I call him back. All the time I am keeping an eye on my watch.

'I can't give you more than ten minutes Testone. Suppose Miele were to ring and didn't catch me and then didn't call back?'

I speak to him in an overwrought voice. He looks up at me with understanding. He knows very well that my mind is preoccupied that I'm imprisoned indoors waiting for a phone call that never comes. He knows I'm in a hurry to get back because by this time my suspense has become transformed into an exquisite pain that both nourishes me and drives me mad.

He tries to get through his business in the shortest possible time urinating against trees against walls against rubbish bins against the wheels of parked cars.

'When are you going to make up your mind to shit Testone?' But he puts off that moment as long as he can drifting from tree to tree with his nose to the ground. When he sees I've reached the end of my tether he finally comes to a decision. He settles down on his hind legs and strains his muscles with such force that his whole neck goes rigid. But he hasn't finished yet because as soon as he gets into that strained position he gets up again and circles round impatiently. He sniffs the grass nervously he pushes back his ears he squats down again and finally with all his muscles contracted and his eyes staring into the void he lets his excrement drop on the grass.

Then he moves away turns his back towards his business and starts to splatter the earth kicking up with his hind legs. Gravel tufts of grass and earth fall anywhere but on his pile of shit. Then he comes back looking very pleased with himself his tail wagging as if to say 'Now we can go'. He barks with relish at the birds trees and passing cars as he trots along in front of me.

Back home I lie on the ramshackle divan with broken springs. I turn on the record player. I put on Don Giovanni and the nordic voice of Sherril Milnes fills the room. I imagine him moving: his agility his white breeches his crimson velvet waistcoat his pointed cap

231

with the triumphant plume of foaming white feathers. I go to the window and try to visualize him down below in the street blond and smiling as he blows me a kiss. The voice of Don Giovanni laughs in my ears.

Testone and I spend the evening on our own. There is not a movement from the telephone. Not a sound. Then suddenly it rings. Testone gives a start. His eyes follow me as I run to answer it.

'Armida – what are you doing?' It is Nico's voice gentle and sad.

'I'm here patching up my play to keep the director happy.'

'Would you like to come out with me this evening?'

'Where's Ada?'

'She's gone off to see her mother in Puglia.'

'And Dida?'

'She's gone away too – with Cesare. He's driving her mad the bastard. All the time he makes love he's bawling that it's not her he loves but Ada.'

'Just like you do with Ada don't you?'

'I don't make love to Ada. Anyway our talking about Dida is quite different. There's no coercion or blackmail about it . . . we just lie in the dark and talk about her.'

'Suppose she falls in love with you.'

'That's just your fantasy. You like things to be planned. But for us it's not like that at all . . . we'd be in a real fix if our paths met: it'd be the finish of this knife-edge that keeps us united.'

'Have you heard anything of Miele?'

'Look Armida . . . you as well . . . you're running after a heart who's only wish is to escape from you. How about having supper so that we can talk about Miele?'

'No Nico. Thanks all the same. I'm sleepy. I want to go to bed early.'

'If you could only settle for loving without being loved in return you'd be happy Armida. Then you'd only want his good and wouldn't think of possessing him.'

'Thanks for your advice Nico. But luckily Miele loves me.'

'Yes you're certainly very fortunate . . .' His voice is full of commiseration. I put down the receiver feeling annoyed. I return to listening to Don Giovanni as he strides across the village square. And Elvira – 'she's quite mad my friends' – has managed to break the eggs in the basket while he was occupied seducing Zerlina.

'Stop villain' she cries. 'I am just in time to save this wretched innocent from your barbarous clutches.' This calamitous Elvira always moralising and punishing resembles all the calamitous Elviras who populated my childhood with their senseless prohibitions.

And Don Giovanni bores into her ear 'My treasure don't you see – all I want is to amuse myself?' But she resents this and flies off the handle: 'Amuse yourself you cruel man I know how you amuse yourself!'

Meanwhile Zerlina does not know what to do. She looks expectantly round her. Don Giovanni catches that look of frailty on the wing. He accosts her and takes her by the wrist. 'Oh poor unhappy one she loves me and out of pity I must feign love in return for it is my misfortune to be goodhearted and generous.'

One cannot fail to love this liar with the perfumed voice who struts boldly trampling heedlessly on the tender hearts of women with his buckskin shoes.

I wait and wait. Finally after midnight I keep myself awake with coffee. I eat a sliver of mozzarella cheese with bread and butter. I drink a glass of milk. Testone has already eaten but he watches me hoping I will spare a titbit for him. So we divide the supper: one piece of cheese for me and one for him. A piece of bread for me and one for him. A few grapes for him and a few for me.

When eventually my eyes are closing with sleep I undress. I put the telephone beside the bed. I slip underneath the sheet. I continue reading but with only the greatest effort. At last I doze off to sleep. But I sleep badly. Every so often I wake with a start under the impression that the telephone is ringing. I grab the receiver and shout 'hullo!' Testone is woken up by the light and he watches me unable to comprehend what on earth is going on. He remains stretched out on the floor motionless except for his restless eyes. I watch him. I am filled with disappointment. I put out the light. I lie down. But I find it impossible to get back to sleep. By now a whole week has gone by and he still hasn't phoned.

233

'A RMIDA my love. I've only just got back. How are you?'
'Fine.'
'Forgive me for not having phoned you as I said I would. The difficulty's been I was always on the move from one town to another. I've been thinking about you so much...'
'Shall we have supper together?'
'I'll come and fetch you later.'

I look in the mirror. I've got thinner. Uglier. My face is hollow and creased. My eyes dark. My hair looks lifeless and droops down over my forehead. I decide to cut it. I hack at it with hard blunt scissors. I put on a bright red dress with a tight waist and a skirt that falls loosely round my legs. I put some colour on my cheeks. I put on high-heeled sandals.

I decide to take Testone. He hasn't been out since the morning. I wash and brush him because it seems only right for him to be clean and smell nice.

Miele picks us up in his red Volkswagon. He puts his arms round me. He kisses me. He rattles on about a thousand insignificant things. I don't question him at all. I sit on the edge of my seat listening to him my thoughts far away.

We go to a restaurant alongside the Tiber called 'I Trenini'. A terrace on stilts overlooks the railway line to Ostia. We sit at a small rickety table underneath a pergola. We order pasta and grilled fish. Testone has remained in the car. Miele didn't want to bring him in with us.

While we eat Miele asks me to talk about myself. I don't know what to say. I tell him that I've had a letter from Ada. That Nico has telephoned to tell me that Filippo has got a girl from Naples pregnant. That she was working for him as a housemaid. I tell him that Dida and Cesare have gone off to Amalfi together. I tell him about Ernesto who pretends that the company insists that I change the distribution of the actors in my play as he doesn't want the women's parts to have too much importance.

He stays silent watching me. I've no idea what he is thinking. His eyes look opaque.

'Go on talking' he says. 'You speak so nicely.' And so I ramble on. My voice falsely cheerful. Suddenly he interrupts me. He puts on the decisive look that belongs to important occasions.

'I want to tell you something Armida.'

'Tell me.' The suspense lasts for centuries. My stomach muscles tense. My throat dry.

'Don't take it badly my love... it's difficult for you to understand... appearances are all against me... The fact is... the fact is that I shall probably have to get married.'

'You're getting married?'

'It's a complicated story... it's to do with a refugee from Guatemala. If she doesn't get married they'll take her passport away and deport her. Then she runs the risk of being sent to prison and being tortured... A poor little fragile delicate creature.'

'Didn't you say you were in love with me?'

'I do love you Armida... that's what I wanted to say... that nothing will change. Even if everything seems to change. I feel you closer to me than ever and I love you so much.'

'So when did you decide to get married?'

'It's a political action my love. You must believe me. An act of courage and support for someone who would otherwise die...'

'And she loves you?'

'I think so. Maybe she doesn't. I don't know. Come to that what is love my dear Armida? A state of ambiguity of weakness... a nebulous explosion in which you can find everything from what's left after a day's work to the memories of a long-lost childhood. Now let's go home together. I want you so much I feel I'm going to burst...'

'I'd rather not Miele.'

'But why?' He is genuinely surprised. He squeezes my hands between his. Almost irritated by my sudden obstinacy.

'Seeing that you're in the mood for telling the truth Miele can you tell me once and for all about things as they really are – where did you get the clap I caught from you?'

'I've always told you the truth Armida. I swear I've never made love with anyone but you. Never. I swear it – never.'

Faithful to himself. Tenacious and stubborn to the point of self-sacrifice. Heroically resisting the temptation to tell the truth so as to follow confidently his grandiose fantasy of love.

And once again I renounce distressing him with the demands of my miserable female logic. It's right he should appear as he wants to appear – even if it is not the truth. What is the truth as he would say? Where is the boundary between the raw delineation of fact and feelings which are so real yet so mixed up with fantasies?

'Armida you must believe me. You're the only one I love. I need you. I can't bear to lose you.'

I watch him skin a peach and put it into his mouth bit by bit with delicate craftsmanship. He looks at me imploringly. Absolutely sincere and absolutely dishonest. Innocent because his impulses are without malice. Like the innocent brutality of those who naively and artfully strip themselves naked and then expect us to accept them as they are through the sheer strength of love.

I hear a distant barking. 'It's Testone' I say. 'Something must have happened. Let's go.'

He doesn't object. He insists on paying all the bill. He swallows the last drop of wine and follows me out.

Testone is on the roof of the car barking furiously. The top has been cut down one side. A long gash with a knife and the two strips of waxed cloth curled up. But the thieves haven't stolen the two suitcases that Miele had hidden underneath the seats. They had been frightened off by Testone.

Miele laughs with relief. He strokes Testone's head and talks softly and tenderly to him.

'Good Testone. You're a genius. You've saved me from being robbed. You're a good dog a very good dog. You deserve a whole chicken.'

We get into the car. Miele starts the engine. We set off with a jerk. He drives furiously going round bends without braking as if he were doing a ski turn on the tarmac. He looks sad. Wretched. He takes my hand and kisses it.

'When shall we see each other Armida?'

'I don't know.'

'Shall I ring you tomorrow?'

236

'No.'

'Am I to take it you don't want to see me any more?'

'Not for the moment. No.'

'But why? I need you Armida. I need you and I love you. Believe it or not. I love you so much. I can't do without you.'

As soon as he stops outside my flat I fling myself out of the car and rush through the entrance without even turning to say goodbye. I hear his voice calling me despairingly through the car window. I don't turn round. I don't reply. I go to the lift. It's broken. I rush upstairs followed by Testone.

IN America they give it a woman's name: Charlotte Nancy Lilly Susy. As if to acknowledge that the dark unpredictable violence of a hurricane can only come from the unfathomable depths of the feminine psyche.

An ordered landscape that seems to be living in harmony with the universe for the brief eternity of its existence: a house a wood a garden a field a few shops a street a petrol pump a school . . .

Suddenly a wind comes from nowhere leaps over the roofs rises up on itself flings the tiles into the air rips off the rafters hurls down chimneys sends walls flying for miles splits trees rips up neat little gardens overturns cars against the rocks demolishes shops floods the street sweeps away the school in an avalanche of mud. In the space of a few minutes nothing is left. The harmony is destroyed. The upheaval is immediate and total.

My far-off eye watches from the corner of my bedroom indifferent to the fury of the hurricane. The tempest shows no sign of calming down for days and days. I am a prey to the lacerating forces of the cyclone. My mouth is parched with fever. My neck is drenched. Waves of turbid water laden with debris shatter against the shoreline that divides my eyelids from the roots of my eyes. Waves succeed waves and I cannot escape from them. I am drowned in a swirling river that sweeps away bricks gates sheets of corrugated iron dead animals signposts burned trees and boats smashed into colanders.

My calm frozen eye watches in silence from the height of the ceiling and awaits the end. There is a certain subtle pleasure in taking part in my own destruction without having to intervene apart from the miseries of my pointless convulsions and death agonies.

When I think that it is all resolved and that I can now sing a requiem to the corpse my eye recognises that something is moving beside the chest of drawers. No – it is not Armida with broken arms and legs. It is Testone who after days and days of waiting at the foot of the bed gets up trembling all over and howling.

Testone's alarm brings me back to the world. I get up. Staggering like a drunkard I take him for a walk under cover of darkness. I don't want to see anyone. I've taken the telephone off the hook. I've let it be

238

known I'm going away. I go out leaving my eye hanging on the cornice. Half blind. With only one eye I stumble I fall I get up I lose my way.

I return home out of breath. I sit in front of the open window that beckons me with the cold empty voice of a siren. Armida throw yourself out. It's so beautiful beautiful taking off in flight. The thought of dizzily swaying swaying down fascinates me. The window opens its arms ready to welcome me and I cling spasmodically to the wicker chair. I put a hand on Testone's wet nose so as to save myself from being lured by the euphoria of flying gently away. It seems almost as if my eye is returning to the socket where it has always lived. I see the houses opposite taking shape and colour.

So our convalescence begins. Testone's and mine. His affectionate breath on my ankles. His soft gaze in my eyes. We live off tinned food. We sleep at the strangest hours.

I stay awake or rather I vegetate in front of the open window in a September that slowly ages with occasional flashes of scorching heat.

Testone and I go out at night like two thieves tiptoing silently fleeing from the sight of any neighbour walking through deserted streets breathing in the damp night air like a medicine.

239

THE potato is still there dripping from my cupped hand. My back begins to ache after standing so long on my feet. The voice that comes out of the small black box has led me through the streets of memory like a blind clairvoyant guide.

How that voice held me spellbound and lost for three whole years! Three long centuries. Two legs with slightly swollen ankles carrying the sharp sensual voice that bewitched me between Scylla and Charybdis one midsummer night eighteen years ago.

Now his clever voice emerges from the small innocuous box of black plastic that usually regales me with beautiful concertos of Bach and Mozart in that sun-drenched kitchen between the window overlooking the courtyard and the steel sink next to the hiccuping dishwasher. His siren voice comes back to twist its scaly tail around my waist.

I sit down pressing my knees against the table. I get close to the radio and turn up the volume. The voice becomes deep and husky. I turn the knob and it becomes the shrill squeak of an ant with sibilant esses.

Miele is talking of peace as if he were talking of love with the intensity and ardour of a great orator. Miele rising to a crescendo over the huge sums that are spent every year on defence – bombs guns fighter aircraft warships submarines torpedoes hydrogen bombs neutron bombs to say nothing of thousands of generals and soldiers all of whom wear shoes uniforms helmets belts machine guns bullets hand grenades that make them sweat like fountains...

If I had a well-ordered calm disciplined memory I would not have been so astonished at this sudden crowding in of the past. Someone who keeps his memories at the ready in the bookshelf of his brain would know how to control them. It would be enough to stretch out a hand to reopen old files new photograph-albums books to consult and return to. But for me it is not like that. As Plato describes it my mind is like a tree on which birds of memory perch whenever they are tired and want to rest. But a breath of wind the least ripple the least suspicion and away they fly – and who can catch them on the wing?

The surprise of suddenly finding for myself the branches of

memory laden with forgotten birds takes my breath away. Suddenly they break out in a frenzied restless chattering. Thousands of birds meeting greeting skylarking bickering pecking squawking in a crescendo that makes my head go round and round.

Eighteen forgotten unrecorded years lost in an underground murmuring Miele has married a beautiful woman with dark hair and he's had two sons. Now he is divorced and lives with a girl twenty years younger than himself. He writes books he organises committees he is a success.

Ada works as an architect designing film sets with as much intelligence and imagination as ever. She lives with a girl from Ferrara with the gentle name of Serena. Dida and Cesare have separated. Cesare has re-married a teacher from Naples. He has got a paunch now and he still grumbles though with less vivacity than he used to.

Dida lives on her own with her son. They are as like as two drops of water. She has never divulged who the father is. He is the son of a single mother. For years she was very poor and she survived as best she could with irregular temporary jobs. Now she earns a living singing and composing songs and doing the rounds of the festivals and folk concerts.

Paolo has married a beautiful Canadian and lives with her in Montreal. They have three fair-haired sons – three little French-Canadians. He paints obsessively. He has exhibitions and his work sells. His face is even more ravaged his eyes anguished the tips of his fingers sprouting buds of colour ever more subtle and beautiful.

Nico the sweet gentle Nico fell in love with the 'armed struggle' believing it is possible to change the world against the will of the people. He went firing into people's houses shooting them at point-blank range 'for their own good'. He took part in two 'actions of war' as he called them. Then he died nobody really knows how. He was killed after having wounded some university professor in the leg during the campaign 'against the deliberate misinterpretation of culture by the multinationals and in an attempt to destabilize the centres of power.'

I went to see him in the mortuary. They had opened him up

241

carving him in half lengthways like a chicken. A deep scar like a furrow from his throat to his pubis covered by a stained sheet which was lifted for just a moment long enough to imprint for ever on my mind his wounded image his pale swollen face the marks of his glasses on his cheeks darkened by a beard a half smile of desperate longing and the certainty that over all those years he had no other love no other pleasure not other desire than what bound him to Dida.

So I am here with that potato in my hand with its solidity so white so lucid so tender which seems to enclose for ever the misery and at the same time the sublime mystery of Miele.

OTHER FICTION TITLES FROM CAMDEN PRESS

CORREGIDORA
Gayl Jones

Blues singer Ursa is consumed by her hatred of Corregidora, the 19th-century slavemaster who fathered both her grandmother and mother. Charged with 'making generations' to bear witness to the abuse embodied in the family name, Ursa Corregidora finds herself unable to keep alive this legacy when she is made sterile in a violent fight with her husband. Haunted by the ghosts of a Brazilian plantation, pained by a present of lovelessness and despair, Ursa slowly and firmly strikes her own terms with womanhood.

'And above all there is some quite extraordinary writing about sex, not just about the coital act, but about the moods, the balances, the feelings of the participants – desire, fear, pleasure, hatred, caught in quite believable and revealing vignettes. I did not know that women could write about sex in quite this way...'
The Guardian

'*Corregidora* is a poem to black men and women. It is an ode, howbeit painful, to all the participants in the American Experience.'
Maya Angelou

£5.95 paperback ISBN 0 948491 43 4

LETTERS TO MARINA
Dacia Maraini

Letters from one woman to another describing their love affair.
Letters that will probably never reach their destination, never
even be posted.
Letters 'to tell you all those things about myself you've never
wanted to know. You were in love with a woman who came to
you without a past, new-born and naked out of the dark
womb of time.'
Letters that awaken Bianca's ghosts: her wounding relationship
with her father, her incestuous desires for her mother, terrifying
dreams, secret loves, a miscarriage, the eroticism of childhood,
the claustrophobic sexuality of a girls' boarding school.

It is the author's most personal and poetic novel. 'I spent four
years writing it', she says. 'I put into it many events, emotions
and memories that were very close to my heart.'

'Maraini has a gleeful but compassionate eye for the grotesque,
surreal and unexpected in everyday life...'
The Sunday Times

'an author of large talent.'
The Guardian

£5.95 paperback ISBN 0 948491 12 4

SPUNK
Selected short stories
Zora Neale Hurston

Novelist, folklorist, anthropologist, playwright, journalist and critic, Zora Neale Hurston (1901?–1960) has been called the heart behind an entire generation of modern black women writers. Named by Alice Walker 'a native American genius', she was born in Eatonville, Florida; where she grew up in an all black, self-governed town.
Hurston's stories celebrate the vitality and exuberance of black culture, whether in 'The Gilded Six Bits', an ironic account of infidelity, the powerful 'Sweat', a story of marital cruelty, or the joyful 'Isis', where a little girl tries to shave her grandmother's whiskers and runs off with the new red tablecloth to dance at the carnival.

A dynamic, witty, flamboyant and outrageous character – she styled herself 'Queen of the Niggerati' to shock – Zora Neale Hurston became one of the greatest figures of the Harlem Renaissance, and was for thirty years the most prolific black American woman writer.

'One of the most significant American writers of this century'.
The Times Literary Supplement

'The stories in Spunk transcend the particular without any sense that Hurston knows how far she's leaping: unselfconscious, exuberant, tragi-comic, they are, to wipe the grime of overuse from a good word, brilliant.'
New Statesman

£4.95 paperback ISBN 0948491 29 9

Camden Press titles are available from most good bookshops.
In case of difficulty, please write direct to
Camden Press at 43, Camden Passage, London N1 8EB